Praise for

JOURNEYMAN

Two intrepid young men set out from Kentucky to retrace the westward peregrinations of Kerouac and Cassady, twenty years after the fact, with tragic results for one and life-changing consequences for the other. *Journeyman* is the survivor's stirring, multi-layered account of their travels and travails, interwoven with recollections of the life he left behind. Rick Neumayer's writing is direct and purposeful, and it propels us through these misadventures as though we were along for the ride.

—**Ed McClanahan**, author of *The Natural Man*, *Famous People I Have Known*, and other books

Journeyman **is an affecting** and well-wrought story told against the backdrop of a war that shaped a generation of Americans. Rick Neumayer's good-natured narrator hitchhikes with his friend across the United States during 1971, and the friendship between these two young men is a lively, steady stream running throughout the book. Both are complex, vulnerable, imperfect human beings who make you ache with their youthful desire to find a meaningful direction in their lives and to create a better, more just world.

If you lived through the Vietnam War era, you will recognize the deep truth of this novel; if you were not alive then, you will fathom the chaos and hope and heartbreak of those years and how they laid the foundation for the world we're living now. This is a timely, generous book that deftly captures a powerful, heady, mind-bending time.

—**Eleanor Morse**, author of *White Dog Fell From The Sky*

Rick Neumayer's *Journeyman* immerses the reader viscerally in the America of 1970-71, with a quixotic hitchhiking pilgrimage from Louisville to a San Francisco commune at its narrative center. It's a moving and provocative story of initiation during a time, not unlike our own, when the energy and possibilities of youth rub up against the complicated realities of a country divided by racial mistrust, generational misunderstanding, political fractiousness, and domestic and international instability.

—**K. L. Cook**, author of *The Art of Disobedience* and *Marrying Kind*

JOURNEYMAN

JOURNEYMAN

a novel by rick neumayer

Fleur-de-Lis Press 2020

Front cover painting: *Almost Home* by Corie Neumayer (2019), with permission
    from Sena Jeter Naslund
Author photo: Corie Neumayer
Book design: Jonathan Weinert

"Our Own Private Walden Pond" appeared in a slightly different form
    in *Falling Star Magazine*, Summer 2018.

Printed in the United States of America
First Edition

Library of Congress Control Number: 2020940624
ISBN 13: 978-0-9960120-4-1

Fleur-de-Lis Press of *The Louisville Review*
1436 St. James Court, Apt. 1
Louisville, KY 40208
02.550.1870
nagingeditor@louisvillereview.org
.louisvillereview.org

contents

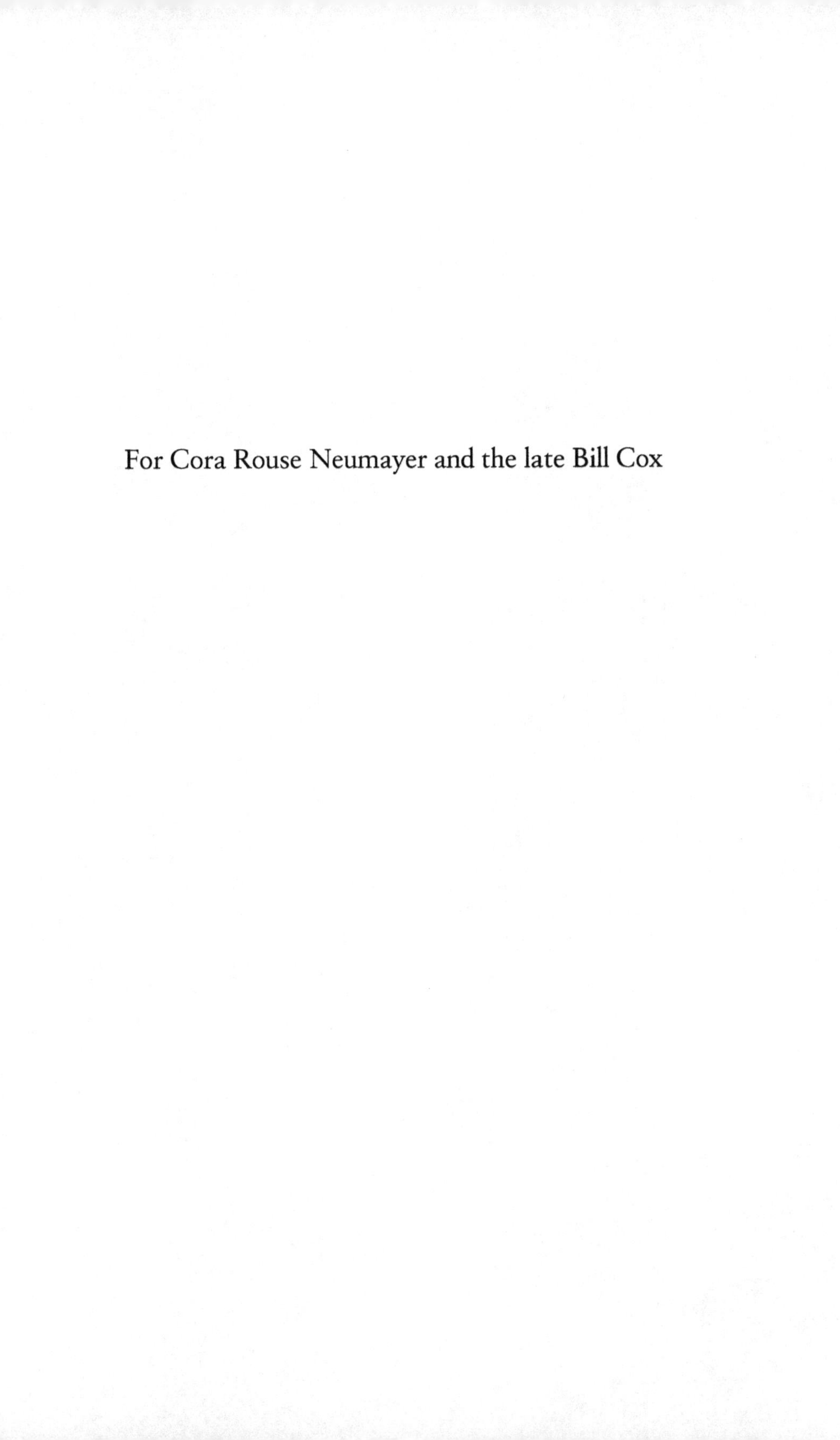

For Cora Rouse Neumayer and the late Bill Cox

our own private walden pond

1

June 1971

King and both Kennedys are dead, Nixon's in the White House, and the Beatles have broken up, anything and nothing seems possible. I'm leaving my old Kentucky home with my friend Stan, waiting beside the already warm blacktopped edge of I-64 with our thumbs pointing westward.

"Hitchhiking is illegal in Kentucky, Stan. Did you know that?"

"Only if you're standing *in* the road. Standing on the side of the road is okay."

"And you know this how?" I say, over the highway noise.

"Have faith, my brother."

A half hour goes by with us still gazing at Louisville's familiar skyline, and my faith tank is sitting close to empty. I ask myself why I let Stan talk me into this. The answer comes almost immediately in the form of a faded green Dodge van with Missouri plates. As it pulls over, I grab the rucksack containing my worldly possessions and rush toward the flashing tail lights.

The driver, a bearded young guy like us with hair down to his shoulders, leans over to the passenger window. "Where you headed, man?"

"Haight-Ashbury," I tell him.

"Far fucking out. I can take you as far as St. Louis. Jump in."

The big heavy side door, which slides instead of opening on hinges, is stuck. I manage to screech it open, but I do not heedlessly climb aboard. There are rules for hitchhiking, perhaps not written down, but rules just the same, and only fools ignore them. Rule number one is never set foot inside a strange vehicle without first checking out the driver and any passengers.

Stan apparently never has learned this rule because he immediately yells, "Shotgun," and jumps into the front seat.

The van's driver is alone, fortunately, which keeps the odds in our favor, and he looks okay, garbed like us in jeans and a tie-dye. Also, I can smell dope clinging to the carpeted floor. I pitch in my gear, duck down, and clamber aboard. There's no back seat, so I just flop in an empty space between the bulging trash bags and cardboard boxes overflowing with clothing.

"Looks like you're moving," I say.

"I just flunked out of UNC Greensboro," he says. "My deferment's gone. I'm going home to find a job until I get drafted. What's your name, man?"

"Pate Merwin," I say.

"Stan Hicks," says my pal.

"I'm Norm."

"Thanks for picking us up, Norm."

"Wish I was going with you guys."

"What's stopping you?" Stan asks.

"My lottery number is seventy-one, so I'm pretty sure my ass is gone. What about you?"

"I was in the Navy," Stan says. "But I'm against the war."

"Cool. What about you, Pate?" Norm peers at me in his rear-view mirror.

"Draft dodger."

"No shit. How do you do that?"

"I have my ways," I say, cagey since I just met this guy.

Norm surprises me by pulling out a joint. He lights it, passes it around, saying, "It's a little harsh, but it'll get you off."

Indeed it does, as the rich sweet scent of burning pot fills the van. We're already away from the city. The low wooded hills and farmlands of southern Indiana have never looked so green to me. I'm fascinated by how the road cuts through shelves of limestone, where rivulets of spring water drip from exposed ledges. Everything is *so* interesting.

Keeping our speed at a steady sixty-five, Norm says to me, "I don't want to go to prison. And I can't get C.O. status because I'm not religious. So what else can I do?"

"Tell them you're a Quaker," I say, as the turbulence from an eighteen-wheeler throws us across the lane line.

"Or a fucking Jehovah's Witness," Stan adds.

"I'm not sure what I believe in anymore," Norm says, "except maybe love."

"All you need is love," Stan says.

"Thank you, John Lennon," I say.

"Why'd you go into the Navy, Stan?" Norm asks.

"I was stupid. If I had it to do over again, I'd go to Canada or Sweden."

"Don't think I could ever leave the country."

"Better than being in the military," Stan says.

A hawk is circling overhead, flapping its enormous wings, gliding smoothly through the air, perhaps hunting for small ground game to kill with its claws and beak. Pointing it out to the others, I say, "Stan and I once were hawks. I was in high school R.O.T.C. He served two years on an aircraft carrier in the middle of the Pacific. Now we're doves."

"Once the military's got you," Stan says, "you're theirs. If you run, you're a deserter. That means they can shoot you or throw you in the stockade. You wouldn't stand a chance in there, Norm, not with those Marine pricks for guards."

We're starting down a long, steep hill that offers a sweeping view of farmland and woods. America, the beautiful.

"You could pretend to be crazy," I say, "or a drug addict."

"Wouldn't be much of a stretch in either case," Norm says grimly. "Wish I'd just passed chemistry and French. How'd you get out of the draft, Pate?"

I'm not sure I want to tell him. After all, we only met fifteen minutes ago. But they can't put me in jail just for *saying* what I did. And by telling Norm, I might just keep him from getting killed. "I took speed and stayed awake for three days."

"Wow." Norm wants more details, which I provide as the miles roll by and the landscape levels out. Norm listens intently. When I finish, he offers heartfelt thanks. From there on, we mostly listen to music until we reach the Gateway Arch. We expect Norm to drop us off at his exit. Instead, he takes us all the way through town and to the corn fields beyond. Before leaving, he writes down his phone number and lays a fresh doobie on us.

"For the road," he says.

"Two hundred and fifty miles," I say, at the foot of an off-ramp. "Not bad for a first ride."

We only have another half hour or so of daylight, so Stan suggests stopping here for the night. I agree. At a nearby 7-Eleven, we load up on supplies, including beer and snacks. Then we cross the two-lane road into a field thick with chest-high rows of corn. In the middle where we'll be invisible, we stop and unroll our sleeping bags. Stan pops the top off a newly acquired beer and lights up Norm's going-away present.

"I thought that dope was for the road," I say.

"This is the road. What, are you saving up for a rainy day?"

"Forget it." I'm still a little pissed at him for jumping in the way he did. "But how about the next time we check out our ride before getting in?"

Twitching his droopy moustache, he dips his head in consternation. He always reminds me of bearded Neptune when he does that. Neither of us says anything for a minute. Then he looks back up.

"You worry too much, Pate."

"Maybe you don't worry enough."

But when he offers the joint, I inhale sharply and lie back with my fingers clasped behind my head and watch the cornstalks turn gold.

"How far is it to Denver?" I say.

"I don't know. Another seven hundred miles?"

"Listen, I know some people there. Maybe they'll put us up."

"Sounds good," Stan says.

As the stalks become dark shapes, I start to wonder what Deborah Johnson, the woman I'd been living with, is doing right now. If she is happy without me. Why things turned out the way they did. She wanted to settle down, but I wasn't ready. Guess I'm still not. I muse on this until a slice of moon appears.

"What do you want out of life, Stan?"

"A little sleep, maybe. What do you want?"

"Man, I've been asleep my whole life. It's time to wake up. I want to think like I've never thought, feel like I've never felt, and do what I've never done." As I listen to the crickets' cries as never before, I imagine the wonders that lie ahead: purple mountains, sagebrush-dotted deserts, and the city by the bay.

When I awake, it's morning and the edge of the sky is light. The corn stalks sway in the breeze. Mosquitoes buzz. I curse and slap at them. Blissful as an old dog under a porch on a hot day, Stan says, "Good morning." When I don't reply, he adds, "What's the matter?"

"I feel like shit." My head's in a vise. It can't be a hangover, not on three beers even with Norm's killer weed. Maybe it's the rolled-up underwear I'm using for a pillow. I start to sit up, but reconsider. Another ten minutes go by before I'm finally on my feet. I stuff my sleeping bag into the rucksack and stumble through the corn across the road to the convenience store. When I ask for the bathroom key, the snippy old man behind the counter says, "Restroom's for paying customers only." It's too early to argue and my head hurts. I buy some aspirin, bug spray, and a felt-tip pen.

"Now can I have the key?"

When I see the throne room, I wonder what all the fuss was about. One grimy toilet, no hot water, and a filthy towel dispenser. I study my reflection in a nicked mirror. If I look this scruffy after one night, I wonder how bad I'll look in another week or two. I strip off my T-shirt and wash up. When I'm clean, I dry myself on the shirt and put it back on. Out in the parking lot, I spray bug repellent all over me like a dog being sprayed for fleas. By the time a scarecrow emerges from the cornfield, I'm having coffee and doughnuts. The strawman drops his rucksack beside mine.

"Man, I got bites all over me." I toss him the spray.

"Ever wonder why we say *man* at the beginning, or end, of every sentence?" I ask.

"Speak for yourself, man." He douses himself.

I grunt. I'm feeling cranky and impatient to get back on the road. While Stan dawdles, I scrounge up a piece of cardboard and make a "DENVER" sign with my new 7-Eleven felt-tipped marker. Standing on the side of the interstate, I hold up the sign for passing motorists to see.

"Smile, so they won't take you for a serial killer," I say.

"You look more like Manson than I do."

Distant cars and trucks grow steadily larger before whooshing by, swaying cattails in their backwash. A half hour passes before a big Mack truck with a bulldog hood ornament stops for us. As I climb up the running board, the window rolls down and a gravelly voice intones, "I'm headed to Topeka, if it'll help youse guys out."

I instantly recognize the east coast accent, having had a roommate from Delaware once. Lots of them came to Western Kentucky U. for the cheap tuition. Grabbing the door handle, I take a quick peek inside the cab. It's roomy. The driver is alone. Good. The only red flag is how bleary-eyed he seems and the reek of stale coffee and cigarettes that nearly knocks me down.

"Stow your gear in the back."

I watch Stan climb up, not believing how high we are. No wonder truckers act like lords of the highway. Our driver revs his engine and the semi jerks ahead.

"Hey, where ya from?" the trucker says. "Louie-ville? I come through there all the time. I'm Frank, from Joi-zee. Trenton. Ever been there?"

Ten gear shifts later, we're barreling down the highway. Frank says he stopped for us because he's been on the road for the last twenty-four hours and needs someone to keep him awake.

"Where youse going?"

When we tell him San Francisco, he says, "Are ya hippies, or what?"

"You tell me what a hippie is," I say, "and I'll tell you if that's what I am."

"You know, people who take drugs, but not baths."

"Har har. You take bennies to stay awake, don't you, Frank?" Stan says.

"So? That's different than pot."

"How? They're both illegal."

"Listen to this guy, will ya? Were you a college debater, or what?"

"I was a masturbator," Stan says.

Frank chortles at that. "Yeah, and you probably still are. You don't sound like no fuckin' hippie, though. Were you ever in the service?"

"As a matter of fact, I'm a Navy vet," Stan says. "Served in 'Nam."

"Yeah?" Frank looks at me. "What about you?"

I'm all talked out about the draft, so I just shake my head.

"I was in Korea myself," Frank volunteers, initiating a discussion of the wisdom of getting involved in Asian land wars.

All through Missouri, I nap. In Kansas, I'm dreaming of Deborah and Donald when something wakes me up. I open my eyes to find our driver asleep at the wheel and the truck weaving all over the highway.

"Frank!" I yell and jab him in the ribs with my elbow.

He startles awake groaning and jerks the wheel, guiding us precariously back into the correct lane. I look over at Stan, who unbelievably is still asleep. After this near catastrophe, Frank's wide awake for a while. But then his eyelids begin to droop again. About that time, I notice a sign reading, "County Fishing Lake." Stan and I exchange glances and immediately I tell Frank to pull over. Even though it's obvious he doesn't want to, he stops and lets us out.

I advise Frank he ought to put some flares out and catch a few Zs. But saying he's all right, off he goes.

Down a grassy embankment and over a wire fence, we exit from the interstate and hike back toward the lake, which takes longer than expected. Finally arriving, we find it deserted with no facilities. This doesn't bother us. In fact, it's perfect, being isolated and tucked away in the woods. The lake itself is small and irregularly shaped. It sits in a little valley of dusty pine, oak, and dogwood. The place is teeming with gnats and flies. When I dip my fingers into the lake, it's cool and inviting.

Stan asks if I want to go for a swim.

"What if somebody comes?"

"Who's going to come?"

We strip and dog paddle around. "Think there's any fish in here?"

"Bluegill, I imagine. Maybe crappie. Want to catch our supper?"

When I ask how, he gives me a pitying look, climbs the rocky bank to get dressed, and thrashes off through the timber.

I linger in the water. It's been two days now, and I'm beginning to get a clearer picture of what life on the road with Stan will be like, even when things go smoothly. Sleeping in a cornfield with its attendant aches and pains and chigger bites. Dealing with surly people. Being careful not to say things that might upset our rides. Surviving on junk food, coffee, and alcohol. We were lucky to find this place. No telling where we'd wind up next time.

I'm dressed when Stan returns, flexing a long weeping willow branch he's found. After testing its suppleness, he strips off the leaves. Then he rummages through his gear and pulls out a paper clip and a roll of monofilament, which he ties tightly around the thin end of the bare branch, leaving about six feet hanging off the tip. Bending the paper clip into a question mark, he sharpens it against a rock.

"Now all we need is bait. Bluegill will bite on almost anything."

Surrounded by Johnson grass and purple ironweed, I crouch, cupping my hands. I catch a brown mottled grasshopper and give it to Stan, who threads his primitive fishing hook between its eyes. This makes me squeamish but doesn't bother him at all. Then he flicks the baited hook into the water along the edge of the lake.

"Wouldn't we do better in deeper water?" I inquire.

"See the weed beds and brush piles? They give the fish cover." He retrieves his line. "Why don't you build a fire while I catch some fish." He casts again, making rapid light movements with the pole.

I gather twigs and dead branches for kindling. When I have enough, I ask, "How are we going to cook the fish? Roast it on a spit?"

"No. Gather up some big rocks and make two stacks," Stan says, all the while keeping his attention on the water. "Build the cooking fire between the stacked rocks. Then put a thin flat piece of rock on top for a cooking surface. Unless you'd rather fish."

"That's okay. You're doing fine." I gather rocks. When he lands our first catch, I observe, "Not very big, are they."

"Bluegill don't get big."

Stan unhooks the writhing fish and puts it on the grass, where it flops helplessly until he bangs its scaly head on a stone outcropping. I snag another grasshopper. Stan re-baits his hook. And by the time I have a decent fire going, he's landed two more bluegill.

"Want to clean them?" He offers me his thin-bladed fillet knife.

I shake my head. "Fishing line, hook, knife. You've got everything, don't you?"

"'Be prepared.'"

"That's the Boy Scout motto. Were you a scout?"

"Son, I was an Eagle Scout. How about you?"

"Only a Cub."

Stan slices the catch from gills to backbone, then all the way along the spine to the tail and pulls out the offal. "Why'd you quit?"

"Had to. We moved."

He puts our fillets on the hot rock and pulls out a doobie.

"I didn't know you were holding. Why didn't you tell me?" I ask.

"I just had the one." He lights it. By the time the joint's half-smoked, the sun has dipped behind the trees, the horizon purple and gray. Tossing a pebble into the water, I hear a satisfying plunk. Bull-frogs croak. Crickets chirrup. Cicadas click.

"Ah," Stan says, flipping our dinner over carefully with a stick, "the simple life. Think how much time people waste working jobs they hate to acquire stuff they don't need. Ever seen a picture of Thoreau's house? It was tiny—just ten by fifteen."

"I guess you could call this our own private Walden Pond."

"Damn straight."

"Thoreau lived at Walden for what? A year? We don't have that much time if we ever expect to catch up with the Summer of Love."

"That was four years ago, Pate."

"Yeah but remember what Mark Twain said about Kentucky. He hoped that's where he'd be when he died because everything happens in Kentucky twenty years later than everywhere else."

"I guess you figure we're ahead of schedule then."

I grin.

The sizzling fish smells wonderful. We eat it with our fingers. It tastes wonderful, too. I put another branch on the fire, stirring up sparks and bits of white ash that rise and float away.

"We should be in Denver by tomorrow night," I say. "My friends there might put us up. We could take a hot shower and sleep on a mattress instead of on the ground. I could call."

"Okay." Stan passes the joint, tilts his head back. "Look at all the stars."

I shift my gaze. "I've never seen so many." We sit quietly, smoking what's left of the marijuana.

"Do you believe in God, Stan?"

"Yeah, I guess. I don't really know. What about you?"

Poking a stick at the fire, I tell him about being dragged to a holy-roller church every Sunday as a kid, where the sermon was invariably hellfire and brimstone. "They were always collecting to send missionaries to Christianize Africans. But when the neighborhood turned black, they moved the church to the suburbs. Bunch of fucking hypocrites."

I toss the stick into the flames and listen to the fire crackle.

After a while, Stan bends and twists his legs into a pretzel shape. He tells me it's a half lotus. A chick named Carla showed him how to do it.

"It opens the central conduit so you can drink the nectar of your essence," he says.

"Opens the *what*?"

"Or some bullshit like that," he says.

"So, you can drink *what*?"

"Shut up," he says.

I obey, inhaling and holding onto the smoke before exhaling. "What happened to Carla?"

"Hell if I know."

"Have you ever had a real girlfriend for more than a week?"

"Once, back in high school."

I'm expecting more baloney, but his tone is deadly serious with a bitter edge.

"Cheerleader named Teresa. She had perfect skin and big green eyes. We dated my whole senior year and broke up on graduation night." Stan explains that he had a basketball scholarship. The plan was for Teresa to go with him. "But I guess down deep she was a practical girl because after we walked across the stage and picked up our diplomas, she told me she'd decided to go to some out of state college on her own. When I asked her about us, she said, 'Oh, Stan, these high school romances don't last.'"

Untangling his legs, he picks up a twig and starts whittling. After a long silence, he says, "Thoreau believed we can't begin to understand ourselves until we're lost."

"Thoreau? Again?"

"Thoreau's the man, man." Stan keeps whittling until that twig is nothing but scattered shavings.

The next morning, the sun rises in orange, gold, and violet layers. I hobble barefoot over to the pond feeling stiff from another night of sleeping on the ground and splash cool water in my face. Part of me wishes we could stay on another day and swim and fish and talk about things that matter. But Stan has grown restless. After some Twinkies and water, we hike back to I-70. I've heard hitchhiking described as a great way to spend hours with people you otherwise might never meet. But you can't meet them if they don't pick you up. Somewhere ahead, I know, there are pink mountains, green mesas, and sand-colored arroyos just waiting for us. But here in Kansas, it's nothing but flat grasslands all the way to the horizon.

An hour later, a red Plymouth Valiant pulls over. The driver, a middle-aged guy wearing a straw hat, says he's only going to the next town. We've been waiting for so long we're a little let down, but a ride is a ride. Asked if there's a good place to eat breakfast here, our bene-factor names Mary Ruth's Café. "Best flapjacks in town."

Twenty minutes later, we're peering through Mary Ruth's front window and smelling hot coffee and bacon. Inside, clean-shaven, short-haired working men occupy half a dozen tables and chrome stools. Plates are clanking, boisterous voices raised. But the instant we step in the door, there's a hush. Everyone turns to stare at us.

"What the hell you want?" says a fat man in bib overalls.

The whole situation has a dream quality, like I've just walked into an old western movie. But what amazes me most is that the man in the overalls bears such a striking resemblance to one Haystacks Muldoon, a professional wrestler who was on TV when I was a kid.

"Breakfast," Stan says with a smile.

"They just ran out," Haystacks says.

"No, they didn't," Stan says.

Haystacks rises, along with his companion, who is no Gorgeous George. Everyone else in the place seems eager for the tag-team match to begin. Me, I'm too busy imagining being head-scissored, hammer-locked, and camel-clutched. I shove my hands into my pockets to hide the fact that they're shaking. But first, there must be the ritual exchange of taunts. Nothing so elegant as, "Thou art like a toad, ugly and venomous." More on the order of:

"We don't like hippies around here." (Haystacks).

"Or faggots." (Gorgeous).

"Which one of us is which, do you think?" Stan says.

It puzzles Haystacks momentarily, but then he says, "What if we just kick both your asses?"

I've seen *Easy Rider*. This is exactly the sort of trouble I've dreaded. Fortunately, we're not out on the highway and they're not toting shot-guns. Otherwise, we might as well be Wyatt and Billy. Nevertheless, I'm measuring the distance to the front door when a stout woman with a smudge of flour on her cheek appears from the kitchen. She's carry-ing pancakes on platters and looks like somebody's maiden aunt, but there's steel in her voice and she loses no time sizing up the situation.

"Lloyd, Boyd, what are you two doin'?" she says.

"Why nothin' much, Mary Ruth," Haystacks says. "Just fixin' to take out the trash."

"Remember what I told you the last time you picked a fight in here?"

"Yes, ma'am, but—"

"Don't you *but* me. You better act like you remember, unless you want to be barred forever. Do you?"

"No, ma'am."

"Then sit down and eat your flapjacks and keep your big mouth shut. Understand?"

Haystacks sits. So does Gorgeous. Everyone else looks disappointed, but soon goes back to eating noisily.

"You boys want coffee?" Mary Ruth asks us. "There's room over at the counter."

Mary Ruth brings us coffee and plastic menus.

"Don't mind those McKutchen boys. They're not bad-hearted, just a little light in the head. You want the special? Most folks do. It's flapjacks with bacon and eggs and hash browns."

She clips our orders to a flat rotating wheel that carries them through an opening to the kitchen.

I glance over at Stan. "What were you trying to do, get us killed?"

Moustache twitching, Stan says in a low voice, "Just the opposite. Only one way to deal with bullies: back 'em down."

"And if that doesn't work?"

"Then we probably get our asses whipped."

"Oh, well, that's okay then. But next time, warn me first."

Mary Ruth's pancakes turn out to be tasty, light brown with darker edges, a pat of butter melting on top, and a pitcher of maple syrup in easy reach. We eat everything, then head to the restroom to clean up. Noticing a public phone on the wall, I consider calling Matthew Duncan, who I heard had married Rebecca Adams, who was putting him through grad school at Denver University. Matthew and I were never close at Western. In fact, the last time I saw him he was so angry he wanted to kick my butt at an after-graduation party out in the country. But we're all a long way from home now, and Matthew might be happy to see a familiar face. I decide to postpone calling until we're closer to Denver.

We're both halfway expecting to get jumped as we leave, but the rednecks have gone.

Up to now, I've put aside my fears, but this incident has reawakened them. As we hike back to the interstate, part of me wants to turn right around and go home. I have no desire to die young, a prospect that suddenly seems to have grown in likelihood. I've been in lots of fistfights, but that was before I became whoever it is that I am now.

A curious farmer gives us a lift to Junction City in his pickup truck. As the highway unspools shiny and black, we tell him about our journey so far, including the recent excitement, which we both downplay, and then a bit about where we hope to wind up—i.e., a commune in San Francisco. In turn, he tells us about growing the crops we see in the fields—oats, soybeans, hay. He says that every little town from Salina to Oakley has its own grain elevator and water tower.

By mid-afternoon, we cross the state line into Colorado. I'm expecting the flat lands to turn instantly into mountains, but of course they don't. The outline of the Rockies won't appear until we're near Denver. The level prairie doesn't even become rolling rangelands until we're west of Burlington, where some heartless rancher drops us off in the middle of nowhere. Stan seems disappointed, but one thing I know—and like—about him is how easily he'll get over it. All we need is one more ride to make it to Denver tonight.

Ten minutes later, a battered old station wagon stops for us. The driver is wearing a suit. I'm surprised he stops because he doesn't look hip at all. But rejecting his help is not an option.

"Looks like we're going to the same place," he says, pointing at my now tattered hand-lettered sign.

Stan is calling, "Shotgun," and climbing aboard. I get into the back seat beside what looks like a sample case, the kind traveling salesmen carry.

"Don Murphy, from Wichita," the driver says. "Call me Murph."

"This is a Country Squire, Murph?" Stan asks, as the car stutters forward.

"Ford's premium station wagon."

"Did you know that's the same model as a Woodie?" Stan says. "Except there's no wood strip in back."

"You mean like a surfer's beach buggy? No, I didn't know that," Murph says.

"Pretty cool," Stan says.

"Merwin," Murph says to me. "Is that Welsh? Sounds like it."

"Yeah, I think so."

"And Hicks?"

"German," Stan says.

"I'm half-Irish and half-German myself," Murph says. "I'm in household products. Cleaning items. Are you guys out here looking for work?"

"Just passing through," I tell him.

"Where you headed?"

"To the coast," I say.

"California?" Murph twists around to look at me. "I used to work a route out there myself."

"Why would anyone leave California for Kansas?" Stan asks.

"Too many wetbacks," Murph says. "Don't get me wrong. I got nothing against them. But I gotta make a living, right? And Mex— they don't buy. If I don't sell, my family don't eat."

"You like being a salesman?" I say, hoping to change the subject before it blows up.

"I love being a road warrior," he says. "The secret of being a successful salesman is you've got to like people. If you don't, they can tell, and you won't sell them a thing. Got a joke for you."

He tells us one about a traveling salesman whose car becomes hopelessly stuck in the snow. "It takes him several hours to make it to the nearest farmhouse. When the farmer answers, the half-frozen salesman pleads for a place to spend the night. 'Why sure, young fellow, I can give you a place to bunk,' the farmer says. 'But I got no daughter for you to sleep with, like you always hear about in jokes.' The salesman replies, 'In that case, how far is it to the next house?'"

Murph laughs heartily at his own joke.

"I'm pretty sure you two are not in sales," he says. "So what's your game?"

"We're panhandlers," Stan says.

"Bums, you mean?" Murph squints at Stan, who nods, deadpan. "How do you manage to keep your self-respect?"

"Oh, that's easy," Stan says. "We're Communists."

Murph hits the brakes and pulls over into the emergency stop lane. "Get out," he thunders. As he drives away, Stan yells, "I served in Vietnam, asshole."

And here we are again, once more standing on the side of the road.

"Goddamn it, Stan. I hope you enjoyed that. Panhandlers? Communists? Where did that shit come from?"

"Guy was an asshole."

"An asshole who was giving us a ride."

Boiling mad, I kick a rock on the shoulder, sending it skittering across the road. It's fifty minutes before another driver stops to pick us up and I am pissed at Stan the whole time. I've started to wonder if we can, in fact, make it to the West Coast together. It seems like we've been skirmishing all day long.

When our next ride turns out to be in another big rig, one that's headed right for Denver, I'm so grateful I sling my backpack into the storage area and hoist myself into the middle seat without giving it a second thought.

"Name's Vernon, from Abilene," the driver says, and spits a greenish-black stream into the foam cup resting between his thighs.

Now I know why the cab stinks.

Stan joins me.

As Vernon shifts into first, he asks who we are, where we're coming from, and what's in Denver for us. We tell him our names, that we're from Louisville, and out here to visit friends in the Mile High City.

"What's that you're chewing?" Stan asks.

"Beechnut." Dark spittle dribbles down Vernon's chin. He wipes it off, then rubs his dirty hand on his jeans. "Want some?"

Not on your life, I'm thinking.

But Stan says, "Sure," surprising me again, and Vernon hands over a little hockey puck-sized can.

"Take a pinch and let it sit between your lip and gum. When the saliva builds up, spit it out."

Soon, what looks like a wad of bubblegum appears in Stan's cheek. I glare at him. Unbelievable. With a sheepish grin, Stan says, "Pate's more the clean-living type."

"Was once one myself," Vernon says, "but look at me now."

He's a wreck. Scraggly gray beard but little other hair, except for tufts sprouting from his ears and nose. Sleeveless flannel shirt apparently tailored with a Bowie knife. He wears red suspenders plus a wide hand-tooled belt. The more I study Vernon, the more he reminds me of the old prospector played by Walter Huston in *The Treasure of the Sierra Madre*.

"Shows what bad habits will do to you." Vernon spits into the cup again. I'm wondering if he ever misses. "Been on the road for ten hours straight. Don't want to be noddin' off."

As we speed along, gaining elevation, paralleling a white rock ridge, Stan and Vernon talk baseball. Not Stan's favorite sport, but to my surprise a subject he knows a lot about. Seems the Oakland Athletics have a rookie southpaw named Blue, of all things, who is off to a ten-and-one start. I pay scant attention to their ramblings, instead focusing one eye on the edge of the road so as not to be blinded by oncoming headlights, a trick my first stepfather taught me. He also taught me to fear and loathe him.

"Behold the Promised Land," Vernon says.

When I raise my eyes, a monumental blue silhouette is visible in the distance.

"The Rocky Mountains," Vernon says. "They run all the way from Canada to New Mexico. Someday I'm going to drive every inch of them."

For now, he confines himself to the stretch leading into Denver, where we arrive two and a half hours later. Vernon lets us off downtown near the state capitol. Like Lewis and Clark, we've reached a landscape of infinite scale and wild grandeur and done it in only three days' time.

2

Eight months earlier, October 1970

I was standing in Deborah Johnson's line at a downtown bank in Louisville. All I knew about her (besides her name, which was printed on a little tented sign at her teller's window) was her shapeliness and the contours and planes of her face, which reminded me of a sculpted African mask—the kind that accompanies a ritual sacrifice, a splashing of blood, permission needed from the tree itself before it could be cut down. Whenever I came in to cash my paycheck, she looked professional—today she wore a beige blouse and a charcoal skirt—and had a pleasant smile for me. But I hoped for much more.

As I stood there appreciating Deborah's curves, an image of a driftwood coffee table popped into my head. I remembered seeing a photo of one while standing in line at the grocery store. The wood had been sanded down and an interesting piece of glass attached to the top. Clever and unusual, I'd thought.

When my turn at Deborah's window came, she said, "Hello, Mr. Merwin."

Pleased that she remembered my name, I said, "Call me Pate," and she smiled again.

While she processed my paycheck, I stared at the wall mural behind her depicting my hometown as a backwoods outpost, which in some ways it still was. We'd abolished slavery a century ago, for instance, but here in 1970 interracial romance still remained taboo. As Deborah counted out my money, her fingertips brushed against mine.

Should I let this moment go by, as if our worlds hadn't just collided? I took a deep breath of dust, furniture polish, and floor wax, all part of the building's slow deterioration, and said, "I was wondering. What kind of furniture do you have in your apartment?"

Deborah looked quizzical, as if I'd suddenly gone out of my head with fever. "What makes you think I live in an apartment?" she said. "Maybe I live in a mansion. Where do you live?"

"In an apartment on Saint James Court."

"That's a good area," Deborah smiled.

"Well, it used to be." Fearing she'd think I was bemoaning the number of blacks who'd moved in, I quickly explained that owners had subdivided many of the old Victorian homes into apartments. "I couldn't afford to live there otherwise, not on a substitute teacher's pay."

"You're a sub? You don't look like the ones I used to have."

"I know at least one principal who'd agree with you. He sent me home today because I didn't look professional." I opened my pea coat. "What do you think?"

Her eyes flicked over my bell-bottoms and U.S. Navy work shirt. "You look fine. I hope you don't lose your job."

"Oh, they need subs too much for that. Like today, I got paid even though I didn't do any work. As long as I'm willing to go anywhere and teach anything, they'll guarantee me an assignment every day. I've taught musical instruments I couldn't play and languages I couldn't speak. Plus, I get to keep my beard."

"I like beards," she said.

I looked around, wondering if I was holding up the line. But I was the only customer in the place. "How do you feel about driftwood?"

She looked puzzled, as well she might.

"Why did you ask?"

"I just wondered what you'd think about a coffee table made out of it. I liked a picture of one I saw in a magazine. It made me think of you for some reason."

"Why?"

"I don't know. Maybe because it's beautiful?"

She didn't laugh or frown, just looked at me thoughtfully.

"I was thinking about making one for you." I glanced at her ring finger. "I mean, if your husband wouldn't mind."

I realized this was the dumbest thing I'd said yet. What husband wouldn't mind? Idiot!

She held up her ring. "This was my mother's."

"You're not married? Would you like to go out with me some time?"

"Is that what took you so long? I thought you'd never ask."

"How about tonight?"

"My, you start slow, but then you go real fast."

Her place was about fifteen minutes from mine, if you knew the way. And I did, though I hadn't been down in the West End for years. Now as I entered the underpass near 15th Street, a freight train rumbled overhead and a steam whistle moaned, sounding sad and beautiful in the fading daylight.

Near Dixie Highway, the industrial look changed to residential, with shotgun houses replacing mammoth warehouses and manufacturing plants. Deeper into the West End, I arrived at 44th and River Park Drive, where stood Flaget High, a storied but declining parochial school, whose football team was once an athletic powerhouse. I turned onto River Park, where the residences were the same kind of California bungalows with covered concrete porches that had been there during the late 1950s when blacks were, in the phrase we'd used back then, *taking over* the area. As if aliens had invaded our shores.

It was reassuring to find that some of the modest one- and two-story brick structures on Deborah's block still seemed well-maintained. But at others plywood was nailed over the doors and windows. Such was the case at Deborah's place, as I discovered after parking out front. I walked around to the side of her house and that door was boarded up, too.

What have you done to your hair? I thought in astonishment when she answered my knock. All that beautiful shoulder-length hair gone, replaced by a short springy Afro.

"Don't you like my hair this way?" she asked, instantly reading my mind. "I only wear the fall to work."

Fall? Oh, she was telling me it was a wig. I'd never known anyone who wore one.

"You look great."

"You better say that." She smiled. "Sorry about the door. Somebody's always breaking in around here."

I didn't much like the sound of that, though I couldn't say I was too surprised, based on the neighborhood's appearance. It was disconcerting to realize, however, that I was concerned not only for her safety but my own. *Get a grip*, I thought, as she led me through a hallway. *Be a man*. In the center of the kitchen a little boy with a big Afro was eating macaroni and cheese at the table. Deborah had not mentioned having any children, but he sure looked a lot like her. I wondered why she hadn't told me she had a child. Had she been afraid I wouldn't show up if I knew?

"This is my son, Donald."

I said hello and offered to shake hands. He didn't respond.

"What have I told you? Remember your manners. And hold your fork like this." Deborah demonstrated.

"How old is he?"

"Five."

"Are you in kindergarten, Donald?"

"He goes to nursery school."

I looked at Deborah. "Quiet, isn't he?"

"He doesn't know you yet."

I crouched down so I could look the kid in the eye. "I hope we're going to be good friends, Don."

"I wish you wouldn't call him that," Deborah said.

"Why? Doesn't he like it?"

"I don't like it."

I felt that I was on shaky ground with her. Maybe this wasn't such a good idea after all. Maybe she was thinking the same thing.

I watched her dab his chin with a napkin and start clearing the table before I asked what she'd like to do tonight.

"Oh, I don't know," she said, and began filling the sink with soapy water. "Why don't you surprise me?"

At this, my anxiety level went up another notch. I'd thought of suggesting a drink at Joe's Palm Room, a cool old jazz club at 18th and Jefferson where our presence wouldn't raise any eyebrows. In fact, it was the only place I could think of. I just had never seen many mixed-race couples around town. What if she didn't like that idea? Then what the hell would I do?

Deborah quickly finished the dishes and marched Donald off to the bedroom, saying they'd be ready in a few minutes, and to wait in the living room, which proved as small and spotless as the kitchen. But what instantly caught my eye was the coffee table, which was small and inexpensive-looking. When I gave it the touch test, it wobbled. I didn't know whether to be thrilled or terrified because it meant I would likely have the opportunity, and the need, to produce one as good as I'd boasted. And my woodworking skills were not exactly tip top. I wished I hadn't made such a dumb offer.

Taking a deep breath to steady myself, I looked over the room's other equally modest furnishings: an armchair, fake black leather couch, and a small bookcase. A twelve-inch black and white TV was on top of the bookcase. No photographs or pictures on the walls. No books in the bookcase, only inexpensive stereo equipment and an array of LP records. I looked through them, hoping to learn something personal about Deborah, but found nothing except a bunch of Motown and James Brown.

By the time she came in with Donald, I'd calmed down a bit and he was already bundled up and ready to go. "Would you mind dropping him off at his grandfather's house at 37th and Market?" she asked.

"Why not bring him along?"

"Not tonight. Tonight, we get to know each other."

That made me smile. When she saw my '61 Falcon parked at the curb, it was her turn to smile.

"Is that yours?"

"Valve clatter, bald tires, and all."

"Oh, it's nice, Pate."

I liked the way she said my name. How she slid in beside me, too. I could feel the warmth of her body.

"Can we listen to some music?" said Donald.

"Ah, he speaks," I said. "Sorry, Bud, but the radio doesn't work. Tell you what, though. If your mom will go out with me again after tonight, I'll get it fixed."

"That's not up to him." Deborah drew a little away from me. "And please don't call him Bud."

Wow, I thought, this chick is an emotional roller coaster. Or a minefield.

I was still smarting five minutes later when we got to her father's house, also a California bungalow, but free of plywood and well-kept. As I started to walk the two of them up to the door, Deborah stopped me and said to wait in the car because her father was "old-fashioned."

Which probably meant he didn't like white people, especially if they were dating his daughter. I'd expected problems from my family, but now I saw there were going to be more. Many more.

Deborah got back in the car. "What are we going to do tonight?"

"I was thinking Joe's Palm Room."

"Sounds good, but I have a better idea," she said, sliding closer. "Let's go to your place."

This seemed almost too good to be true. Almost.

"Okay," I said.

No girl had ever suggested going back to my place on the first date. The thought of it gave me goosebumps. This was the stuff of dreams. Maybe my fevered ones of Deborah were going to come true after all. I could hardly believe it. She was so good-looking and so far, race had not proven much of a barrier. I wondered how long this could last before my good fortune ran out.

My place, which I shared with a roommate, was a two-bedroom apartment on the third floor of a fine old Victorian brick house located near downtown. Built around the turn of the century, it had been partially restored by my landlord, who occupied the first two floors. I proudly pointed out the fluted columns, odd angles, and arched windows as we circled the long grassy esplanade in the middle of Saint James Court, a street that I remembered had impressed her, while I tried to find a parking place.

"Do you live there all by yourself?" Deborah asked

"No, I share it with my old college roommate Stan Hicks."

For whom I was conducting a surreptitious search at that very moment, hoping his yellow VW bug wasn't around. As the Victorian gas lamps came on, a space by the elegant fountain opened up and I grabbed it. The fountain was located in the center of the court. In it, a bronze sculpture of Venus rose from the sea. Half a dozen houses south, we came to a brick pathway leading to my front porch. Deborah expressed her admiration for the climbing roses and porch swing, and inside the carpeted foyer, the elaborate woodwork and stained glass windows.

We went up to the third floor, entering my place through the kitchen. Deborah walked from room to room, noticing everything from the mirrored mantel over the fireplace to all the polished hardwood floors. My bedroom, formerly the parlor, overlooked the court. She paused to take in the view. Stan's bedroom, which she checked out next, faced the alley.

"This is beautiful, Pate." Her big brown eyes gleamed. "But where's your coffee table?"

That again. "Did it seem weird for me to offer to make one for you?"

"Maybe a little bit. Did you mean what you said? Or was that just a line?"

"More of a spur of the moment idea. I noticed you already have a coffee table."

"Yeah, but you're not off the hook. I've always hated that rickety old thing. Tell me more about the one you're going to make for me."

"Handmade, naturally curved, unique. How does that sound?"

"Good enough to drink to, if I had a drink."

"Sorry."

I opened the bottle of chardonnay I'd chilled for just this occasion and poured us each a glass.

"To you," I said, and sat beside her on the sofa, which was really a love seat, in front of the fireplace. I craved being closer to this exciting, remarkable woman.

"To us." We clinked glasses.

"Nice wine," she said.

"Glad you like it." As all true Louisville natives must, I next asked her if she was "from here."

"Does being born here count?" She'd grown up in Detroit, she said, and only moved back recently. "What about you?"

I told her I was a Louisville native and had lived here most of my life. "How about some music?" I put John Lennon on the turntable.

While he was singing about giving peace a chance, Deborah said, "Speaking of peace, I noticed your peace symbol bumper sticker. So, I take it you're against the war?"

"Oh, yeah."

"Me, too," she said. "Are you worried about getting drafted?"

"No."

"Why not?"

"I'm 1-Y. I flunked my draft physical."

"I see." She drank some wine.

I could tell she wanted to know why. Everybody did. It was no secret, except from the draft board, of course. But I was careful about enlightening strangers. Deborah was no stranger, however.

"High blood pressure," I said.

"You have high blood pressure?"

"No, but they think I do."

"Why do they think that?"

I had to explain.

Three weeks before my college graduation last May, when I should've been focused on final exams, all I could think about was my draft physical. If I passed, it would be goodbye Bowling Green, hello Saigon. And for what? I didn't believe anything that Richard Nixon said. He'd promised to end the war. Then after he was elected, he'd widened it by invading Cambodia. And the four Kent State students shot to death by the Ohio National Guard had convinced me that the government would kill any of us, even right here, if they thought it was in their interest. So thanks, but no, thanks, to serving in the military.

"When the doc saw my blood pressure, he told me to lie down," I said. "He was afraid I was about to have a stroke. What he didn't know was that I'd dropped speed the night before and stayed up, not getting any sleep."

"Wasn't he suspicious?" Deborah asked.

"If he was, he kept it to himself."

I told her I thought I'd fooled them by cutting my hair and beard off, wearing preppy clothes, and not doing anything stupid—like pretending I couldn't hear during the hearing test. For the next three nights, I'd stayed up, taken more speed, and failed all the follow-up blood pressure tests. Now I was home free.

"Does it ever bother you, knowing what you did?" Deborah asked.

"Sometimes," I admitted. "But why should it? I couldn't get conscientious objector status because I'm not religious. My only choices were to either dodge the draft, go to prison, or leave the country. Which one would you have chosen?"

"Honey," she smiled, placing her hand on mine, "I'm with Muhammad Ali. Why would I shoot brown people in Vietnam when I get treated like a dog in Louisville?"

I guess she read the white guilt in my face—she was really good at that, I realized, very intuitive and sharp—because she placed her hand on my shoulder and smiled. "Not your fault, Pate. Well, maybe some. You are white." Then she turned serious. "I'll tell you one thing, though. They'll never get their hands on Donald."

Our talk was interrupted at this point by the sound of footsteps on the stairs. A few seconds later, the door to the apartment swung open, and there stood a lanky six-feet-five inches of untrimmed whiskers and shaggy light brown hair, in cut-off green camos and a Navy T-shirt, clutching a six-pack under each arm.

"Want a beer?"

I held up my wine glass. "No thanks, Stan."

"Sorry, Pate, didn't realize you were having company tonight."

"Deborah, my roommate Stan Hicks. Stan, meet Deborah Johnson."

"You're tall," she told him.

"And you sound like a northerner," Stan said.

"You think I'm the one with the accent?"

Grinning, he flopped on the floor. After yanking a beer from the six pack's plastic ring, he produced a joint. "If you don't want any beer, how about smoking some dope?"

My heart started hammering again, but I didn't really think someone as urban savvy as Deborah would freak out over a little grass. As a matter of fact, I'd intended to offer her some weed myself later on this evening when we were better acquainted. But I was displeased with Stan for forcing the issue. He got the jay lit and passed to her. She inhaled deeply.

"You've done this before," Stan said.

"Are you serious? I'm from Detroit."

"Well, I'm from Shively," Stan said. "Lively Shively."

He meant anything except lively, but she seemed to know that already.

"How did you two meet?" she asked.

"On the basketball court in a pick-up game down in Bowling Green at Western Kentucky University. I was going to college to collect on my GI Bill after 'Nam."

"You were in Vietnam?" Deborah said.

"On a ship off the coast. Seaman First Class Stanley J. Hicks, U.S. Navy, at your service, ma'am." Stan saluted.

"But what about the war? Pate's against it."

"So am I," Stan said, "now." He explained that he'd enlisted to please his old man, who was a quartermaster during WWII. But the longer he was in the service, the less sense the war made to him. "We couldn't win," he said. "Never should have gone there in the first place." By the time Stan figured this out, it was too late. He was in the middle of the ocean. It was fight or go to the brig.

Smoke hovered near the ceiling. I felt we'd covered the subject and I wanted some time alone with Deborah. "Don't you have somewhere else you need to be, Stan?"

"If you mean the VFW, it doesn't open till eight."

"No, that's not what I mean."

"Are you talking about the Veterans of Foreign Wars?" Deborah asked. "You're against the war and still go there. You must have a death wish."

"Nah," Stan said. "It's cool. We're all brothers in arms, though I try to show them the error of their ways."

He launched into a story about a vet who wouldn't shut up the other night about how much he loved the service.

"I told him I loved the Navy, too," Stan said. "Where else do you get plenty of chow, a warm bunk, and a roof over your head just for risking your life to prop up a corrupt dictatorship?"

The vet told Stan that if he'd ever served on an aircraft carrier, he'd see things different.

"But I had served on a carrier," Stan said. "The Ranger, in '67, five months on the line, Yankee Station off North Vietnam. I told him our planes hit everything from ferries and bridges to airfields and sur-face-to-air missile sites. Sometimes at night, you could see the fire. We were that close."

I'd heard this story before, so I got up and, giving my roommate the evil eye, lit the gas logs. He didn't seem to notice.

"Most of the time, though, I just typed requisitions," Stan said. "Closest to actual combat I got was in the hangar bay, mask-taping holes in the wings of shot-up A-4s."

"Well," I said, lighting incense which I put on the mantel, "that's all been very interesting, Stan. But now don't let us keep you."

"Well, nice meeting you, Deborah," he said. "No, Pate, don't ask me to stay."

After using the head, he left, taking all his beer with him.

"What do you think of my roomie?"

"Seemed like a nice guy," Deborah said.

I laughed. We smoked.

"You know, this is really good dope, baby."

No woman had ever called me that before. I liked it. Putting Cros-by, Stills & Nash on the stereo, I poured some more wine. "So, what's your story, Deborah from Detroit?"

She tucked her feet under her. "Not much to tell."

Her mother had died when she was thirteen. From a heart attack, she said. Her father couldn't take care of her and lay track for the L&N Railroad. So, he sent her to live with his wife's sister in Michigan. Deborah didn't see him again for another four years.

"What was it like up there?"

"Lonely," she said, "being by myself all the time."

"Didn't you have any friends?"

"One, but my auntie wouldn't let him come over."

"Why not?"

"Auntie didn't trust him."

"Was she right not to trust him?"

"She meant she didn't trust me."

In the background CSN were singing about helplessly hoping, a feeling I knew all too well.

"Why didn't your auntie trust you?"

"Well, she did catch me sneaking him upstairs one time."

We laughed.

After a pause, she added, "I was seventeen when the baby started showing."

I couldn't imagine how that must have felt. I wondered if this baby was Donald. He was the right age.

"When my auntie tried to put him up for adoption, I brought him back to Louisville. We stayed with my father for a while, until he started trying to run my life. Then I got a place of my own. But enough about me. Let's talk about you. Did you always want to be a teacher?"

"Does anyone? It was something to fall back on."

"Why did you need a fall back?"

I told her about wanting to be a journalist. How I'd been promised a reporting job at my hometown paper after college. But then I'd resigned from the campus newspaper because our faculty adviser refused to publish anti-war editorials. When I came back to town to interview, the new managing editor, a colonel in the National Guard, declined to employ me. She asked what about other newspapers around the country. I said I'd applied to practically every one of them. They all wanted to know why I wasn't going back to work for the Louisville papers.

"Hence, teaching."

"Are you going to stick with it?"

"Who knows?" I got a candle out of a drawer and stuck it in the now-empty wine bottle. "Maybe I'll write a novel instead."

"You going to write one about me?"

I lit the candle. "Depends on how interesting you turn out to be."

"Honey, you have no idea."

We kissed, and kept on kissing, until the candle wax was dripping on the hardwood floor.

Pulling back, she said, "Is this the first time you've ever dated a black girl? You're not just experimenting with me, are you?"

I thought about it, trying to say something honest, but I couldn't decide on a response.

"I should go," she said.

"What's wrong?"

"I have to work tomorrow morning."

Bitterly disappointed, I blew out the guttering candle and got to my feet, every nerve in my body prickling.

I didn't know if I'd ever see Deborah again after that. But when I called, she said yes.

This time, I told her, I'd pick up the two of them and bring them over to my place.

Driving down West Market Street, I passed Shawnee High. At one time, I'd lived behind the school and I recalled many happy hours of playing on the grounds with my friends. But as I got closer to Shawnee Park, I noticed dismaying changes in the neighborhood. Medical and dental offices were now boarded up and the old corner grocery store had been burned to the ground.

The biggest change came at the end of Market Street by the river, where Fontaine Ferry amusement park had stood for over half a century. Two years ago, rioters had burned it down, too. No more

Ferris wheel, or roller coaster, or swimming pool. Just a huge vacant lot was all that remained. I thought I understood why it had happened. Tension over segregation at the park had built up in a series of small seismic shocks, and finally erupted in an explosion of rage. If they wouldn't let me in the park because of my race, I'd probably have wanted to destroy it, too. But I still felt a sense of loss, as if someone close to me had died.

Back at my apartment, I vowed there would be no more mistakes. This time, I was burning everything—candles, incense, dope, bridges. I'd already made sure Stan wasn't going to barge in on us again. A basket-wrapped bottle of Chianti stood breathing on the table. On the stereo George Harrison was singing about the pain we cause by breaking each other's hearts.

It hadn't taken long for Donald to fall asleep in my bed after dinner, and now Deborah and I lay on the floor across the room on a sleeping bag.

"What if he wakes up?" I said.

"He won't. He's exhausted from watching *Spider-Man* and *Lost in Space.*"

"Yeah, but what if?"

Deborah put her finger to my lips, unbuttoned her blouse, and took it off. In the shimmering candlelight, her skin was the color of burnt sugar.

3

June 1971

Since the Mile High City was founded during the gold rush, I picture drunken prospectors gambling away their hard-won nuggets, cowboys driving cattle through the streets, and outlaws robbing the transcontinental railroad. But what I see is a sprawling metropolis, the capital of Colorado. On a sunny day like this, Denver is a rumpus of color. Blue skies, red earth, white mountains. Terracotta tile roofs, silver skyscrapers, brick planters of purple and red geraniums. Dos Equis orange umbrellas.

If I'm ever going to look up my friends from school, now's the time. I got their phone number and address from a mutual friend before leaving Louisville on the off chance that we might stop by and see them. But taxi fare is out of the question and I don't want to call them and have to ask for a ride. Better to stretch out our legs by hiking to their neighborhood and then calling. We start through older densely populated areas of the city. Eventually, they give way to modern post-war neighborhoods. Finally, we reach the university district, which proves larger and more high-toned than expected.

I'm having second thoughts about this surprise visit. Will Matthew Duncan still be mad at me? Even if he isn't, will he and Rebecca be glad to hear from someone who was only on the fringes of their group? I had no theatre background. In high school, actors were bullied by athletic goons. In college, though, theatre students were envied for their wild parties. As I gravitated more toward the bohemian scene,

I started getting invited to those parties. But will I be welcome here now?

With the sun silhouetting the skyline, I pick up a pay phone in a smoky cantina on Evans Avenue. It's Mexican in every way, but the crowd around me makes it look like a college hangout, funky and low-rent, with mismatched bar stools and chairs, terracotta floor, and light shades of hammered tin. Bullfight posters, sombreros, and Tecate beer signs embellish bright yellow walls. I dial the number and Matthew answers. He surprises me, first, by recognizing my voice even though I have to yell to make myself heard over the blaring mariachi trumpets, violins, and classical guitars; and second, with his enthusiasm after learning that Stan and I are in town. Of course, he was always enthusiastic.

"Where are you?" Matthew asks.

"At the El Matador." I read the name off a big garish sign over the bar. "Do you know it?"

"Yeah, place on the corner with the pea green bar. You're close by. See you in ten."

I tell Stan that they're on the way. Although we're starving, we refrain from ordering any food until they arrive.

I've just finished my first Modelo Negro and am munching on a basket of corn chips in a back booth when Matthew and Rebecca walk in. I stand and wave. They smile and wave back. When Matthew gets to the booth, he grabs my hand.

"Pate, you old dog, you," he says as if I were his long-lost brother. This is the same old Matthew, who can be the nicest guy in the world when he chooses. He's slimmed down, though, and trimmed his wildly tangled hair and beard. He reminds me of a young Richard Harris playing King Arthur in *Camelot*.

"Pate." Rebecca gives me a heart-stopping hug.

"Wow, you look fantastic," I say, and introduce Stan.

We slide into the booth, facing them.

"You guys just got in?" Matthew asks.

I tell him yes, we hiked here from downtown.

He whistles. "That's a helluva long walk."

"You should've called," Rebecca says. "We would've come and picked you up."

Touched by this unexpected gesture of friendship, I say we didn't want to impose.

The talk shifts to people we know and how their situations have changed since college. Stan can only listen, but I notice him admiring Rebecca.

"How's married life, Matthew?" I ask.

"Great," he says.

"Yeah, great," Rebecca says.

"Where do y'all live?"

"*Y'all*. Haven't heard that for a while," Rebecca smiles.

Her light brown hair is pulled back into a wispy knot. Unlike Matthew, she hasn't changed her appearance much. The knees of her skinny bell bottom jeans are just as worn through. But why would anyone who looked like her want to change?

Plastic menus arrive on our vinyl tablecloth. We order drinks.

"Where are you staying?" Rebecca asks.

I tell her we don't know.

"We have a cottage right off campus. You guys are welcome to crash with us tonight," she says.

"We don't want to be any trouble."

Stan kicks me under the table.

"It's no trouble," she says. "You have sleeping bags. One of you gets the couch, the other the floor."

"Housing is part of my fellowship," Matthew says.

"He got a full ride," Rebecca explains.

"Not bad." I'm impressed. I know Matthew's a talent, but somehow never saw him as grad school material. "Maybe I should go to graduate school."

"I'm surprised you haven't," Rebecca says, making this sound like a compliment.

Flustered, I change the subject. "Speaking of sweet deals, Stan goes to college on the GI Bill."

"How does that work?" Matthew asks.

Stan gives them the usual spiel.

Our server comes back to take our food order.

When that's done, I say, "Matthew, you're the only one I know who's in grad school right now. What's it like?"

He sits back, as if giving the matter serious consideration. "Guess I was lucky to get in after my sorry-assed undergraduate grades. But now every class is theatre, so I've become a scholar."

"What's the toughest part?"

"Studying."

"Matthew's profs actually had to introduce him to the concept," Rebecca says. "But now, when he's not in class or rehearsal, he's burning the midnight oil."

He's also traded in his ragged T-shirt and cutoffs for twill pants and a silky shirt. I assume this new look is part of his new grad student identity.

"So, Rebecca," Stan says, "what do you do while Matthew's off being a famous actor?"

"I'm a secretary in the theatre department. It's okay," she says, a bit wistfully, "but I'd like to get back into theatre."

"You were really good at Western," I tell her.

Matthew slaps my arm. "Boy, do I envy you guys."

"Why? You're the one in grad school, who's married and actually doing something with his life."

"Exactly the problem," Matthew says.

"Well, honey, you can always quit and get a job," Rebecca says.

"Only thing I can imagine that would be worse is getting drafted," he says.

Rebecca abruptly slides out of the booth and heads for the restroom. Watching her go, Matthew gulps down his drink.

"In two years, I'll have my MFA. Then I can get a job teaching in college," he says.

"I always figured you'd end up in Hollywood," I tell him.

"Horseshit." But he grins with pleasure.

Lucky bastard, I think. If Rebecca was my wife, I'd be praising her, both for her talent and her self-sacrifice on my behalf. Not Matthew. I wonder what's going on. If they're fighting, should we stay with them? The possibility of moving on right away deeply disappoints me.

When Rebecca gets back, she asks what I've been doing since college.

I tell her about the perils of being a substitute teacher.

"Hey, hon," Matthew interrupts, "did Tom Sanders ever call for me again?"

"Who?"

"Tom Sanders, that guy from California."

Rebecca shakes her head. "What does he want?"

"Some bull about summer stock." Matthew looks at me. "So you're traveling around the country. How cool is that?"

Before I can respond, Rebecca touches my arm. "Why are you doing this?"

"Isn't it obvious?" Matthew cuts in. "Kicks, right?"

I want to agree. He has that effect on people. "We're trying to catch up with the Summer of Love, even though we're four years too late."

"Whoa, I can dig that," Matthew says. "Pate, my man, I didn't think you had it in you."

"Actually, the trip was Stan's idea."

"No, shit?" Matthew looks at Stan.

While they talk, Rebecca leans so her mouth is close to my ear. "Now tell me the real reason."

She's always been a smart girl, one who likes being valued for her mind, as well as her body. But I don't know if I can explain it.

"Rebecca, every damn thing I've done up to this point in my life has been planned. I feel like I need to just let life happen for a change. Yesterday, we camped next to a little pond, caught fish for dinner, and saw a million bright stars. We talked about Thoreau for hours. It was all so . . . liberating."

Giving me her most radiant smile, Rebecca says, "Sounds great. You aren't cynical at all, are you? Wish I could be more like that."

"What's stopping you?"

She glances over at her husband. "Wish Matthew could be more like you. Ever since he got cast in *Endgame*, everything's either absurd or meaningless. I prefer your way of looking at life."

After we've eaten, Matthew says, "Time to go, guys. I've got class tomorrow."

They live in typical married student housing, a one-bedroom wood-frame cottage in a neighborhood with everything from apartment buildings to impressive upscale homes. They've gone to some trouble to fix it up. Walls are freshly painted in bright colors, fixtures and hardware spiffed up.

While Rebecca gets us blankets and pillows, Stan and I flip a coin for the couch. I win and find it comfortable. Stan tries out an oversized chair and ottoman before settling down on the hardwood floor in his sleeping bag. As I'm dozing off, Matthew sticks his head in the door.

"Hey, guys. If you sleep late and Becca and I are gone when you wake up, help yourselves to breakfast."

Becca? I've never heard her called that before.

"And feel welcome to stay with us another night or two. In fact, stay as long as you want. We like company. There's plenty to see in Denver. We'll show you around."

He says good night. Alone again, Stan asks how long I want to hang around here.

"A few days? We're in no hurry, right?"

"Okay," he says, "but if I hear any moaning or headboard-banging coming through the wall, I'm out of here. Why didn't you tell me Rebecca was so gorgeous?"

"You think she is?"

"What, have you been struck blind all of a sudden? Were the two of you ever . . . ?"

He lets the question hang in the air.

"Keep your voice down. Rebecca has always been Matthew's girl."

"But you had a crush on her, didn't you?"

He won't leave it alone. Finally, I tell him about a party at somebody's farm right after graduation.

"People were wild, dropping acid, skinny-dipping like it was Woodstock. But when I ran into Rebecca at dusk, she was all alone."

"Where was your buddy Matthew?"

"He wasn't exactly my buddy."

Rebecca didn't know where he was. I could tell she was really pissed off about it, too. The theatre crowd was considered pretty loose in those days, so I assumed Matthew was off somewhere getting laid. Rebecca asked me if I'd like to take a walk, something not many girls as good-looking as her ever had done. I accepted. We strolled through the fields, not talking much at first, but she had a way of putting people at ease. She brought up the war, leaned close enough for her chest to brush against my arm, and said how much she admired me for protesting.

"Then what?" Stan demands.

"While I was standing there, trying to figure out what to do, Matthew showed up and went nuts because she was alone with me. He acted like he wanted to punch my lights out, but took it out on a tree instead and broke his goddamn fist."

"What a maniac," Stan says.

Pot meet kettle, I thought. "Anyway, as Rebecca led him off to get medical attention, she called out to me and said how much she enjoyed our walk. Matthew says, 'Better watch out for that guy, Rebecca. He's hornier than a two-peckered billy goat.' He was probably right."

"How come I've never heard this story before?" Stan says. "If it was me, she'd have dumped him and come back to my place."

"Yeah, probably." I roll over and try to sleep, but I'm tormented by the suspicion that he might be right.

Sunlight steals through the kitchen blinds as I'm drinking coffee the next morning. The refrigerator door is covered with magnets, notes, photographs, a calendar, and a D.U. button. When Stan comes in yawning and scratching, he asks if I've eaten yet. I have, but there's granola and O.J. in the fridge. After helping himself, he joins me at the table.

"Rebecca left us a door key, and a note," I tell him.

"What does it say?"

"That while Matthew's in class this afternoon, she wants us to go swimming with her."

"Is that a good idea? You and Rebecca alone together?"

"We won't be alone. You'll be there."

"I don't think so. I'd rather explore the town."

We've been cooped up together for days now, so maybe I shouldn't be too surprised. And who knows? Being apart for a while might do us both good. When Stan takes off, I phone Rebecca, who doesn't seem to mind Stan not joining us. She says she'll meet me at the house when she gets off work.

Still tuckered after being on the road for three days, I spend most of this one lazing around and reading a Kurt Vonnegut novel I brought along. In the story within the story, this science fiction writer decides to free his characters and one of them shoots him in the leg. That's enough for me. If I ever write a book, I'm not freeing anyone.

Around four o'clock, Rebecca arrives with an auburn-haired young woman, whom she introduces as Katy Palmer, a co-worker and her best friend. Rebecca tells her I'm an old chum from college.

"I've invited Katy to go swimming with us," Rebecca says.

"Hope you don't mind," her friend says.

Although my immediate reaction is to feel disappointed that I'm not going to be alone with Rebecca after all, I quickly answer, "Of course not. Sounds great." I mean, how bad can two women instead of one be?

While Rebecca goes inside to get her swimsuit, Katy and I wait for her on the front steps. Katy's heard that I'm traveling with a friend and asks where he is today. I tell her that Stan found something else to do.

"I'd love to hear about some of your hitchhiking experiences," Katy says.

I give her a colorful account until Rebecca reappears moments later with a pipe in her hand and asks if anybody wants to get stoned. We all do. Back in the living room, we smoke hash until we're buzzed out of our gourds. Then we set out for a ten-minute ride in Rebecca's Saab to the pool, which appears to have been a quarry at some point, with high stone cliffs around the edges.

Still feeling very high, we thread our way warily through rows of sunbathers until finding a place to spread out our striped beach towels. While the women remove their cover-ups and start smearing coconut-scented suntan lotion on each other, I reluctantly tear myself away to climb the high dive ladder. The peaks and low-hanging clouds in the distance seem crystal clear and close enough for me to reach out and touch them. That's how ripped I am. While tempted to try some fancy, hard-to-do dive, I settle for jumping in feet first with a tremendous splash.

"How's the water?" Rebecca asks when I surface.

I tell her it's fine and that she should come on in.

She dives gracefully from pool side, barely making a splash, but comes up screaming at me. I'm a big fat liar and the water's ice-cold, she says, but it doesn't keep her from swimming laps.

By this time, I'm sitting on a towel beside Katy, who in answer to my question says that she's originally from Lima, Ohio, and came out here so her husband could go to medical school. After she put him through, they divorced. She changes the subject, asking me why I am hitchhiking across the country. Instead of sticking to my usual pat answer about chasing the Summer of Love, I tell her, "It sounded like an adventure. It was Stan's idea," and let it go at that. She looks at me thoughtfully.

Rebecca climbs out of the pool, teeth chattering and gooseflesh all over. While toweling off, she asks what we've been talking about. We give her a capsule summary.

"Glad you two are getting better acquainted," she says, and dries her hair with the towel.

We chat about nothing for a while, as the effect of being stoned gradually diminishes.

"Want to go up to Ward with us on Saturday?" Rebecca asks.

I inquire what that is.

She describes it as an old mining town in the mountains where hippies have taken over. "Matthew wants to drive all of us up there."

"Cool. I'm up for that," I say.

Katy is, too.

"Great," Rebecca says.

Talk turns next to how Rebecca and I first became acquainted.

"Rebecca was a star, who I admired from afar."

"Hey, that rhymes," Katy notes. "Are you a poet, Pate?"

"It's just the dope," I say. "Remember when you were in *Oliver*, Rebecca? You should've seen her, Katy. She was great."

"I'd like to hear more about that," her friend says.

"Well, Matthew played Bill Sykes, and I was Nancy, his woman. Matthew seemed so menacing I was a little afraid of him—until I realized what a big pussycat he was. That was our first show together."

"I thought you brought a lot of complexity to a character for a musical," I say.

"Don't discount musicals. There are plenty of great ones."

"I just meant that you really seemed to get into your part."

"So, you're saying I'm good at playing morally ambiguous characters?"

She's teasing me, I realize.

"I'm saying you're good, period. Now what was your big musical number?"

"'As Long as He Needs Me.'"

"Yeah, that's the one. Do you still know it?"

She sings softly about her abusive lover, for whom she will always care *if* he continues to need her.

"My God, Rebecca, you have a wonderful voice. You're the one who should be on stage," Katy says.

Rebecca shrugs and lies back, one leg gracefully bent at the knee. "Matthew's the one with talent."

I'm not entirely sure that's true, but she doesn't seem to want to talk about it anymore. I ask if they're thirsty and make a snack bar run for overpriced chips and drinks. After paying up, I find myself low on cash. I'll need to fatten my wallet somehow as Stan and I continue traveling westward.

The sun is sinking behind the mountains in a fiery burst of color as Rebecca drops Katy off and drives me back to her place.

"How do you like Katy?" she asks.

"Seems like a nice girl. Think I should ask her out?"

"Why not? But you need to understand that she's a little fragile."

"What happened to her marriage?"

"Well, she put her old man through med school, and then he split and married someone else."

"Sounds like a dirty deal." I wonder if Rebecca ever worries Matthew might do the same to her.

She shakes her hair loose. It blows in the breeze as we speed down Iliff Avenue.

"She's been pretty torn up ever since her divorce. I don't think she's even had a date."

"Maybe it's time she did."

"I think so, but she may not be ready."

"Thanks for telling me."

"I thought you'd like each other," Rebecca says.

I hum a few bars of her tune from *Oliver.* "Katy's right, you know. You should go to graduate school in theatre."

"I hope to, as soon as Matthew finds a job."

"Guy's crazy about you," I say, as we pull up in front of their house. How could he not be?

"He'd better be, or I'll slice his gonads off."

On Saturday, four of us drive up to Ward just as Matthew wanted. Stan isn't with us, having met someone and made other plans. He wouldn't have fit into the car anyway. Over the past few days I've seen less and less of my pal. He's gone all day, comes in during the wee hours, and sleeps late. I don't think much about it. This is not all that different from our usual pattern of living together.

Since we're going to see hordes of hippies and want to fit into the scene, we're all wearing flowers in our hair and sporting peace symbols. Katy's peasant top is draped over bell bottoms. Rebecca's dressed like Roger Daltrey in a long-fringed leather vest, Pocahontas headband, and knee-length boots. And Matthew's got on a beige caftan sort of thing, leather pants, and granny sunglasses. Me? I'm seriously under-dressed because my usual T-shirt and jeans are all I brought with me.

It's about a forty-five-minute drive from Denver to Boulder, Matthew says. Then another forty-five-minutes to Ward, elevation 9,450 feet, population one hundred and fifty. Instead of music, we're listening to the Saab's distinctive rumble and I wonder what Matthew is doing with this little upscale Swedish car anyway. Seems jarringly inconsistent with what I assume are our shared counterculture values. I wonder again how much he's changed since the old days, which was only a year ago, I realize.

"Why a Saab, Matthew?" I ask. "You've always struck me as an old Jeep type kind of guy."

"I still am." He grins at me mischievously. "But this baby's got cool European styling, and it will go from zero to sixty in twelve and a half seconds."

"Oh."

I ponder how the hell they can afford this car on a grad student's stipend and a secretary's wages. I know Matthew's family doesn't have any money. I assume that Rebecca's parents must be helping to foot the bills. Well, it's none of my business.

First chance Matthew gets, he revs the engine up, pops the clutch, and lays a patch of rubber.

She scowls at him. "Matthew, those tires are expensive."

"Sorry," he says, and winks at me over his shoulder.

I try to break up the sudden tension by asking what it's like to be a secretary in the theatre department.

"Oh, it's great," Rebecca smiles sardonically. "We know everything that's going on there, don't we, Katy?"

"Right. Everybody thinks we're Dear Abby. Between personnel problems and doing actual work, we stay pretty busy."

Might help if Dear Abby were here now, I'm thinking. But things settle down as our steady climb through the foothills inspires Matthew to recount Ward's history. The old silver mining camp was once among Colorado's richest towns, he says. But around 1900, a fire destroyed most of it. Since then, it's been almost a ghost town. But the recent influx of hippies has changed that.

"What's the big attraction?" I inquire.

"Natural beauty? Clean air? Lax drug law enforcement?" he answers.

The last twenty-six miles snake up four thousand feet. We're on a two-lane road, and my heart shudders at each drop-off. This is the only way in, or out, Matthew claims. When we arrive, the place seems deserted.

"So where are all the hippies?" Katy asks.

It's like we've come to the zoo only to find the animals are missing.

"Don't worry, Katy," Matthew says. "They're around here somewhere. Probably hanging out at the café in the general store drinking weed tea and eating cannabis-laced brownies."

We find he is correct. The restaurant is packed with long-haired young people dressed a lot like us, "Up on Cripple Creek" is playing on the sound system, and there's a faint odor of marijuana in the air. Mecca, we're thinking. But from the moment we walk in, conversation dies down. The sudden change is eerie, as if we pose some sort of threat or maybe just don't belong here. When the wait staff makes no move to greet us, Matthew approaches a server. She responds by shaking her head.

"She says she doesn't know how long the wait might be," Matthew says.

"Let's go," Rebecca says. "I don't feel comfortable here."

We leave, disappointed and confused.

But after our long drive up here, nobody wants to just turn around and go back. Hippies or no hippies, this place is beautiful, with pine forest covering the mountainside. Matthew spots a footpath gently sloping up into the trees and suggests taking a hike. Nobody has a better idea, so off we go. We walk on for ten minutes before our path is blocked by a massive tree that has fallen across it. Rather than skirting around it, we climb up onto the trunk and catch our breath.

"I'm sorry, guys," Matthew says. "I feel like I've let you down."

"It's not your fault," we all say.

"Maybe this will help make up for it." Matthew pulls out a joint. We begin smoking it.

"What was up with all those people back in the café?" Katy asks.

"I don't know," Matthew growls. "They weren't so clannish last time."

"Maybe they're afraid we're narcs," Katy says, and gets a laugh.

"Why would they think that?" Matthew says.

"Well, we did drive up here in a fancy European car," says Rebecca.

"It was the same at a diner back in Kansas," I say, "except there it was the rednecks making us feel unwelcome. Here, it's our fellow freaks."

"Rednecks and freaks," Rebecca says, exhaling. "It's like only the costumes have changed."

"Rebecca understands the importance of wardrobe and props," Matthew says.

"Is it all theatre to you?" I ask him.

"Everything is theatre," Matthew says.

"You don't believe there are any real hippies?" I say.

Blinking rapidly, Matthew says, "Sure, I do. We just saw a whole café full of them. Aren't you one?"

I shrug. "I'd like to think of myself as a nonconformist, but that's hard when I look like everybody else."

"Life's full of contradictions," Matthew says.

"Maybe it just means picking a side," Rebecca says.

After a moment of silent contemplation, Matthew says, "Real hippies or not, I wouldn't mind moving up here someday."

"Why?"

"Natural beauty. Clean air. Lax drug law enforcement."

Rebecca shakes her head. "You're just high, Matthew. You'd go out of your mind up here in a week."

"I would not. The blood of the pioneers flows in my veins."

"THC is more like it," she scoffs.

"You believe I could make it up here, don't you, Katy?" Matthew asks.

"Sure," Katy says. "You can make it anywhere you want."

Matthew grins. "Hear that?"

"Time to go," Rebecca says.

Nobody disputes this and we make our way back down the path to the car. I'm not sure about the subtext, but there's an unmistakable undercurrent of tension now that's magnified by our intoxication and surroundings. Before Matthew can climb behind the wheel, Rebecca grabs the keys from him. "I'll drive. You're too wrecked."

"Like you aren't? Give me the damn keys."

"Fine. Kill us all." She tosses them at him.

I'm alarmed, but it's a long walk back to Denver.

"What are you doing?" Matthew says as Rebecca slides into the back seat with me.

I freeze, startled.

"I'll be safer back here," she says.

But will I? I wonder as Matthew's face reddens.

"Fine." He looks at Katy. "You can sit up here with me. We'll have a nice chat."

He starts the engine. As we pull away, Rebecca leans tight against me. "I'm feeling a little drowsy. Do you mind?" she says and, without waiting for an answer, presses herself against me and puts her head on my shoulder. Oh shit, I think, knowing instantly that I should move away. But there's not much room on this seat and I'm thrilled by her touch.

"Uh, are you sure this is a good idea?" I ask.

"Why wouldn't it be?" Rebecca smiles.

Because your husband's glowering at us in the rearview mirror? Not much doubt what she's up to, but I am—as they say—putty in her hands. It's a terrifying moment. I'm half expecting Matthew to try to kill us on the spot. Instead he floors the Saab and it roars off like a bull out of a chute. As we pick up speed going down the mountain, everyone is yelling at him to slow down. But Matthew's gone deaf.

He takes us on a twisting, turning, suicidal roller-coaster ride, swerving repeatedly toward the edge of the abyss. It's horrifying when the pavement drops away and it feels like we're flying off to our doom.

But Matthew wrenches the wheel and we touch down, only to go through it all over again and again. How we make it down the mountain in one piece is a mystery to me. Through it all, Rebecca has clung to me and now I feel we're both emotionally exhausted and completely sober.

Nobody talks.

Ninety minutes later, we're back in Denver. Our mad driver drops Katy off at her apartment. Eyeing us in the mirror, he says, "Okay, Rebecca, fun's over. Now get your sweet little ass up here beside me where it belongs."

She barely opens her eyes. "No thanks. I'm fine where I am."

This time, he doesn't react at all, which is more worrisome than his fury. Back at their cottage, he sits with the motor running while we exit the Saab. It's still not too late for him to attack me physically or try to slap her around, in which case I wonder how I'll react. Fortunately, I don't have to find out because he just drives off, leaving her alone with me, a guy he once called "hornier than a two-peckered billy goat."

Rebecca hugs me. "Come on in, Pate. Keep me company for a while. Don't worry about Matthew. He's just being an asshole. He'll get over it."

She lets go of me and saunters into the house, while I wonder how long he'll be gone and whether I want to still be here when he comes back. Maybe I should grab my stuff and split. Who am I kidding? Of course, I should. But I'm like a bloodhound hot on the scent and powerless to behave rationally.

I follow Rebecca inside. She heads straight for the bathroom, unbuttoning her blouse as she goes. She leaves the door standing half ajar. I can hear the water running and drums throbbing in my head. I know that all I have to do is go in there and let nature take its course. The prospect is dizzying, but so is the realization of the danger I've put myself in. Not to mention knowing what a rotten friend I will be to someone who gave me shelter and more.

I force myself to sit down on the couch and breathe in the fragrance of her bath soap. I don't know what I would have done if Stan hadn't shown up just then. One look at me and he knew everything.

"Why are you still here?" he says.

"I'm worried about leaving Rebecca alone. Matthew's so pissed off he might hurt her."

"He might hurt you, too," Stan says.

I know he's right, but I still can't leave.

"All right," he says. "Have it your own way. But I'm out of here. I'll be at the VFW post if you need me."

He gives me directions and leaves.

To steady my nerves, I go to the kitchen for a beer even though this means walking past the bathroom door twice. The sight of Rebecca pouring water over herself is almost more than I can stand. But I'm back on the couch when Matthew walks through the front door.

4

December 1970

Over the next six weeks, I spent my days subbing and my nights with Deborah. I visited a succession of middle and high schools. If the permanent teacher I subbed for had left a lesson plan, I tried to follow it. Otherwise, I made up one of my own. After a while, I'd gotten good enough at this to wonder about having my own class, something I'd never before considered seriously. Some days were so easy I could kick back and read a book. Others I fought for my life. But even the bad days were easier knowing the evening ahead included Deborah.

We alternated between her place and mine. Sometimes Donald would stay with his grandfather when she spent the night at my apartment. She listened to me, sympathized with my troubles, cooked for me. She even bought me clothes. But though I sensed she was welcoming me to her world, the zippered jumpsuits and long-collared shirts only pointed up our differences. Deborah was smart, savvy, a true survivor. But she didn't read a lot or follow politics.

Every time we stepped outside together it was a risk. In public, I always feared that strangers would taunt or menace us. But they never did. I couldn't explain, other than to call it dumb luck. But maybe me being six-three had something to do with it. Most other people ignored us, which was fine with me. On nights we spent apart, I sometimes accompanied Stan to bars. He didn't say much about Deborah, never wisecracked or complained about how often she was in our apartment. He was no longer there much himself.

One night, Deborah brought up the driftwood coffee table again. Was I still going to make it for her? Of course, I was. When? Soon.

I told Stan about it. He said, "What's the problem?"

"The problem is that I'm a lousy carpenter."

"Then why did you make such a dumb offer in the first place?"

"Guess I was desperate to connect with her and said the first thing that popped into my head."

"That was the first thing that popped into your head?"

"I know, it's stupid."

"Not necessarily, but it is a little weird. Worked, though, didn't it?"

"That it did."

We were sitting on our front porch watching the leaves swirl around in the wind. I told him about seeing a driftwood table in a magazine and how it reminded me of her.

"You must've come up with some super slick salesmanship to close that deal," Stan said. "I mean, I don't see the comparison at all. A beat up, dried out, aged chunk of wood nobody wanted that's been floating around like a corpse in the river for god knows how long? How did you ever sell that to a good-looking woman like her?"

"I may not be much of a carpenter, but I'm a decent wordsmith."

"Meaning bullshitter par excellence."

"I guess that's fair—except that I really meant it when I said it."

Stan shook his head. "So, what are you going to do?"

"I don't know. That's why I'm asking you."

"You want my help?" he said.

"Do you know anything about woodworking?"

"I know enough."

It had to be more than I knew.

"We're going to need some tools and some driftwood, obviously," Stan said.

Buying anything in Old Louisville posed a challenge. There simply weren't many stores that sold anything other than booze and lottery tickets. The closest hardware store was on Preston Street. We went there and bought a saw and several grades of sandpaper that Stan picked out. I knew there was always plenty of driftwood below the Falls of the Ohio, so that was our next stop after crossing the bridge to Clarksville, Indiana.

It was a gray, wintry day as we hiked down below McAlpine Dam to where the driftwood collected by the fossil beds. Not an angler was in sight, though the fish were supposedly plentiful there.

"When I was a kid, my uncle brought me along when he wanted to fish," I said.

"Ever catch anything?"

I laughed. "Not me. Not him, either, although he always brought a rod and reel and a coffee can full of worms. Mainly, he just liked it here and so did I."

It was another world, a prehistoric kind of place where rushing water was king. At the shoreline, small, close-spaced waves rolled in. Whitecaps broke over white rocks, depositing twigs and wood chips. Clumps of river-grass grew waist-high, and trees with silver-gray bark sprouted from flat wedges of limestone pockmarked by wind, waves, and sun.

We had it all to ourselves, except for a coal train that was rumbling across the river on what I knew was once the longest iron bridge in the country. I suddenly realized that although we had only driven a short way to get here, the distance we'd traveled through time seemed vast. Geologic. I mentioned this to Stan.

"Why do you say that?" he asked.

"Well, for one thing, those fossil beds you're looking at are about 386 million years old."

"Really? How do you know?"

"I read a book once. You should try it some time," I said.

Stan ignored that, knowing I was just being a smartass. He loved to read.

"The fossils were exposed when they dammed up the river a hundred and fifty years ago. Before that, this was rapids where Indians and buffalo crossed."

We made our way along the bleached rocks to a place where the current had heaped up great piles of driftwood, all ours for the taking.

Finding exactly the right size and shape proved a challenge, though.

"How about this one?" Stan toed a tangle of detritus on the shore.

"Not good enough," I said.

Next he pointed out a large spidery-shaped clump of root. We looked it over.

"It's perfect," I said.

We toted it up the riverbank and back to Saint James Court, depositing it in our landlord's mostly unused, poorly heated basement.

"One of the great things about driftwood," Stan said as he examined this piece, "is that it has no right angles or straight lines. So, what others might call poor design or construction, we can call art."

Encouraged, I went to work, cutting and sanding for hours despite the cold. To my surprise, I found the labor satisfying. Unlike teaching, it provided immediate, tangible results. It never talked back or misbehaved, either.

A week later, half asleep as rain clattered on Deborah's roof, I heard someone hammering on the back door. "Who the hell is that?" I said and started to get up.

But she placed her hand on my chest.

"I'll handle this."

"Handle what?" I felt that it was my place to do so. Still, as a naked white man in the middle of the ghetto under cover of darkness, I deemed discretion to be the better part of valor and let her do it. She clicked on the lamp, slipped on her robe, and went to the door.

"Who's there?" she said.

"You know who it is," came the reply. "Open up."

"No, go away."

More hammering. Again, I started to rise. But she shook her head, so I stayed put.

When Deborah opened the door, a threatening presence stood there outlined by the lamp's faint glow. A man of average size, wearing a yellow rain poncho. I couldn't make out much more about him, but from the sound of his voice I could tell that he was black.

"What do *you* want?" Deborah said.

"You know what I want," he said.

"Thought I told you not to come around here no more. Now go away, Eddie, before I call the cops."

Eddie.

But he came on in and pushed past her. That's when I saw the straight razor flash in the dimness.

Holy shit.

"Uh-uh," Eddie said, brandishing the blade as I attempted for the third time to get to my feet.

"Who the hell are you," I said, "and what do you want?" though both questions had already been asked and answered.

"Tell him what I want, baby."

"What you can't have any more," Deborah said. "Now get out of here before you wake Donald up."

"Nothing gonna wake up that boy. He dead to the world." Eddie nodded at me. "Tell lover boy here about us."

Looking more weary than afraid, Deborah said, "A long time ago, we used to live together. Then this fool got busted for robbing a liquor store."

"Fool?" he said. "You still think you're too good for me, don't you?"

She pleaded with him, calling him by his name.

"You think whitey's going to marry you?" he said. "Did he take you home to meet his kin? Did you take him home to meet yours? Yeah, that's what I thought."

"You don't know anything," Deborah said.

"I know you'll come back to me."

"Never."

"Maybe you would if I cut this fool out of the picture."

He took a step toward me. Deborah came between us.

I jumped out of bed and yanked the lamp from the wall. A pitiful weapon. Eddie laughed at it. But he backed away and out the door. Deborah slammed it shut and locked it.

"Did that happen? Or did I dream it?"

She leaned her back against the door. "Put the lamp down," she said. "He won't bother us anymore."

"How do you know?"

"He knows I'm with you now. Come back to bed."

Shedding her robe, she lay down and was reaching for the baby oil on the nightstand when I asked if she used baby oil on him, too. She slapped my face. When she tried to do it again, I grabbed her wrists and held on.

"I guess I deserved that, once."

"Let go of me and get the hell out of here, Pate."

After she curled up into a ball and rolled as far away from me as she could, I got dressed and left.

Stan dribbled twice, jumped, and swished a shot from deep in the corner. It was Friday afternoon and we were playing Horse at busy Seneca Park, an East End hoops hot spot where the has-beens often met the never-wases in mortal combat. But today we had this court all to ourselves. We'd come here in Stan's VW because there was nowhere to play where we lived. Saint James abutted Central Park, which had tennis courts, swings, and a summer Shakespeare playhouse but no basketball goals.

"Why do you suppose that is?" I asked, lining up the shot I had to make or lose the game.

"Maybe they're afraid it'll bring in the wrong element," Stan said.

"The wrong element? *We're* the wrong element. We live there, for chrissake."

Keeping my shooting elbow parallel to the ground, I launched the shot. I gave it plenty of arch and followed through, but still missed. "Good game," Stan said.

"I got an interesting phone call today," I said. "From an administrator with the city school system. A teaching job has opened up. They offered it to me."

"Where?"

"At Parkland Junior High."

"Yikes. You aren't going to take it, are you?"

I understood the question all too well. The school was located in the middle of the ghetto. Three years ago, part of the neighborhood around it had gone up in smoke following the assassination of Dr. Martin Luther King, Jr. Even after all this time, many businesses and homes in the area remained boarded up or abandoned. Parkland still seethed with anger and frustration with whites. The crime rates were high and there was a significant police presence.

On top of this, the job I was being offered was one nobody else wanted. I knew this because the administrator had told me so. If I took the job, I'd be teaching students with severe behavior problems in something called the Star Unit.

"They're supposedly the worst kids in the building, Stan—in fact, they aren't even *in* the building. They're so incorrigible and disruptive that the principal had to put them in a portable out behind the main school building."

"Sounds great," Stan said facetiously. "Why is it called the Star Unit?"

"It's a euphemism, I guess. Something to not harm their self-esteem."

"Bet that works. So, what's the downside?"

"Well, it's a permanent sub position."

Stan chuckled.

I bounced the ball hard against the pavement. "The last teacher quit after finding another job. Everything else aside, the principal might insist that I cut my hair and shave. I don't know if I'm willing to do that."

"Conformity's not all bad."

"Really? That from the guy who quotes Emerson on being yourself is the greatest accomplishment?"

"Yeah. I'm also the guy who joined the Navy. Sometimes bending to authority has its benefits."

"Very philosophical, considering you're so good at it yourself."

He scratched his beard. "The world wouldn't work without some degree of conformity."

"Yeah, to what degree, though?"

"Guess you'll find out," he said, "otherwise you wouldn't be talking about it."

I told him he was right. I had agreed to try it. But I'd left myself an out. If after a week it didn't work out, I'd be reassigned. Stan said that seemed fair to him.

We started a new game. With the wind whipping through our hair, we rapped about politics and music. Eventually I got around to what I really wanted to discuss: Deborah and Eddie. I told Stan what had happened and asked if I'd screwed up.

"I don't see how." He dribbled twice. "You didn't get stabbed and neither did anybody else. This guy Eddie left without even breaking anything."

I took my turn and shot a free throw.

"Does Eddie know where you live?"

I shook my head.

"Is there any way he can find out?"

I told him I didn't see how. Deborah wasn't going to tell him.

"In that case, you came out way ahead, Buddy."

"But now I'm not sure where I stand with Deborah."

Stan made the free throw. "Where do you want to stand with her?"

"I'm not really sure anymore. What would you do?"

"I'd find another girl."

I thought about that as I missed my next jumper.

On Monday morning, I waited for half an hour in Parkland's principal's office before he showed up. According to his secretary, the boss was off attending to some minor crisis. She looked at me a little askance, doubtless because I had not shaved or cut my hair. My only concessions toward having a "professional appearance" consisted of Bass Weejuns, a blue Oxford cloth shirt, and pressed jeans.

Behind the principal's desk, I saw photographs of a young man who I figured was him in a college football uniform. The photos vied for wall space with framed degrees and bromides like *When the go-*

ing gets tough, the tough get going. I hadn't heard that one since high school. It meant even less to me now than it had then.

I recognized Byron Bloom when he came in. He looked about twenty years older now and had traded in his football uniform for a coat and tie. He was still brawny with a shaved head—and an intimidating presence.

"Well, you've got size," he said, looking me over. "Good. We don't have much time. First period starts soon."

He pulled a manila file folder from a desk drawer and flipped it open in front of him.

"Says here you went to college at Western Kentucky. Play any ball?"

"No, sir."

"Why you want this job?"

"I'm ready for a change, Mr. Bloom. I'm tired of moving around all the time. I want to feel more connected to my students. And I'm up for a new challenge."

"Well, the Star Unit will provide one. It's not a normal classroom situation, as you know. Except for Mr. Thresher, you'll be alone in a portable with thirty-five of our most difficult students. Think you can handle that?"

"I don't see why not. I've taught at almost every school in the system and nobody's run me off yet."

"First time for everything." Bloom fingered my file. "Tell me what happened at Iroquois."

He'd checked up on me. Probably a good sign. Some of the other Grand Poobahs I'd worked for wouldn't even have bothered.

"The principal there said I looked unprofessional."

"I see what he meant."

"This is pretty formal for me."

"I believe he said you had an attitude problem, too. I don't care about that, though, or how you look, *if* you can keep your students under control."

"I'll do my best, Mr. Bloom."

"Teacher before you couldn't, and he was black. That's why you're getting hired in the middle of the school year."

"If you wanted somebody black, why am I here?"

"You're what they sent me." Bloom closed the file. "Remember this, though: If I hire you, I don't expect to have to come out there every day."

"You won't have to."

"Okay. Do you know Mike Thresher? Thought you might, being a local. When I was coaching at Manual, Mr. Thresher was a mean little nose-guard. He's only been back from Vietnam a couple of months. Good man to have around. He'll teach math and science. You'll handle English and social studies. Okay?"

I said it was.

"Then let's go inspect the troops."

To reach them, we went through noisy halls and out the back door. After cutting across a playground glittering with broken glass, we came to a portable about the size of a double-wide house trailer. A heavy metal mesh covered all the windows. To keep people in or out, I wondered? Standing at the door was another burly black man.

"This is Mr. Green, our paraprofessional," Bloom said.

Mr. Green's hands were tucked into his overcoat pockets. He nodded gruffly, exhaling clouds of breath.

Inside the portable, we found overturned chairs and desks, and pages ripped out of textbooks scattered across the floor. The "troops," who were all black males, were chasing each other around or shooting dice against the back wall. A clap like a pistol shot startled them to silence. Bloom had smacked his palm on the desktop. He began by collecting the dice in silence.

Then he said, "Pick those books up off the floor, put your desks back where they belong, and get your butts in them."

There were not enough desks to go around, so some students doubled up. Others leaned against the walls or squatted in the aisles. Bloom glanced at his watch.

"Where's Mr. Thresher?"

"Search me," Mr. Green shrugged. "That's why I'm out here."

"Been better if you'd been *in* here," Bloom said.

Green looked away.

Bloom told me I'd have to keep an eye on them all until my "teammate" arrived. The wall phone was my lifeline. Mr. Green had a lot of ground to cover, but he'd come if I needed him. I could already see how much help he was going to be.

Bloom returned his attention to the students. "All right, this is Mr. Merwin, your new teacher. You've already embarrassed yourselves in front of him. From now on, I expect you to behave. Believe me, you don't want to see me again today." He waited a moment, as if daring anyone to speak. When nobody did, he and Green left.

My first job was to call the roll, but before I could manage it, something crashed into me, wrapping itself around my knees and squeezing like a boa constrictor.

"Get him, Reginald," students yelled.

The thing gripping me had long arms and legs, dark brown eyes, and skin the color of hardwood mulch. It was slim and apparently could bend itself into any shape it wanted, like a balloon animal. Nothing in my experience had prepared me for this.

"Let go," I said.

I tried to pry him off, but he was too sweaty for a proper grip. The harder I tried, the tighter he clung. I don't know why, but I got the notion that what he wanted was a hug. So I gave him one, cradling him like a baby. He smiled up at me, let go, and scampered off. Knowing I had about five seconds before there was bedlam again, I resumed calling the roll. But you cannot control students whose names you do not know. They'll simply ignore you, or pretend they think you're talking to someone else. Sure enough, some masqueraded as others, while a few answered to many names. Subbing had taught me a strategy for this: bribery.

I said we were going to play a game. If they cooperated, I'd give them each a candy bar. What kind of candy bar? Whatever kind they wanted.

"I want a Snickers," one yelled.

"No, Almond Joy."

Then it was M&Ms, Peanut Butter Cup, Milky Way. I said all would be provided, if they cooperated.

"Where the candy?" a big kid in the back row asked.

"Don't worry," I said. "You'll get it. I'll bring it tomorrow."

"Hell, man," he said, shoving away the chair he'd been leaning on, "you won't even be here tomorrow."

"Watch your mouth. What do you mean I won't be here?"

"None of y'all ever come back."

I asked how many teachers they'd had this year.

"Countin' you? 'Bout thirteen. I'm good at math."

As the class hooted, I said, "I'll be back tomorrow with a big bag of candy bars. And you can write that down. Now, when I point at you, I want you to say your name—*your* name—out loud. It won't count if it's not your real name, and you won't get a candy bar."

They went for it.

Each time a student said his name, I repeated it, along with all the others I'd already heard, in order, until I'd memorized them all. When the kid who'd needed a hug wouldn't say his name, his classmates identified him as Reginald Sheckles.

At this point, the door to the portable swung open and a buzz-cut man wearing a suit and tie with cowboy boots waltzed in. "At ease, gentlemen," he said.

"Thresher!" the students yelled.

When they settled down, he said, "Mr. Merwin? I'm Mike Thresher, in case you didn't hear."

I glanced at the wall clock. He was seventeen minutes late. "Principal's been looking for you," I said.

"Already saw him. You okay? Then I'll take my half." He looked at them and barked, "All right, you know who you are; let's go. Move your lard ass, Leroy. You, too, Darrell."

As students began moving out, Alonso, the big kid who didn't think I'd be back, muttered something under his breath.

"Speak up, son," Mr. Thresher said, "if you got something to say." He waited. "No? Okay, Mr. Merwin. If that one over there gives you any trouble, send him to me. We're having a pushup contest, aren't we, Alonso. How many you up to now, four? Five? Well, good luck on the English and social studies. These recruits aren't exactly what I'd call avid readers."

Thresher was right about that. When a student read aloud, his peers ridiculed his stumbling attempts. By the time we got around the room, I knew none could read at grade level. It didn't help that the authors had aimed our textbook at white suburbanites. I stuck my head in Thresher's door. "Where are they in history?"

"The Mexican War," said Thresher, whose students were sulky but on task, studying a math handout. "But anywhere will do."

Since we were self-contained, Thresher said we could arrange our schedule any way we wanted, except for lunch. We agreed to start by alternating groups every ninety minutes, with five-minute breaks. With their brief attention spans and hyperactivity, a shorter interval would've been preferable. But every time we uprooted them, they'd become more rowdy and harder to control.

Back in my room, students wouldn't stay in their seats unless I yelled at them. As the day wore on, it was all I could do to keep them from tearing the place apart.

the biggest mistake of my life

5

June 1971

Matthew glances at me while sweeping past and into the bath-room, where the yelling commences.

"What the hell's going on?" he says.

"You tell me."

They lower the volume. I stare out the window into the darkness. Something falls to the floor. I hear glass breaking.

"Are you in love with her?" Rebecca says, her voice rising to a wail.

"In love?"

Then I can't distinguish their words anymore. But with the situation seeming calmer, it appears to be a good time for me to go. I grab my rucksack from its resting place in the corner. I open the door, but not without some regrets, and am halfway down the block when a car pulls up beside me. I dread that it's Matthew, but when I turn I see Katy driving a red Corvair.

"Pate," she says.

I go over and lean on the car.

"Going somewhere?" I smell coconut. Must be her scented sham-poo. Her eyes seem bigger somehow and there's black mascara on her eyelashes that I hadn't noticed before.

"Fleeing the scene's more like it. What are you doing here?"

"Forgot my compact," she says.

"Best leave it until later. Now might not be the right time."

"Are they fighting again? Not that I'm surprised after what went down at Ward. Where are you headed?"

"To find Stan."

"Let's talk first. Get in."

I toss my bag in, then me. We go a couple of blocks until she spots a closed Texaco service station. She pulls in under the sign with the big red star and switches off the engine.

"What's up, Pate?" she asks, but doesn't press me, waiting patiently with her hands on the faux wood steering wheel.

I stare blankly at the gas station and the traffic passing by. It's a grimy old filling station with two pumps. The cube-shaped building is painted white. A glass door is flanked by large windows and oil can pyramids. The space is divided between two car-sized bays, one marked "Washing" and the other "Lubrication." A small red star is painted over each bay, along with three horizontal red stripes.

"All right," I say. "You saw how Rebecca was acting in the car, right?"

"Kind of hard to miss."

"Well, it didn't stop when we got home."

"Really? What happened?"

I blurt out how she'd left the bathroom door partly open for my benefit, and Matthew's untimely arrival.

"Oh, my god," Katy says.

"What do you think is going on?"

"I don't know." She puts her hand on my wrist and leaves it there. "But now you need somewhere to crash, right? Better come home with me."

"That sounds great, but Stan's waiting for me at the VFW post."

"He won't leave town without you. You can sort it all out in the morning."

I think she's right.

Six blocks later, we're at her place. As we're getting out of the car, my previous dread comes true as Matthew arrives in the Saab.

"What the hell are you doing here?" he says to me.

"I might ask you the same question. Why aren't you at home with your wife?"

"Fuck you."

"Look, Matthew, if you didn't like the way Rebecca behaved with me in your car, you should've said something. Why didn't you?"

"I think that's a very good question," Katy says.

"Here's another." Matthew faces her. "What's he doing here with you?"

And suddenly everything is clear to me.

"He needs somewhere to stay," Katy says.

"But not here," Matthew says.

"We'll talk about it tomorrow."

"No, we'll talk now."

She looks at me. "I'm sorry, Pate. Maybe you should go."

"Yeah, I should."

I grab my bag and sling it over my shoulder. According to Stan, the VFW post is located downtown several miles from here. I start walking in that direction.

Hard to believe that only this morning we were all still friends and four of us were in Ward together. At the time, I felt close to everyone and happy we'd come. But now I cringe sadly knowing I've been used in their treacherous little game of deceit and betrayal. A far cry from peace and love. More like life in the suburbs I'm so anxious to avoid.

The roar of a motorcycle and shrieks of laughter interrupt my musings. It's Saturday night, after all, and the streets will soon be full of revelers. I keep putting one foot in front of the other. To avoid being thrown out of the VFW, I'd need to find Stan right away. Otherwise, I wouldn't be able to pry him loose, and that could mean more hours of waiting. So, when I get there, I look around for him frantically. I finally spot him on the other side of the room drinking and laughing by the famous photo of the Marines raising the American flag over Iwo Jima.

"Well, hello, Sherlock," he says, sounding a little drunk, as I plod over and tap him on the shoulder. "How'd you manage to track me down?"

Before I can respond, someone else claps me on the shoulder. I turn around to find myself standing face-to-face with a soldierly figure: head up, chest out, stomach in, shoulders squared—with a regulation military buzz cut.

"I don't think I've seen you in here before," he says. "You a vet?"

"Harry," Stan interrupts. "Meet my old shipmate, Pate Merwin." We shake hands.

Before I can speak, Stan rushes on. "Pate's usually a regular blabbermouth but he's got laryngitis right now. Otherwise, he'd bore us all to death."

Catching on, I clear my throat and point at it.

I don't know if Buzz Cut's really convinced, but he lets me stay.

"What are you doing here?" Stan pours me a beer from a pitcher on the bar.

A Patsy Cline song is playing on the jukebox as I briefly outline the events at Ward—being shunned by the locals, getting high in the woods, Rebecca and Matthew's quarreling, and the ride down the mountain. He doesn't ask any questions, which is okay.

"As I was saying," the guy sitting next to Stan at the bar says, and I realize I've interrupted their conversation. "You swabbies always have it easy compared to the Marines."

"That's what all jarheads say," Stan replies. "Don't forget that whenever one of you grunts gets hit, it's a Navy corpsman who bails your sorry ass out."

The Marine's hands move restlessly on the bar top. "When I was in 'Nam," he says, "we lived for months in the dirt. We slept in holes, burned leeches off our legs. Humping the boonies once, we were about to hit our LZ when our chopper came under heavy ground fire. It must have been twenty—or even forty millimeter—real heavy automatic stuff. Chewed the crap out of us."

He pauses to knock back a shot, then calls to the bartender for another.

"A lot of my friends didn't make it home. Some who did think they're still there. I got hit, but only a few scratches. One night while I was in Oak Knoll Naval Hospital in Oakland, the evening news showed a big antiwar protest. That hurt, man. It was like the whole country was against us."

The whole country's not against you, I want to say, it's against the war. I want to say I'd protested because I thought the war was wrong. The soldiers were not wrong; the war was.

I study the rusty rifles and other wartime memorabilia on the walls.

In some ways, I admire men like this haunted Marine. My choice to evade the draft was illegal, but to me it was simply the lesser of evils. Still, he'd done the fighting and I hadn't. Part of me would always feel guilty about it.

Somebody drops a coin in the jukebox and a few seconds later the country song is replaced by "God Bless America."

"Well, what do you think of the VFW now?" Stan says, as we step lively along darkened downtown streets.

"It was not exactly what I expected. By the way, that was a nice save back there, shipmate."

"He could've carded you," Stan says. "But I've been in there every night this week, which is why he let me vouch for you."

I start to mention the wounded ex-Marine, but Stan interrupts: "There are no ex-Marines. Once a Marine, always a Marine."

"Okay, I stand corrected. Anyway, that guy still seemed stuck back in the past, experiencing it all over again. It made me wonder if you ever feel that way."

After being quiet for a moment, Stan shakes his head. "You mean am I over following orders without question? Or dehumanizing the enemy so it's not people I'm killing? Man, when I enlisted, I was pig ignorant about Vietnam. Couldn't spell it or find it on a map. If I knew then what I know now . . ."

I notice he hasn't answered my question. "When exactly did you get out?"

"My enlistment was up in November of '68. I got liberty at Hong Kong in May, then we steamed for home. After refitting at Bremerton, the ship I was aboard went on across the bay from San Francisco to

Alameda. A few months later, I was a civilian again."

We trek on.

"Where are we going?"

"We can't go back to your friends' place," Stan says, "so I guess that means we go to mine. You can crash there tonight on the sofa."

His place? I gather he's referring to the mystery woman he's been spending so much time with lately. I'm glad to finally meet her. I notice a sign for Larimer Street and point it out to him.

"We're walking on hallowed ground, man. This is where Sal gets dropped off among the old bums and beat cowboys in *On the Road*."

"Well kiss my Kerouac," he says, already miles away. "Tomorrow, let's head north to Cheyenne. It's a straight shot from there to Salt Lake City on I-80, then on to Reno and San Francisco."

"What about your lady friend?"

"I've been honest with her."

"How about this instead? We go south to Colorado Springs, then west. They say that high desert country in the Four Corners area is beautiful. We might scare up some sacred mushrooms."

"Magic mushrooms?"

"Whatever you want to call them."

The rest of the way to his friend's place we jabber about peyote, the spirit world, and our greatest highs and worst bummers.

Even before the skinny long-haired girl opens the door of her apartment, I smell patchouli, incense used to cover weed, dirty clothes, or body odor. In this case, it's the only thing covering this woman, whose features are long and drawn as if she's forgotten how to smile. I could count her ribs, though I politely try to look only at her eyes.

"Who's this?" she asks, in a soft, dusky voice, seeming surprised to see me.

Stan tells her my name, that we're hitching together, and that I need a place to sleep tonight.

"Is he mellow?" she asks.

"Very mellow," Stan says. "Pate, this is Felicity."

"Want to get naked?" she asks me.

"You're beautiful," I tell her. "But I just want to sleep on your couch. Or on the floor."

"Thought you said he was mellow." Felicity is clearly disappointed, but rallies to take Stan's hand and leads him into her bedroom.

It's been a busy night. That must be why I'm so hungry. I quietly prowl through Felicity's icebox but there's nothing in it but celery. Only some dried apricots in the cabinets, too. No wonder she's so emaciated. She reminds me of a poster for starvation victims. But I know there is a god because eventually I find half a box of Cocoa Puffs on the top shelf. It reminds me of Deborah and Donald, who loved that damn cereal. I wonder where they are now.

When I've eaten it all, I throw away the box and douse the lights and try to go to sleep. But I'm too wired. If everything hadn't gone to shit in Ward, I'd still be sleeping at Matthew and Rebecca's house. I should have steered clear of their mess like Stan. How does he manage to do that?

Next thing I know Stan's shaking me and it's time to go. I yawn, feeling slightly hung over, and propose stopping somewhere for coffee and donuts, my treat. Except I haven't got any money. In fact, when I reach for my wallet it's gone. I check between the couch cushions. On the floor. Everywhere. No wallet. I try to envision the last time I saw it and realize it must've fallen out of my pocket at Matthew and Rebecca's house.

When I inform Stan that we'll have to go back, he says, "Jesus Christ, Pate. Get your shit together."

I tell him I'm sorry. That no one will be around since Rebecca has to work and Matthew will be in class. He's still not happy about it, however. In fact, I've never seen him so grumpy.

"How will we get in?" he says.

I show him the house key I'd forgotten to return. It takes us nearly an hour to get there. When we finally do, I search the living room but there's still no sign of my wallet anywhere.

"Where the hell can it be?" I'm saying when Matthew shows up.

"What a surprise," he says. "How'd you get in?"

"Rebecca gave me a key to the front door." I flip it to him. "I'm looking for my wallet."

"Oh, this?" Matthew pulls it out of his back pocket.

"You found it." I hold out my hand, but he does not give it to me.

"You're leaving Denver, right? Where are you headed next?"

"Colorado Springs," I say. "What do you care as long as we're out of your hair?"

"Take me with you," he says.

Generally, I like surprises, but this one floors me. "What?"

"Cut the bullshit, Matthew," Stan says, "and give Pate his wallet back."

"No bullshit," Matthew says. "I really want to come with you guys."

"After all that's happened, you can't possibly be serious," I say.

"But I am."

"Look, I'm sorry for my part in this," I begin.

"You mean in the car?" Matthew laughs. "Don't flatter yourself, Pate. We're actors. Rebecca and I have always done exactly what we pleased, right from the start. If she'd wanted to screw you, she would've. And you wouldn't have been the first."

Can this be true? I am flabbergasted.

"Since coming to DU," Matthew continues, "I've heard a thousand lectures, gone to countless rehearsals, and hit the books harder than ever before. I am sick to death of it all. Packing up everything we owned into a U-Haul and coming out here was the biggest mistake of my life."

"You're going to quit school? I can't believe you. You're turning your whole life upside down."

"Exactly. Look, the idea is to come out of here a well-rounded theatre artist. That means you have to try everything. But I'm an actor, and that's all I ever wanted to be. Graduate school was a mistake, which is why I'm leaving."

"What about the play you're in?"

"Screw *Endgame*," Matthew says. "My understudy can play my role."

"What about Rebecca?"

"And screw Rebecca, too."

"Don't you even love her?"

"Always have, always will," Matthew says. "But it's just not working out. Nothing's working out like I thought it would. Anyway, Rebecca will be fine. Her parents are loaded."

"This is crazy," I say. "Why the hell do you want to go with us?"

"I want to be out there on the cutting edge, Pate, not lecturing a bunch of bored college kids. We could have a blast traveling together."

"We don't need you," Stan says. "We don't want you."

Matthew waves my wallet. "Take me with you, and I'll give this back."

"You'll give it back anyway," Stan says.

"What if I don't?"

Stan lunges at him and they crash to the floor, grunting, knocking over furniture. I try to stop them, but I'm just in the way. Stan wraps Matthew up in a wrestling hold. But Matthew sinks his teeth into Stan's ear until he lets go. They keep fighting. Stan swings a roundhouse punch at Matthew's head, but when he misses, Matthew kicks him in the knee. Stan goes down. The fight appears to be over. They're both gasping and bloody. The living room is a ruin. In the melee, Matthew has dropped my wallet. I pick it up and shove it in my pocket.

"Good fight," Matthew says. "You're tougher than you look."

"Fuck you," Stan says.

I pick up an overturned chair and set it upright. I grab a towel to stanch Stan's bleeding ear and help him to his feet. We hobble out the door.

Six hours later, we're seventy-five miles from the Great Sand Dunes, where we hope to spend the night. The weather had seemed promising at the outset this morning, but the Rockies are notorious for sudden change. Now the weeds are bent along I-25 and thick clouds blot out the scenic western peaks.

"If you'd listened to me," Stan shouts, "we'd be in Cheyenne by now, instead of stranded in the middle of nowhere with gale force winds bearing down on us."

It's not like him to carp and second-guess, but I know he's right.

"What do you want me to say, Stan? You wanted an adventure. We've got one."

"Not exactly what I had in mind," he says.

I can barely hear him as flashes of forked lightning are followed closely by booming thunderbolts.

"Look at *that*," he says in awe, pointing at the horizon where a line of black rumbling clouds towering up thousands of feet is racing our way.

"Jesus. We need shelter."

"Yeah. Where?"

Nothing but grassy open space and irrigated cropland surrounds the interstate. And the cottonwoods growing on the median are only good for attracting lightning, according to a farmer who gave us our last ride. There's nowhere to go. No escape.

"Here it comes," I say, as a few drops of rain strike my face and arms.

Then a sudden gust nearly lifts me off my feet. The sky soon becomes a roaring, heaving sea of blackness as the storm settles in directly overhead. We hunker down as low as possible, but rising water is collecting in the roadway. Flash flooding may come next. I'm starting to fear for my life, knowing we wouldn't be the first to simply vanish in the Rockies, as hazardous and remote an environment as any found in the U.S. I'm cursing myself for guiding us here when headlight beams suddenly appear out of the gloom.

"Look!"

"Thank God."

Buffeted by the storm, the approaching vehicle seems to take forever to reach us. At long last, its shadowy form emerges from the murk and pulls up beside us. With its windshield and windows steamed up, I can't see who's inside. But we're desperate to get a roof over our heads, so I'm willing to skip Rule One in favor of Rule Two, which is any port in a storm. Besides, it's a pink Cadillac Eldorado, of all things, and it's towing a silver slipstream trailer, the kind often favored by retirees who winter in Florida. But I've never seen a snowbird trailer painted quite like this one before. Even in this monsoon's greenish dimness, those psychedelic Day-Glo swirls stand out as unmistakably as neon on black velvet. I immediately flash on Ken Kesey and the Merry Pranksters from *The Electric Kool-Aid Acid Test* and wonder what have we here?

Meanwhile, a back window has been rolled down enough for someone to stick an arm out and they're waving us around to the other side if we want to get in. All this has taken about ten seconds. In ten more, we've hauled ass and our military surplus luggage around the front grill and piled in through the open back door. There's a white-haired woman who's probably in her seventies sitting on the other end of the wide back seat. She's wearing a bright yellow headband.

"Welcome aboard, boys," she says pleasantly.

"Thanks for picking us up, ma'am," I say.

"Yeah, you may have just saved our lives," says Stan, who looks more presentable having discarded his bloody T-shirt and cleaned himself up. But he still has a bandaged ear and she notices.

"What's wrong with your ear?"

"It's nothing serious."

"Sorry about dripping all over everything," I say.

She'd sent us to the other side so she wouldn't have to open her door and get drenched, I figure. But that didn't keep the Caddy's plush interior from getting soaked. The crushed velour seats and shag carpet would need a good drying out after serving water-filled sponges like us. Of course, these folks—this woman and the pair in the front seat—surely knew what was bound to happen when they let us in the car—which is all the more reason for us to be grateful.

"It's okay," the woman says generously, as the Caddy slowly accelerates. "Always happy to assist tempest-tossed souls in need."

This seems an odd way of putting it, almost . . . mystical. Who are these people?

"Where are you headed?" Stan asks our driver.

All I can see is the back of his head and his gray ponytail.

"Right now, I'm focused on getting us through this storm," he says in a deep rumbling voice while keeping his eyes on the road. This, I find reassuring.

I can tell even less about the guy riding shotgun, except that he's got a dark hoodie pulled over his head. So far, he hasn't said boo or looked around once. I wonder if he's a hitchhiker like us, or maybe a family member.

We ride on quietly for a while, hoping the storm will pass or at least abate. But outside the wind squalls like a suffering infant, while the rain beats on the roof with the desperation of a drowning man. The Caddy is heavy, which helps keep us grounded. But the trailer is lighter and yaws. The effect is unsettling.

"Man, I don't know what we would've done if you hadn't stopped," I say.

"It really wasn't our idea, though," the driver says.

"I don't understand. Whose idea was it?"

"Mine," says a familiar voice, and Matthew turns around to face us while removing his hoodie. "How's your ear, Stanley?"

"What the hell? How's this possible?" Stan says, bewildered.

Matthew grins like a wise man who knows all. "We've been on the lookout for you guys. I told Nick and Iris to pick you up if we found you, and I thought we would."

"Pull over," Stan barks, clearly ready to bolt. Fortunately, a timely thunderclap drowns him out.

Grabbing him by the wrist, I hiss, "Shut up. We need this damn ride." I've never seen him this angry before. He's shaking with rage. I'm afraid I might have to literally restrain him from popping Matthew in the jaw. Soothing Stan is going to be like softening rocks or bending oak, as the poet says. He starts to say something, but fate is on our side for once and the woman interrupts.

"At first, Nick didn't want to stop," she says.

"No need to go looking for trouble. It'll find you soon enough," the driver says.

"But then Matthew spotted you two, so we had to stop," the woman says.

I'm about to ask her name when she says, "We're the Paraprosdokians, Iris and Nick from Boulder. We buy and sell rugs."

"Guess you already know our names," I say. "But how do you know Matthew?"

"We were grabbing a bite at a taco stand just before leaving Denver when he came up and asked us for a ride. He was so charming that we couldn't say no. We like to be hospitable and we have plenty of room," Iris says.

Nick chimes in: "Hospitality is making your guests feel at home, even when you wish they were."

"Nick," Iris reproaches him.

We laugh. The rug merchants' geniality seems to mollify Stan, who asks for the second time where they are headed.

"The Great Sand Dunes," Nick tells us, clenching an unlit cigar in his mouth.

"Great," I exclaim. "That's where we're going."

"Me, too," Matthew says.

I'm ready to spring into action if necessary, but Stan just sits stewing. There will be hell to pay, but it must wait until we've reached our destination. Then we can deal with Matthew and his curious insistence on going wherever we do.

At U.S. 160, Nick leaves the interstate. This proves a winding two-lane mountain road, which unfortunately reminds me of our headlong descent from Ward.

"We'll be crossing the Continental Divide later on," Iris says excitedly. "This is supposed to be the scenic route, but we're not going to see much unless this gully washer lets up. I told you we should've started earlier, Nick."

"Iris," Nick yells as he pulls off to let faster traffic pass us, "shut up. *Please.* I'm trying to get us through this storm in one piece."

After going through a tunnel, we climb from valleys to wooded slopes, and up a long, steep grade full of zigzagging switchbacks and safety ramps for runaway trucks. At one point, there's a nearly perpendicular pass through this range with no guardrails between us and a bottomless canyon.

"Holy crap," I say, "we could just fly off the road."

"Don't worry," Iris says. "Nick's an accomplished driver."

I shut my eyes. When I open them, the storm has passed and we're descending into a wide, mountain-ringed valley. As the landscape starts to flatten out, I take a stab at starting a conversation.

"Is your name Greek?" I ask. "It sounds Greek."

"It's Greek," Nick says

"How did you two meet?"

Iris says they took a yoga class together.

"Yoga is cool," Matthew pipes up. "It's good for relieving stress."

This the first I've heard anything about yoga from him.

"But it's so much more than that, Matthew. When I met Nick, he was making a lot of money as a CPA, but he was unhappy."

"And Iris was a frustrated professional management analyst who thought she wanted a corporate career."

"In pursuing success, we often forget about what really matters. Yoga reminded us," Iris says.

"So, what really matters to you?" Stan asks.

It's not a question Stan would ask casually, and when he does, it's because he thinks the person he asked might have a good answer.

"Living life more intimately, more deeply, I'd say," Iris replies, looking at him.

"Not easy," Stan says.

"No, but the limitations others put on us are nothing compared to the ones we put on ourselves."

I wonder what she means by that, but don't ask. Iris tells us anyway.

"By trying to hold on to what's familiar, we limit our ability to experience joy in the present."

"Heavy," Stan says. "I need to think about that."

"How does yoga help?" I ask.

"It stills the mind by focusing on our breathing."

"Smoking weed does that, too," Matthew says.

"Yoga's legal," Nick says.

"Ever get high?"

"Sure, Matthew, all the time," Nick answers.

"Then would you mind if we . . . ?" Matthew pulls a joint out of his pocket.

"Not right now," Iris says.

Matthew shrugs and puts it away.

Intrigued by this conversation, I look over at Iris and this time really scrutinize her. She's at the age where women become invisible to younger people, especially men. Her skin looks a little dry and blotchy with some spots. She's wrinkled, has crow's feet, and wears thick-lensed glasses. Nevertheless, she seems far from having one foot in the grave.

Maybe it's the trailer's Day-Glo paint job. Or her bright headband. Or the very feminine outfit she's wearing, which suggests she is more secure about her body than many women her age. It's a loose-fitting breezy lace cardigan top over a long T-shirt and jeans. The top has a pink and gray floral pattern. It's flowing and graceful and probably flutters in the breeze when she walks. She seems good-humored and wise. In fact, she reminds me of a seer, a perceiver of hidden truth. Or am I letting my imagination run away with me?

Nick pushes the Caddy toward a dark ridge on the horizon. I feel that things are back on track somehow. Iris turns on the radio news. We listen for ten minutes. After hearing stories about war, pestilence, and famine, Nick says, "The evening news is where they begin with *Good evening,* and then proceed to tell you why it isn't."

Always a quip, I think.

Everything Paul Harvey reads on air sends Nick into a rant. American society has been corrupted by capitalism and materialism. The government is repressive. Churches are filled with self-righteous hypocrites. Marriage is a loveless prison.

Nick is preaching to the choir, as far as I'm concerned. But it seems yoga has brought him less tranquility than Iris.

6

December 1970

I came home to Saint James Court feeling stressed out and looking forward to nothing more than a shower and a nap. But I was surprised to find Stan waiting for me on the front step even though the mercury had dropped into the forties.

"What are you doing out here?" I said.

"Chilling."

"Yeah, I can see that."

"Sit down."

He had a can of beer in his hand and five more on a plastic ring. He offered me one of them. I took it and joined him on the frigid concrete.

"I want to hear about your first day of teaching in the Star Unit. How did it go?"

"Lousy," I said. "It's like being the only lifeguard in a sea of drowning children."

I told him about my principal's stated preference for a black teacher instead of me. My classroom's condition. The students who had torn it up. My incompatible teaching teammate.

"Sounds rugged," he said.

"Yeah, I may be in over my head." I took a deep breath. "If I'm this beat after one day, how am I going to feel after a week? Or a month? If I last that long."

"Tell me about this teacher you're working with."

"Mike Thresher. He's a former Marine, just back from Vietnam.

He treats the kids like he's their drill sergeant."

"How well does that approach work?"

"Sometimes, I have to admit that it does. The principal's a big fan of Thresher. To me, the guy's just a militaristic bully who doesn't really give a shit about the students. He just wants to collect a check. He's probably a racist, too."

"He's a jarhead. What do you expect? Just be glad he's not armed." Stan grinned over his beer can. "We should go out to the VFW post tonight."

The segue threw me. "Are you kidding? Could I even get in?"

"You could, if you were with me."

"Thought you had to be a member."

"Or be with a member. Depends on the chapter. Good-looking women can always get in, of course."

"Is that why you go? For the women?"

"It's one reason."

"I've got planning to do," I said. "And the last thing I'll need tomorrow is a hangover."

Stan finished his beer, set down the can, and opened another.

"Sometimes at the VFW you'll run into somebody with an interesting story. Like I did the other night when this old guy claimed to have witnessed the first kamikaze attack of WWII. It was in 1944. A Jap fighter holed the flight deck of the *Santee*, an aircraft carrier. They took a lot of casualties."

"I never fully understood the kamikazes," I said, wishing for my nap. "What did they hope to accomplish by becoming suicide bombers anyway, other than prolonging the war?"

"The kamikazes considered themselves part of Japan's samurai warrior tradition that surrender is dishonorable. Better to commit *seppuku*—disembowel yourself with a sword—than to surrender."

"That's crazy."

"Maybe, to us. At least they believed in something that was worth dying for. Look at some of the crazy shit Americans believe in. That money can buy them love. Aliens. Jinxing a free throw or a no-hitter. Tell me that stuff is not nuts."

"But why is it dishonorable to surrender when you know you're beaten?"

"It goes back to the 13th century when Japan was about to be invaded by the Mongolian hordes. They were saved by a timely typhoon that destroyed the Mongolian fleet. They called the typhoon a 'divine wind.' That's what kamikaze means."

"They believed it was divine intervention?"

"Yeah. Anyway, getting back to the story, thirty seconds after the first kamikaze attack another one came in low over the water. They splashed it with AA fire, but then a third one came out of the clouds, rolled over, and dove at the ship. It hit a torpedo bomber parked on the flight deck and blew up eleven planes. The old guy said for half a day, it was like wading in the fires of hell."

I pictured the destruction and shuddered. "You're right, that's quite a story."

"It shows you the warrior mindset, Pate, which means putting yourself in harm's way. It has for thousands of years."

"Is that why you enlisted? To become a warrior?"

"Hell yeah. But a warrior needs something honorable to fight for, which WWII provided but not Vietnam, as I learned too late."

"Plus, life is short."

"Amen to that, brother. Which brings me to the question: Why are you teaching in the Star Unit?"

I shrugged. "Maybe I've got a little of that kamikaze spirit myself."

"Then you better have another beer," he said. "You'll need it."

But I didn't. And I didn't accompany him to the VFW that night, either.

Later, a storm blew in from the west and the sky turned green, the way it sometimes does before a tornado. Rain tapped on my windows so noisily that I nearly missed hearing the phone ringing. It was Deborah calling to tell me that someone had broken into her place.

"Are you and Donald all right?"

Yes, but they'd stolen her TV and trashed her apartment. Could I come over?

"I'm on my way."

I shrugged on my poncho and went out into the storm. The rain fogged up my windshield and did its best to overwhelm my wiper blades. The storm sewers were backed up in several places along the way, creating lakes on the pavement. I plowed on through them, hoping my engine wouldn't stall, but avoided the flooded railroad underpasses where the unwary had been known to drown.

When I arrived at Deborah's, rain was streaming through the cracks in her splintered side door. Stepping over the puddles on the kitchen floor, I followed a swath of destruction to the living room, where I found Deborah, who threw herself into my arms.

"Oh, Pate, just look at this mess."

It looked as if a mini funnel cloud had ripped through here. Furniture was knocked over, bureau drawers ransacked, closets emptied out on the floor.

I didn't see the kid. "Where's Donald?"

"He's in the bedroom."

I asked if any other valuable items, such as a camera or jewelry, had been taken.

No, she said. She didn't have any.

This made me surmise at first that the burglar had been frustrated not to find more stuff he could easily remove and dispose of, triggering his wrathful destructive behavior.

"Did you call the police?"

"Waste of time," she said.

"How do you know?"

Her look said *how naïve can you get.* "They won't do shit."

Maybe she's right, I thought, as I looked around, absorbing the full impact of this invasion of her home. That's what it seemed like, whether she was present or not. How would I feel if this had happened to me? I'd only experienced one break-in in my life, and that was back in college when I was living in a rundown apartment downtown. I hadn't called the cops, either, because I knew the culprit was a disgruntled former roommate. That made me think.

"Do you know who did this?"

"I can't prove it, but I believe it was Eddie who broke in."

Ah. "Thought you said he wouldn't come back."

"I was wrong."

She looked down miserably at the chaos surrounding her.

"I'm so scared, Pate. I don't know what I'm going to do. I need a decent place to live and raise my son, but it seems so hard."

"It will be all right."

Before I got another look like the last one, I added, "Why don't you and Donald crash at my place tonight?"

"Could we?"

"Sure."

"Thank you." She hugged me gratefully.

Her damaged entrance was now an invitation to other looters. I asked if she had some plywood and plastic sheeting. She said she always kept some on hand "just in case."

While she continued cleaning up the wreckage and restoring order, I nailed plywood over the splintered door panels and duct-taped plastic sheeting over the plywood. It might not keep all the rain out, but it would help.

When I was done, I waited while she packed a suitcase and got her son ready. Then we all sloshed through an ankle-deep quagmire to the car.

"This is so messed up," Deborah said. "I work hard, but this is all I can afford. I can't move. We're barely getting by as it is. What kind of environment is this for Donald to grow up in?"

I tried to comfort her by saying things would work out, but her highly expressive features warned me that it would take more than mere words to make her believe that.

We made it through the downpour and back to my place without incident but soaked to the skin. Stripping off our outer garments, we hung them up in the bathroom. Deborah made hot chocolate for Donald, and I poured two snifters of brandy for us. He'd barely uttered a word the whole time. I guessed he was traumatized by events. I tried to be quietly reassuring as we all curled up on the love seat.

"Thanks for rescuing us, Pate."

"Hey, you haven't heard the news," I said. "I got a full-time teaching job."

"Wow, that's fantastic." She sat up straight, smiled, and continued making eye-contact. "I'm so pleased for you. What school?"

"Parkland."

"That's wonderful."

She asked me to tell her all about it.

Thrilled by her positive, excited response, I launched into a lengthy description of the ups and downs of my first day, including the candy bar trick.

"Donald would like that, wouldn't you?" Deborah said.

He remained solemn and expressionless as she kissed him on top of his head.

"You sound like a magician," she said. "What do you have up your sleeve for tomorrow?"

"I've been trying to come up with some interesting assignments. If I don't want them to be disruptive and disrespectful, I'll have to show them I'm not just another sub there to collect a paycheck."

"But a paycheck *is* nice," she said.

I grinned. "Yeah, but as their permanent teacher, I need to show that I care about them."

"You will." She snuggled closer. "I hope Donald gets a teacher like you someday. Hell, I wish *I'd* had a teacher like you."

"You do now," I said.

"Do I?"

"Yeah. How about I give you a little homework assignment after we put Donald to bed?"

"That would be nice." Her dark, scintillating gaze lingered in the air between us.

But after a beat or two of silence, she shook her head and changed the subject.

"That Eddie. Fool can't have me, so he takes my TV. Oh, I wish I could get away from him once and for all."

Eddie had tested our relationship. Now I got the feeling that Deborah was doing so. And I sensed that unless I acted at once, that doubt might worm its way into us until there was nothing left.

I looked over at her child, who was sound asleep.

"Why don't you and Donald just move in here with me?"

She leaned away. "You mean like the real thing, only minus the ceremony? Listen, Pate, it's great of you to take us in like this. I don't know what else we'd do. I appreciate it. And I'm sure you think you're doing the right thing by asking us to live here, but—"

I had to make her understand how I felt. "Look, Deborah, I've never lived with a woman before. This would be a big step."

"I understand, but it would be a big step for us, too."

"I don't know if I'm ready for more than—"

"What? Living together. Maybe Eddie was right when he said this would happen."

"What's happened? Nothing."

"Exactly."

I stared out the window at the rain, thinking she had a sharp tongue and that her gratitude had a short shelf life. She didn't want much, did she? Just *everything*. And right now.

I brooded.

But my resentment didn't last. These Victorian homes, this park-like setting, would be a grand place for her and Donald to live. It was understandable that she wasn't willing to settle for less than marriage. What single parent wouldn't want security and a father for her child? Now that I had a steady job, my suitability as a prospective husband had grown rapidly.

I rubbed my face and thought hard about it. But what if I wasn't up to the task yet? Or ever? And I had qualms about Deborah's readiness, too. Even putting aside racial issues, I foresaw other challenging problems ahead. I didn't know if we could trust each other enough to survive them. Or ever learn to compromise.

When the silence grew too heavy, I took her hand and kissed it.

"I've asked you to move in with me, Deborah. I'll ask again. Why not give it a try? If it doesn't work, you can always move out."

"But so can you. That's the point, isn't it?"

"Look, I care for you, Deborah. I just need a little more time. Can you give me a little more time?"

"What happens to Stan if we move in?"

"He will be the least of our problems."

"How do you know?"

"I know Stan."

In truth, I didn't know any such thing.

On day two at Parkland Junior High, I came to work early, intending to read the morning paper while sipping convenience store coffee. But as soon as I saw the room's condition, I knew all that would have to wait. Although I'd straightened the furniture up when I left yesterday, the floor still had not been swept nor the trash emptied. Worse, the place stank of mildew, rank sweat, and urine. It was probably more noticeable this morning because the portable had been shut up all night. When I opened the door to air the place out, frigid wind rushed in and I shivered as I went around picking up the trash.

When the kids showed up, I greeted each of them by name, and would not let them in until they were quiet and well-behaved. They seemed surprised to see me again, but I was ready for them, having lain awake half the night scheming about how to deal with their misbehavior. But now a new problem presented itself.

Fifteen minutes after class was supposed to start, my colleague Thresher still hadn't arrived. While his students were his problem, leaving them alone would've been tantamount to fomenting a riot. I had to keep them all with me. As I was trying to figure out what to do with them, Reginald blindsided me again. I couldn't help noticing that he was still wearing the same smelly clothes as yesterday. I made a mental note to bring all this up with his counselor.

When my teammate finally arrived, I ignored his half-hearted apology and remained silent as he herded his group next door and immediately began yelling. I hoped I wouldn't do the same thing if my carefully laid plans fell apart. At least now I knew all their names and where they were supposed to sit.

Lamont, however, immediately tested my resolve by complaining about his desk.

"It all messed up," he shouted.

The surface was indeed scarred and notched like an old prize fighter's face. But all the other desks were defaced in some way, even my own. I pointed this out to Lamont, who sighed. Curtis was next, claiming his desk wobbled, so I wedged a shim of folded paper under one leg.

"Curtis' desk," Braxton yelled, "squeal like his mama."

After taking Braxton to task, I tried to calm an outraged Curtis by showing him how my own swivel chair groaned. Braxton offered to trade seats with me. Alonso shouldered his way to the back and flopped, refusing to take his assigned seat in the front row. He said he always sat in back. I told him not anymore. Yesterday, he'd had a nice nap back there. Those days were over.

"Today, you sit up here, son."

"I ain't your son."

"I won't ask you again, Alonso."

"Don't make me no never mind."

"Have it your own way. Mr. Green will get you a ride down to Juvenile Hall."

"Man, you just selling wolf tickets," Alonso said.

"You think I'm bluffing?" I picked up the phone.

"Hold up. Hold up. Just like that you gonna throw me out? Not even send me to the principal first?"

"Not when you're being insubordinate."

"Okay, so I get suspended, but no juvie."

"With a record like yours, you already have one foot out the door." I hadn't looked at his file yet, but he didn't know that.

"Send me to juvie 'cause I won't sit in the front row?"

"Mr. Green?" I said into the phone.

"Aw right, aw right."

No sooner was Alonso sitting where I wanted him than Harold

was asking where their candy bars were. "You promised," he said.

A promise was a promise. Despite the fact I didn't want to issue them all a huge dose of sugar, I pulled the candy out of my desk drawer. The class cheered.

"Hold on," I said. "First, we have to take a quiz."

"Over what?"

"Yeah, we ain't even learned nothin' yet."

"A test of your general knowledge. Get out pencil and paper."

Nobody had any. I told them they all deserved a zero for coming to class unprepared. But I was aware that if they cared about their grades, they wouldn't be in the Star Unit in the first place. Praying they wouldn't stab each other, I handed out stubby orange golf pencils and lined paper that I'd purchased out of my own pocket in anticipation of such problems.

"I'll help you today. But next time come prepared. First question: Who's the president of the United States?"

"Aw, that's easy," Curtis said. "Nixon."

I shushed him. "Don't say the answers out loud. Write them down. That's why I gave you the paper. Question number two: Who's the governor of Kentucky?"

They stared at me blankly.

"Three: Who's the mayor of Louisville?"

More stares.

I told them to put their names on their quizzes.

"Man, we didn't know nothin'," Braxton said.

I felt pretty sure he was right about that. How do you teach people who know nothing? Maybe this was beyond me. We would see.

"Hey, why you got that beard?" Harold said.

The question didn't surprise me. What surprised me was that it took so long for them to ask.

"Cause he a pirate," Lamont said. "Red Beard the pirate."

The other kids screamed with laughter.

"Red Beard, Red Beard," Alonso chanted.

"You 'posed to call him Mr. Merwin,'" Reginald stammered.

I couldn't believe he was defending me.

"'You . . . 'posed to call him . . . Mr. Merwin,'" Alonso mocked.

"Shut up," Reginald said.

"Sucka. I'll mess you up."

Alonso jumped up and the chase was on. Until a hand protruding from the sleeve of a navy blazer grabbed him by the scruff of the neck, quick-marched him to his desk, and jammed him down in it.

"You're welcome," Mr. Thresher said.

The Marine continued on his way outdoors "for a smoke break," which was why he'd just happened to show up when he did.

It pissed me off that he'd interfered in my classroom. I intended to tell him so in no uncertain terms. But that would have to wait. Right now, I was too busy pulling Reginald aside and thanking him for defending me, but also telling him not to do it again. To restore normalcy, I handed out the promised candy. I also passed the garbage can around, urging them not to make a mess. To my surprise, most of the empty wrappers went into the can. Encouraged, I decided to try something new with them in English instead of relying on the text.

"I always loved being read to when I was a kid," I said. An image of my Dad's parents, who'd raised me, flared through my mind. "Did any of your parents, or grandparents, ever read to you?" Two raised hands. "Well, I'm convinced this is how we learn to read—by first experiencing that pleasure."

"What you gonna read to us?" Braxton said.

"This." I held up *Little House in the Big Woods*. Seeing the cover illustration of a little girl with a doll, they hooted. It was understandable. Nothing could've been further from their experience than Laura Ingalls Wilder's frontier tales. I remembered what a spellbinding effect it had on me as a youngster, though, how it had inspired my first attempts at telling stories of my own.

I began at the beginning. By the time I'd read the first three pages about a little girl who lived in a log cabin in the Wisconsin woods many years ago, they were hooked. They loved the cabin, Laura, and especially anything about food. It would be lunchtime soon; maybe they were hungry. When Eugene heard about Pa smoking venison in a hollow length of tree trunk, he asked why it didn't all burn up.

"Excellent question." I explained the hickory chips were too green to burn and would only smolder.

Braxton, upon hearing Laura's Pa had caught a whole wagonload of fish in a net at Lake Pepin, said, "I like to go fishing. My cousin take me down to Cox's Park."

Curtis said his favorite part was when Pa and Uncle Henry butchered the pig. Scalding it and scraping off its bristles with a knife. Hanging it in a tree, taking out its insides, making a balloon out of the pig's bladder. Curtis said his relatives liked to barbecue pork, too.

"But not the whole pig."

Obviously, my miscreants loved Laura and her family. But when they stampeded out for lunch, someone knocked over the garbage can. Candy wrappers spilled all over the place.

Feeling hazy at eight o'clock on Saturday morning, I stepped onto black and white bathroom tiles probably as old as my grandparents and couldn't find the bathmat. When in due course I did, it was wadded up underneath the sink where someone had kicked it. I dragged the mat out and straightened it out on the floor. After showering, I reached for a towel, but they weren't where they were supposed to be. They'd been moved. While searching for a clean one, I discovered that Deborah also had claimed a shelf for herself and spread out possibly every beauty product known to man, or woman. In due course, I found a clean towel and used it to dry off.

I was a little miffed by this presumption, feeling that house guests should leave things as they found them. The cosmetics also reminded me of Mom's makeup hodgepodge when I was growing up. I'd heard it said that some men unconsciously seek out women like their mothers for marriage partners, a thought which horrified me. I glanced at my image in the fogged mirror and realized that I was conflicted about hosting Deborah and Donald. I wanted her here, and I didn't want her here.

While this would seem to confirm Deborah's fears, I told myself to give it a chance. Maybe I was feeling like a spoiled brat, an only child whose space is being invaded by a newcomer. Not by a new *sibling* perhaps, but I was entering a period of adjustment that threatened my world. Both of us were. It was too early to predict if this show would be a Broadway hit or close after only a few performances.

With my spirits buoyed by a familiar earthy aroma, I went yawning into the kitchen where I found a vision in pale pink awaiting me at the table—Deborah in her robe and matching house shoes. Donald was there, too, eating Cocoa Puffs while his mother sipped coffee from a mug with my name on it. For some reason, I didn't mind that intrusion.

"Good morning, little guy," I said, gently running my hand over Donald's dome-like afro hairstyle.

I knew that I'd made a mistake from the annoyance on Deborah's face and the way she pulled back when I leaned over to kiss her.

"Why'd you do that?" she said. "Now I'll have to fix his do all over again before we can go out."

"Sorry. I didn't think," I said awkwardly, at the same time pondering where she might want to go. This was something we hadn't discussed last night.

"No, you didn't." Deborah used a wide-toothed afro pick to sculpt Donald's hair into the shape she wanted.

"I said I'm sorry."

She sighed before relenting. "Don't worry about it—this time."

"What do you mean 'this time'?" I chuckled softly as I took a seat at the table. "I only get one second chance?"

"That's right, buster." She smiled, but I got the feeling she wasn't kidding. "Do you want some coffee?"

"Did you save me any?"

"Of course I did." She poured a cup.

"You look great," I said, to make up for my failure to say, or do, anything right up to this point, and it worked as the downturned corners of her mouth turned into a smile.

Thereupon, my roommate's bedroom door was flung open and he emerged—haggard and bloodshot, hairy and bare—in only a pair of cutoffs.

"Well, hello, Deborah," he said. "I wondered who was out here having such a good time and drinking up all the coffee."

He walked over to the cabinet and pulled out a plain mug. Then he picked up the pot and poured himself a cup of brew.

"Mm, good."

Nodding at Donald, he said, "Hey, kid. How are they treating you?"

The boy made no reply.

Stan caught my anxious expression and said, "Oh, am I interrupting?" With that, he pivoted and returned to his room, cup in hand.

"When are you going to do it?" Deborah asked the instant the door shut behind him.

"Do what?"

"Tell him to move out."

It was a terrible moment. How do you tell a friend that he's no longer welcome in his own home—especially when you're not even sure that's what you want?

"Well?" She looked exasperated.

"Today."

Monday evening when Stan breezed in, the apartment was silent.

"Hey, man," he said, with that careless, wild expression he always wore. "What's going on? Where's Deborah and Donald?"

"They went to her father's house."

"When are they coming back?"

"Tomorrow."

He opened the fridge to grab a beer. As he opened the can, he said, "Got something on your mind?"

I looked him in the eye. "I've been meaning to talk to you."

"What about?"

When Deborah asked me how I was going to tell him, I said I could always remind Stan that the lease was in my name, not his. If it came to that—which I hoped it wouldn't. But this was even harder than expected. Stan was a great friend, and I owed him. But he had to understand,

and I thought he would, although that didn't make me feel much better.

I told him about the break-in at Deborah's place. How her neighborhood wasn't safe.

"Sounds bad. What are you going to do about it?"

That was vintage Stan, assuming I was going to try to solve her problem. He knew me too well.

"The only thing I can. I'm going to ask her to move in here with me."

"I see. Does that mean you want me out?"

"I'm afraid so."

"Okay, you want me out, I'm out."

"I'm sorry, man. I don't know what else to do."

"Don't sweat it. A little more warning would've been nice, though."

"I realize this is sudden."

"She going to pay part of the rent?"

"We haven't talked about it."

"Can you afford it if she doesn't?"

"We'll work it out," I said.

"Okay. Just tell me this: Did you plan to let me know before, or after, she moved in?"

"Aw, Stan," I said, hanging my head a little.

"No big deal. I'll be gone by tomorrow afternoon."

"Where will you go?"

"Not your problem, bro. I just thought we were better friends than this."

He chugged the rest of his beer and wiped his mouth on his sleeve.

Next day, as he'd promised, Stan moved out.

I told Deborah when I picked her and Donald up.

"Hear that, Donald?" she said. "Now you can have your own room."

Donald seemed nonplussed.

"It'll be all right," she told me. "Was there any trouble about it?"

I shook my head.

"That's great," she said. "Makes me like Stan even more."

Me, too, I thought.

Deborah said she'd found a new day care center that was within walking distance of my place, and not too expensive.

"You're going to love it, Donald. You'll have so many new friends to play with. What do you think about that?"

"Can I watch *Spider-Man*?" he said in a tiny voice.

He looked downcast when she reminded him that they didn't have a TV anymore.

"We will soon," I said. "That's a promise."

Deborah made a promise of her own—to cook us a great meal if I entertained Donald. So, I took him along with me down to the basement. He got a little wide-eyed when he first saw the gloomy, cobwebbed cavern. Crates and boxes lined the dark corners. A couple of bicycles were stored there, along with a gas-powered lawn mower, and assorted garden tools. I showed him the driftwood coffee table I was still working on, but that was not why we'd come.

I'd remembered how much fun I had in my grandparents' basement when I was little playing with simple home-made toys, like wood blocks. I wanted Donald to have some, too, plus the fun of helping to make them. I sawed up several two-by-fours into hand-sized cubes, then showed him how to smooth out the rough edges with sandpaper. He seemed fascinated. In no time, we'd finished a dozen blocks. He couldn't wait to go play with them up in his room with a few of his other toys he'd brought over.

When we got back upstairs and Deborah saw how happy he seemed, she smiled radiantly at both of us.

After we ate, I did the dishes and she gave Donald his bath.

"Maybe I'll give you one, too." She winked, I waggled my eyebrows.

First, though, I had to read Donald a bedtime story. I'd picked up a copy of *The Little Prince*, intending to read it aloud to my Star Unit students. But maybe this would be good practice, I thought. At first, Donald didn't seem interested in the yellow-haired boy depicted on the cover as standing between two palm trees on a globe, peering at the stars and sun. I explained that, while the story was make-believe, it had been inspired by the writer's real-life experiences.

"Okay, Pate," he said, using the name I'd told him to call me for the first time, "you can read it to me."

I explained that the author, Antoine de Saint-Exupéry, had crash-landed into the Sahara Desert while attempting to break a flying record. Antoine and his navigator became lost, without any water, and began hallucinating.

"Do you know what that means?" I asked.

He said he did. So, I told him that both flyers were near death when a man riding a camel found them and saved their lives. Then I began to read. The narrator related seeing, at age six, a picture of an animal being swallowed by a boa constrictor. Frustrated with adults for thinking the snake was a hat, he gave up drawing. He found it a waste of time since they never understood anything anyway. This assertion seemed to resonate with young master Donald.

It occurred to me that I'd felt the same way at his age. The grownups in my life had been screwing it up. The first time I ever saw my new stepfather, I was repelled by the coldness in his eyes. *Oh, no! Oh, no!* I'd thought. When I glanced at Donald, he'd drifted off. Hoping his mother wouldn't catch me in the act, I ran my hand through his soft springy hair before tiptoeing out of the room.

Back in the basement I continued using some coarse grit sandpaper on the driftwood I was shaping. I was anxious to move up to a medium, and then a fine grade, and feel the wood's smoothness with my hand. As I'd shown Donald, I sanded with the grain, removing as many scratches as possible. Then I wiped the sanded surface clean with a tack cloth. As I held it up to the light to admire its beauty, I saw how the basement was swirling with sawdust motes and thought maybe next time we should wear masks to protect ourselves.

7

July 1971

As we cross a broad valley between two mountain ranges, Nick spots the dunes looming ahead in the distance. At first, they seem dwarfed by the thirteen-thousand-foot mountain peaks rising behind them, but as we get closer, their true scale emerges. There's thirty-five miles of them, according to a tourist brochure. They are the tallest in North America, up to seven hundred and fifty feet.

At the park, we agree to go our separate ways. But Iris and Nick, who sign up for an RV campsite, invite us to come over after dinner for drinks.

At Stan's insistence, we register for a primitive campsite separate from wherever Matthew winds up. Matthew indicates he doesn't like it, but there's not much he can do about it. Like every campsite in the park, ours has a fire grate and picnic table. There's a large cottonwood tree for shade. We're told to pitch our tent within the rock wall boundaries of the site. But since we don't have one, we simply drop off the rucksacks containing our sleeping bags and head for the dunes.

While they don't seem that far away, we soon learn how deceptive distances out here can be. It takes ten minutes of determined walking to reach the dune field. Once there, each dune seems monumental. At the closest one, there's a group of junior high school kids screaming and tumbling down the steep slopes. I've had enough of that age group to last me for quite a while and suggest we move on to the next dune.

During the day, the rangers have told us that the sand can be scorching. But it's cooler now and the air is clean and dry. As we climb, we must squint due to the particles kicked up by the wind. But we don't mind. This is a fabulous way to stretch out our legs and end the long day of travel. At the top, Stan pulls out a joint he's picked up along the way and fires it up. The view of distant snow-capped peaks, pine forests, and grasslands is breathtakingly spectacular. We sit there, entranced, as the minutes fly by.

After a long while, I say. "I can't believe Matthew tracked us down. What do you think we ought to do?"

"Dump his ass."

"Okay, but I doubt that will be that easy. He must be out of his mind to do this."

"Hard to disagree with that. We're not responsible for what he does or what happens to him."

"Not our brother's keeper, huh?"

Back at camp, we make a fire and heat up some canned corned beef hash for supper. We eat it right out of the cans with convenience store plastic forks and it tastes great. We talk about it. Stan says it's mostly due to the effect of the dope. But I argue that it's even more a product of the clean air and the beauty of where we are, coupled with the exertion required to scale the dunes.

"Not that it's all that important," I concede.

There's a fifty-gallon trash drum for our site chained up to a post. After policing up the area, the old Eagle Scout props open the bear-proof lid of the garbage drum and launches a couple of trash can jump shots that *clang!* into the bottom of the barrel.

"Nothin' but net," Stan says, as if there was one.

As the sharp-edged mountains slowly fade and the purple velvet sky turns gray, we stroll through the sagebrush to the Paraprosdoki-ans' triangular-shaped camp. The air is already thick with burning piñon and Nick is adding more wood to the fire pit as we arrive. Iris is mixing drinks at a weathered picnic table. She waves us over. We sit under a conifer tree on folding aluminum lawn chairs. Everything seems perfect until the trailer door opens and out comes Matthew Duncan with a fifth of gin in his hand.

"It's a gorgeous twilight, isn't it?" he says.

We grunt. We knew he'd be here, of course, but didn't realize he'd beaten us literally to the punch, which Iris continues to mix up as we drain our red plastic cups.

Over the campfire's hiss and the rattle of ice in our drinks, Nick tells us how he's developed relationships with the West's finest weavers. Then he unrolls an armful of small rugs stored in the trailer. I run my hand over the top one, which has a complicated zigzag pattern resembling an eye.

"Very soft," I say.

"It should be," Nick says. "It's one-hundred percent Churro wool, and all-natural dyes. Hand-woven on traditional upright looms."

The next pattern he shows us incorporates stalks of maize, sprouting flowers, and foliage. This represents the Navajo holy people celebrating corn as the tree of life.

"Think about where we are. The Pueblo dwellers along the Rio Grande are still linked to their ancestors' spiritual life by the Great Sand Dunes," Nick says.

"Does that include using peyote?" Stan wants to know.

"Sure," Nick says. "But that was only a part of the simple back-to-nature kind of existence they wanted."

Now in full sales mode, he shows us more rugs. One is priced at $1,500. Another is "a steal at seven-fifty," he says. "But since we're friends, I'll take seven hundred for it."

"Nick," Stan asks, "what's the difference between a rug that costs fifteen hundred and one that costs fifteen *thousand*?"

"Over thirteen thousand bucks," he grins.

"Enough with the rugs," Iris says. "Put them back in the camper, Nick."

While he's doing that, she asks if we're going hiking tomorrow. We confirm this. She wants us to go over our plans with her.

"I have no plans," Matthew says.

We do. We also have canteens and head gear. There's a baseball cap from a hardware store in Louisville for me, and a denim railroad engineer's hat for Stan.

"Good," Iris says, "but you need to set a time when you'll get back and make sure someone knows. Then you need to be back by that time. Otherwise, the park rangers will have to go find you. They hate that."

"Think we're going to get lost, Iris?" Stan says.

"It can happen, don't kid yourselves. Especially if you go out too far, and don't pay enough attention."

Not only are the dunes more physically challenging than we might expect, she tells us, they're always changing. "The Ute word for them, which I can't pronounce, means 'the land that moves back and forth.'"

Nick returns from the trailer in time to quip, "Change is inevitable—except from a vending machine."

Shaking her head at him, Iris relates a story about the time Nick ignored the rangers' warnings and wound up lost in the middle of a thunderstorm. "Should've taught him a lesson," she says, "though I'm not sure it did."

"You're never too old to learn something stupid," Nick says.

"Paraprosdokians have thick skulls," Iris says.

They should hike with us, I propose.

"Thanks," Iris says, "but I'm afraid we'll have to pass. You guys go on. It's an experience you'll never forget."

"Only trouble with that plan," Matthew interjects, "is that it sounds like we'll all have to find another ride."

"No, you won't," Iris says. "We'll wait here for you."

"Really?" I say, amazed. "That's incredibly generous. But don't you have an itinerary?"

"Not always," Iris says. "That's the beauty of our lifestyle. We've got all the time in the world."

Then she insists that we not only write down our plans but leave them with her and Nick for our protection. So, we do.

Before we make our way back to our own camp, Matthew asks me—begs me—for a moment in private. I want to say no, but what's the point of holding a grudge? We'll soon be rid of him anyway. Besides, he's whetted my curiosity. I follow him over to an empty campsite, where we won't be overheard.

"I know you don't want me along," he begins. "But remember, I did put you two up at my house and showed you a good time. Doesn't that count for something?"

It does, I nod.

"Everything was fine except for at the end there," he says. "Don't tell me you didn't enjoy spending time with Rebecca and Katy. Sure, I was a little pissed at Rebecca, but I'm over it. Why can't you let it go?"

"We're talking about *yesterday*, Matthew. That's how long it's been since you not only left your wife but threw away your career. Why do you want to go where you're not wanted?"

"I told you before that Rebecca wanted out of the marriage, too. Only I went first. And I'm not throwing my career away, I'm embracing it. Someone I know from summer stock has connections in Hollywood." He holds up his thumb and index finger half an inch apart. "I'm this close to landing a role on a daytime soap opera."

"Then why the hell do you want to go with us?"

"The part I'm up for doesn't begin for a couple of weeks. Until then, I'm free. We could all have a blast together if you'd both just let bygones be bygones."

I'd wanted Matthew's friendship desperately when he was the cool guy back in college. Now he's begging for mine. Very satisfying.

"Even if I agree, Stan won't."

"Talk him into it. When we get to California, I'll introduce you to everyone from Dustin Hoffman to Julie Christie."

"Really? How do you plan to do that?"

"I understand this celebrity shit. If you're an actor, it gives you an entree into their world. I'm telling you we're going to have a *bitchin'* great time, Pate. We'll do everything, try anything, stop at nothing. Then we'll say, 'Yes, by God, we've lived.' Now are you in or out, goddamn it?"

He's got charisma, this bastard, this heel. There's no denying it. I should reject his ridiculous proposition out of hand. But I'm still thinking it over long after Matthew and I have said goodnight and returned to our own camp laden with Iris's sun lotion and Nick's magnetic compass, which they have insisted we must take.

It's not quite dark, and as we arrive, we're startled to find animal tracks all over the place.

"Holy crap!" Stan says. "What made them?"

I have no idea. But a bit later, a patrolling ranger comes by in a Jeep and we flag her down. We show her the tracks.

"Mule deer," she says. "Don't worry. Aggressive wildlife isn't much of a problem this time of year. But you should make sure all your food is stored in bear-proof boxes."

"Many bears around here?" Stan inquires.

"Black bears. If you see one, stay calm, or it might get excited."

"Excited?" I say.

"On the other hand, snake season's about over." The ranger asks if we're hiking tomorrow. Hearing that we are, she advises us to go early and wear shoes. "The sand gets up to 140 degrees by early afternoon. It's easier to climb after a good rain when the sand's packed down firmly. Unfortunately, it hasn't rained here for days now."

The ranger departs.

I'm carefully unrolling my sleeping bag, alert to possible creepy crawlies, when Stan says, "What did that asshole Matthew want with you?"

"You won't believe it."

"Why?"

"He still wants to come with us, and I think we should let him."

"You can't be serious."

I explain Matthew's argument, his soap opera role, and Hollywood connections. "If we let him tag along with us, he'll see that we get invited to some Hollywood parties."

"And in spite of all he's done, you believe him?"

"Actually, I do."

Stan stares up at the blue-black, star-filled sky. "You say it would only be for a couple of weeks?"

"Yes, but I realize you probably wouldn't be interested in something so superficial as meeting movie stars or going to great parties."

He scratches his chin whiskers. "I might. But if no parties, we dump his ass."

"Deal."

After conjuring bears and snakes in my dreams, I open my eyes to a hazy band of light arching across the night sky. It is seemingly within easy reach. By the time I actually worm my way out of my sleeping bag, though, it's light and the temperature is beginning to rise. I dress quickly and fill up my canteen. Then I go to collect Matthew.

He's ready when I arrive, with a full canteen and headgear he refers to as, "an authentic Australian fishing hat."

When he says he has some money we can spend on groceries for the three of us, I'm encouraged but remain resolved that he must earn my trust. This hike promises to be a real physical challenge, the kind that you feel good about after. We collect Stan, whose ear has healed up enough so that a bandage is no longer needed. He's stopped limping, too. In fact, he feels so good he leads us up the first dune in single file.

Climbing proves easy enough in the beginning when we can walk upright. At the visitors' center, I read about the cavalrymen who explored these dunes back in the 1850s. I wonder if their lungs burned and their thigh muscles cramped up like mine are right now. I can't imagine trying to ride a horse up these things. According to the book I sampled, their hooves would be half-buried on the windward slopes and sink up to the knees on the leeward. For every two steps forward, they'd slide back one.

We push hard, not talking, and scale three dunes, including one so steep we have to go on all fours. As we press on, the dunes seem more and more indistinguishable. At the ridges, we can see back to our campground. But down in the troughs, nothing but sand and sky. When I ask Stan for our heading, he aims our borrowed compass at a line of pink and gray striped cliffs.

"Two-hundred seventy degrees, due west."

Matthew says he needs a rest, but Stan won't hear of it. Matthew stops anyway, so I do, too. He unscrews his canteen, drinks, and lights up a jay. When he offers the marijuana to me, I decline, which is very unlike me. I don't want to be stoned in case we get lost. Moreover, the physical environment is intense enough for me.

"Stan's awfully quiet." Matthew exhales and the wind carries away the smoke.

"What do you expect, Matthew? You two had a brawl yesterday. You're lucky to be with us at all."

"Yeah, I guess. Man, this place is awesome."

I can't disagree.

We watch in silence for a moment as the wind ripples the sand.

Such a seemingly limitless landscape, lonely, barren, arid, harsh, and hostile to human habitation. Yet these same punishing expanses of sand possess a stark grandeur that's irresistible. I assume that Matthew's thoughts are similar. But the next pivot in our halting conversation confounds me.

"You know, Iris and Nick are driving me crazy with all their talk about yoga," he says.

"I thought you liked yoga."

"I might've overstated that. They just go on and on, you know?"

"You shouldn't disrespect people who've been kind to us. Besides, I thought you were seeking some deeper meaning in life."

He shrugs. "Actually, I find life a meaningless farce."

The light has changed. Now the desert's warm browns, golden corals, and muted reds appear even more vivid. Whatever the cause—an aesthetically minded God or a jubilant and random Nature—it's stunningly magnificent.

"Here you are, Matthew," I say, "getting stoned on a sand dune, discussing absurdity in a place where eleven thousand years ago nomads hunted mammoths with spears. Where four hundred years ago Apaches collected tree bark for food and medicine. How can you possibly find life meaningless in such a place as this?"

He stubs out the joint on the sole of his hiking boot.

"You're familiar with *Endgame,* right? As Beckett's play begins, there's been a holocaust. The only people left are an aged blind master who can't stand up and his oppressed servant who can't sit down. Now what would you call that?"

"A play, Matthew. I'd call it a play. Look, most people would prefer to believe in something rather than nothing, even if it's tough figuring out what."

"Yeah, we all need meaning and reassurance whether there is any or not."

"What kind of meaning are you expecting?" I ask. "An external flash of insight? Some new-found inner conviction? Maybe a return to faith, honesty, and true companionship plus no more broken hearts?"

"Any, or all, of that would be good," Matthew says.

I notice Stan's getting too far ahead of us. In fact, as I watch, he dissolves into fragments of white light over the next dune. "We gotta go before we lose Stan," I say, and scramble to my feet.

I take off running down the slope, assuming Matthew will follow. But when I reach the base and glance back over my shoulder, he's gone. There's nobody else in sight and suddenly I'm all alone in *Death Valley Days* without the Old Ranger to guide me. I yell for Matthew, but my cries are lost in the wind. I must decide whether to go forward or backward, but it's an easy choice. First, I can't abandon Stan. Second, I want to push on anyway. And third, Hollywood be damned, we want to get rid of Matthew, who I can only conjecture has turned back toward camp, the self-centered prick. Good riddance.

I try to pick up the pace, but the base area is softer sand, which slows me down. It's one step forward, half a step back. Each one creates an impression in the soft sand. When I look behind me, there's a trail of my own footprints. But they don't last long in this wind-blown shifting sand. It fills them in quickly and they disappear.

Up the steep slope. It's a windy day and fine, fast flying grains of sand sting my bare flesh. The breeze seems to cool the sun, but the rays reflecting off the sand are blinding. To climb faster, I try using both hands and feet. And quickly learn that the park ranger last night was right about how the sand heats up. We're all taught as kids not to touch a hot stove, but that's exactly what my bare fingers feel like they're touching right now.

Up and down, up and down. At long last, I reach the top of a giant sandpile where I can see Stan one ridge ahead of me, sitting on his heels. I yell his name across the divide, but it's all in vain because he can't, or won't, heed my call. I hustle down and up again, hoping he'll still be there when I arrive. And he is.

"Stan," I say.

He waves one hand to shush me. "Do you hear that?"

I still my heaving breath and listen. And there it is—a sound like a sustained bass note played on a pipe organ.

"The sand is singing," Stan says, and for some reason I think of *The Little Prince.*

Maybe it's the dunes' similarity to the Sahara. Or maybe it's something innocent about the way Stan says it.

I'm about to tell him that, yeah, I read about this phenomenon in a tourist brochure, too. That the "singing sand" is triggered by small avalanches going down the dune, caused by wind or hikers like us. But before I can, Stan says:

"I think it might be the sound of infinity."

This idea pretty much takes my breath away, what's left of it, and it's a long moment before I reply. I'm thinking that he hasn't had any weed this morning, as far as I know. And he does have a hat on, so it's probably not sunstroke. I watch cloud shadows twisting over the wind-sculpted ridge and it comes home just how spooky a place this is.

When I find my voice, I say, "I don't know about that, Stan. But you're definitely weirding me out."

When he doesn't respond, I study him more closely. He seems calm. Or maybe hypnotized.

"Got any water left?" I ask.

He hands me his canteen. Mine is already empty. His remains half-full. Maybe that's it, I surmise, drinking deeply. He's dehydrated and that's making him loopy. I set down the canteen.

"I think we've gone far enough, man." I gaze up at the sun. "Time to turn around and go back."

"Not done yet," Stan says.

"Done with what? This dune field is thirty-five miles long. We're never going to walk all of it."

He gets to his feet.

"What are you doing? You'll get heat stroke."

"No, I won't. You can go on back. I'll be along in a while."

"Has everybody around here gone nuts? First, you rush ahead of us. Then Matthew turns tail and leaves us. Now you want to keep going when it's obvious you're half out of your head?"

"It'll be okay, Pate."

"Snap out of it. I'm not leaving you. We need to go back. Now."

I grab his arm, but he shakes me off, upending his canteen in the process. I make a grab for it, but I'm too late to keep it from draining out on the sand, which sucks it down greedily. I look up and Stan's walking toward the next dune.

"What are you doing, you moron? Do you want to die out here?"

Apparently so since he keeps going without another word. Short of using physical force, I don't see any way to stop him. If I tried, we might both end up dying of thirst out here.

An hour later, I'm back at the visitor center where we started, refilling my canteen and emptying it down in one gulp. I fill the canteen again and this time pour the water over my head to cool off. Feeling more human, I head for the Paraprosdokians' place, where I find them playing cards in the shade.

When I ask if they've seen Matthew, Iris says, "Isn't he with you?"

I tell them how he left us out there and then how Stan refused to come back. "Now I'm afraid he's in trouble."

"We'd better get a search party started. I'll tell the rangers," Nick says, and departs in the Caddy, which has been disengaged from the psychedelic trailer.

"How could you abandon your friend in the desert, Pate?" Iris says.

"Which one are you referring to?"

"Both of them."

"I don't consider Matthew a friend."

"Then do you always treat your friends just like the people you don't give a shit about?"

I see her point and feel ashamed. I never should have let Stan go on alone. I was weak. I need to make up for it. Maybe that's why I yell at Matthew as he strolls into camp and feel so relieved not to have answer Iris's question.

"Where the hell have you been?" I demand.

"At the store." Matthew holds up some beef jerky.

"Stan's in trouble," Iris says to him. "Nick's gone to alert the rangers, but I don't think we can afford to wait for them. You and Pate need to get right back out there and find him."

"I don't know," Matthew says. "He's a big combat veteran. He'll be all right."

I get nose to nose with him. "Listen to me. You wanted to come with us, and now you're going to be even if I have to drag you out there by the throat."

"Okay, okay. No threats necessary."

"Glad to hear it. Bring your canteen."

Although our footsteps have been obliterated by now, we re-trace them more or less through half a dozen dunes. They're easy enough. But there's no telling which way Stan might have veered off, and he's the one with the compass. We spread out along a ridge in order to cover more territory. I'm hoping Stan's military training will have prepared him for this, as Matthew sarcastically predicted.

But the deeper you go into them, the more confusing the dunes become. And without water, I'm aware that Stan could keel over at any time. That would make it harder to spot him in the seas of sand particularly down at the base where he'd be completely hidden until right up to the moment he was found. I'm trying not to be melodramatic about it, but I'm truly afraid we might be too late.

Memories of my friend flood through my mind, from when we first met up to hitching out here together. We'd been relying on each other for quite a while now. Even if he was being a butthead about it, how could I have abandoned him in the middle of this desert? If I get another chance, I vow to become a better friend.

I keep trudging onward, scanning the horizon, waving occasionally at Matthew. We've been at it for well over an hour before I see someone sprawled on his back two ridges away. Waving to Matthew, I run through the sand. It takes a while, but when I finally get there it's Stan. I drop to my knees and listen to see if he's still breathing.

"Is he all right?" Matthew asks a few moments later.

"He's breathing. I'm trying to get some water into him."

I aim my canteen into his mouth. He chokes and coughs and spits the water out. His eyes flutter open. "Are you trying to drown me?" he croaks.

I tell him he's going to be okay and help him to sit up. Now he grasps the canteen himself and drinks slowly.

"Not too much at one time," I caution.

"You scared the hell out of us," Matthew says.

"You sure did," I say.

"Sorry," Stan mutters.

Shading his eyes, Matthew peers off into the distance. "You know, I think I can see Hollywood from here."

"Shut up, Matthew. This is no time to joke. Stan could have sunstroke."

It's midafternoon. I don't know how far we've come, but it's going to be a long slog across the now cocoa-colored sand back to the campground, which from here looks tiny. And people are mere specks. After a rest, we help Stan up. I'm hoping he's sufficiently recovered to help us get him back to camp. Draping his arms over our shoulders, we head back.

It feels like many hours and we're all exhausted by the time we emerge from the dunes. Iris and Nick are waiting for us back at their camp with several gallons of water. We park Stan in a lounge chair in the shade, then collapse on the ground. Nick, bless him, pours jug water over our foreheads while Iris removes Stan's shoes and shirt and wipes his forehead with a cold compress made with melted ice. We're all sitting on folding aluminum lawn chairs around Stan when the same park ranger shows up again in her jeep and kneels beside him.

"You had everyone worried about you," she scolds. "How are you doing?"

"Weak and nauseated," he replies.

The ranger turns to us. "It's dangerous to stay out on those dunes too long. We've been looking all over for you guys. You shouldn't have put yourselves at risk by going back out there. You could've gotten lost, too. Then we'd have three of you to find. Next time leave it to the experts."

We promise next time to leave it to the experts.

"You're dehydrated. I'll call emergency services," she tells Stan.

But he stops her from reaching for her radio, saying that isn't necessary.

"Look, you may feel like you're hanging in there," the ranger says, "but you could go into shock. You need to see a doctor."

"My friends here are taking good care of me," Stan says, and flatly refuses further medical assistance.

The ranger keeps trying to persuade him, to no avail.

"All right. Elevate his feet. Put more cool wet rags on his neck. If he starts feeling faint or dizzy, or complains of cramps, let us know right away, okay? Someone will be on duty in the main ranger station if you need us."

After the ranger drives away, I hand Stan a wet cloth, which he puts over his forehead. Iris and Nick are in their trailer. Matthew has gone off to buy the promised supplies at last. So it's just me and Stan now.

"Thanks for saving my ass out there today," he says.

"Why did you do it?"

"Guess I just wanted to see if I could."

It's not much of an answer and that worries me, but I don't feel like haranguing him about it. Still, he had crossed a line today that put our lives in jeopardy. For all I know, he might even be suicidal. It's a question that will hover over the rest of our trip.

"I never should have left you."

"You came back. That's what matters."

I wonder if he's right about that. Maybe I should've gone ahead and tackled him, if that's what it took. Wrestled him to the ground and kept him there until he saw reason. But I didn't and that, coupled with his own inexplicable behavior, almost cost him his life.

The setting sun turns the dunes from gold to red, purple, and orange. As I hand him the canteen and he tilts back his head and takes a drink, I think maybe beauty should always be approached with caution because beauty and danger seem to go hand in hand.

Matthew reappears in the twilight holding a grocery bag. After dropping it off with Iris, he wants to speak with me in private. I agree, though it's the last thing I want to do.

"Make it quick," I say, after walking over to a vacant campsite.

"Look, I'm sorry, Pate. Sorry for everything. Can we just start over?"

Matthew has always been a disarming bastard, that I'll give him. As apologies go, it's not too bad. No self-justification, rationalization, or accusation. But I tell myself to remember that he's an actor. How do I know whether he means it or is just reciting lines? It would be churlish to refuse his request, however.

"All right. Against my better judgment, a fresh start."

We shake on it.

Back at their camp, Iris and Nick inform us they've decided to wait here an extra day before pulling out in order to give Stan more time to get back to normal. We're appropriately grateful.

8

March 1971

By the calendar, it was already spring. But winter lingered on: cold, gray, and uninspiring. As the weeks went by, I'd been learning a lot faster than my students. Misery can produce that effect, and I was often miserable at work. But the situation improved as I remembered more lessons from student teaching. As a temp, I didn't need to put myself out. All I had to do was get through the day. But I was a permanent teacher now with much more at stake.

One tactic I'd tried was phoning the parents of any student who caused trouble. Time-consuming, but it usually resulted in improved behavior. I also recognized the wisdom of speaking slowly and never attempting to talk over the students. Not until everyone was quiet would I move on with the lesson. If students had to strain slightly to hear me, they'd be forced to pay attention. That was the theory, anyway. More often than not, it proved true. It also seemed to have a calming effect on the kids. I tried to keep it simple. Used short sentences. Double-checked to make sure they understood me. If they got off-task, or weren't following instructions, I stopped until they were.

All this helped. Still, after weeks of conducting class fairly normally, I was unsatisfied with my students' overall level of achievement. I had to try something new. One day on the way to work, I picked up a stack of *Courier-Journals*. Newspapers supposedly were written on a sixth-grade level, which was better than any of my students could read, but maybe stories about real life would interest them more than our dull text. As usual, the kids slouched in, bumped into each other, and made rude remarks. Several of them surprised me by politely greeting me as "Mr. Merwin." Small victories, but they all counted.

When the tardy bell rang, I arranged them in groups of three and was handing out the newspapers when the day's first disturbance occurred.

"You stink, Reginald," Curtis yelled.

Lamont held his nose while pretending to gag. Reginald put his head down. And I felt a little ache in my heart, not knowing what to do. Trying to force the others to work with Reginald would only stiffen their resistance and humiliate him even more. His body odor, in fact, had grown much worse. I'd noticed it when he hugged me. Small wonder, since he still wore the same clothing he'd been wearing now for weeks. At first, I'd ignored it. But now something had to be done.

After moving him away from the others and next to me, I started today's lesson with the comics section. The students seemed to like that. When we finished reading *Peanuts*, I persuaded Lamont to read *Beetle Bailey* aloud. Then the other kids took turns. By the time we'd finished the funnies, I was feeling good. We were about to move on to the sports section, and to complete paragraphs, when the outside door screeched open.

"Sorry to interrupt."

Principal Bloom entered, followed by a pair of uniformed city cops. At the sight of their white faces, the room buzzed.

"I need Braxton and Lamont. Let's go, fellas," Bloom said.

The barrel-chested, broad-shouldered cop cuffed them in front of the whole class.

"Hold on," I said. "Why are you arresting these young men?"

"Heisting TVs all over the West End, that's why," said the older cop, who was ruddy-faced and beak-nosed. "This is a real den of thieves. I wouldn't want your job."

Unable to see his eyes, I stared at his tinted glasses. "I wouldn't want yours, either."

He glared back at me but said no more. They hauled Braxton and Lamont away.

"This is what happens to people who think taking shortcuts is smart," the principal said. "This is what happens when you aren't willing to do the hard work it takes to become a man. What's so funny, Alonso?"

"Nothin'."

"You won't think it's funny when they come back for you."

Alonso stared at his desktop.

"That could've been any of you," Bloom continued. "Think of how their mothers are going to feel when they hear their sons have been arrested."

Some flashed hard looks, others hung their heads.

"A word before I go, Mr. Merwin."

I stepped outside with Bloom.

"We depend upon the police. We don't want our faculty members antagonizing them. The next time we need police, they might take their sweet time—or not come at all. Understand?"

"Mr. Bloom, all I said was—"

"I heard what you said. You made a bad situation worse. Next time, keep your mouth shut."

I felt like telling him off. But he was probably right. Also, I had responsibilities now. If I lost this job, my new family—as well as my students—would be the worse for it. I'd already blown several other opportunities. Who knew when another might come along?

"Better get back in there before they tear the place apart," Bloom said.

I found Thresher standing with his arms folded over his chest in the doorway between our classrooms. He was conventionally clad in khaki slacks, a pale blue shirt, and a tie. Though not tall, he was a strapping figure.

"Too bad they didn't roust Darrell and Alonso along with the other two," he said.

I walked on without answering.

At lunch time, I found him in the faculty dining area at a table with several other teachers. A half-eaten sandwich was in front of him. I didn't bother to ask for a private moment. I just let him have it, saying I didn't appreciate what he'd said in front of my students this morning.

Wasn't it enough the police had to come in and disrupt my class?

Thresher said, "You should be grateful they've been taken off the street and out of your hair, Merwin. It's a win-win."

"Don't you think that's a little harsh, Thresher, coming from their teacher?"

"Those two belong behind bars."

"I knew you were a hard-ass, but I didn't realize you hated the kids."

Thresher picked up his sandwich and bit into it. "I don't hate 'em. I just want some of 'em gone."

"If that's how you feel, why are you even here?"

"I want to be a high school football coach," Thresher said. "After this year, it might happen. Now here's one for you: Ever serve in the military?"

"No."

"I didn't think so," he said. "They almost ran you off last week. You can't let them get out of control like that. It makes Big Byron very unhappy."

I told him I could handle my class without his help, and from now on to stay out of my room.

"Are you sure about that?" he said, adding that we were all alone out on that island. Might be good to know somebody had our back.

"Not if it's you," I said.

Thresher shrugged and went on eating.

That afternoon, I resumed reading *Little House in the Big Woods* to the kids. They loved the part where a huge panther pursues Laura's Grandpa through the woods, finally leaping at him but landing instead on his horse's back. They were spellbound when Grandpa shot the panther dead and said he'd never go into the Big Woods again without his gun.

"Don't go *anywhere* without your gun, man," Eugene said.

Not the lesson I'd meant to teach, nor what I expected to hear, but after what I'd seen so far I wasn't surprised. The bell rang. I caught Reginald before he got out the door.

"How come you're wearing the same clothes every day?" I said softly.

"My g . . . grandma sick," he said. "She c . . . couldn't do the wash."

"What's wrong with her? Does she need help?"

"She all right. I take care of her."

But the next day, Reginald didn't show up.

My other scholars pushed and shoved and picked on each other, but at least nobody else was arrested. I wondered if Lamont and Braxton would get expelled, and what effect incarceration might have on them. Would they come out rehabilitated and determined not to stray again? Or as utterly broken human beings with drug habits?

I'd already lost two of my flock. I was probably kidding myself to think I could keep any of them safe and out of trouble. But teaching only allows a minimum of time for such reflection, and if I didn't want bedlam, then I'd better offer a better alternative. I handed out a timeline showing that the first African slaves had arrived in Virginia in 1619. I wondered what they were thinking. Who was I to bring this up? What gave me, a white man, the right to talk about slavery to the descendants of slaves?

And yet I had to.

"In 1746," I said, "a slave named Lucy Terry Prince composed a poem about an Indian attack, which makes her our first Afro-American poet. How many of you knew that?"

No hands were raised, no comments offered. I wasn't surprised. It was the same at all the other schools. Few, if any, of the kids had heard of Nat Turner or Harriet Tubman. But at least now I had their attention.

"How you know?" Eugene said.

"By reading about them on my own."

"You only saying that 'cause you a teacher."

"Well, yeah, Alonso. That's what they pay me for."

The other kids laughed at him.

"He got you, Alonso. Gimme five!" Curtis held out his palm. Harold slapped it.

"Bet you don't know the words to that poem," Alonso said.

I smiled and recited all twenty-three lines, which told of brave heroes who sadly had met with untimely ends. When I finished, the room was quiet.

"Damn, Mr. Merwin," Eugene said, "you memorized the whole thing."

"Want to see if you can?"

"No."

I asked if any of them wrote poetry. "You noticed the rhyme, of course. That's what holds the poem together. Sounded like a song, didn't it? It's called the oral tradition, what we had before things were written down. It's possible in the beginning all poems were sung."

"Why don't you sing it then, man?" Curtis said.

"They don't pay me enough for that."

Harold wanted to know how anyone could know the words to the song if they weren't written down. After complimenting him for asking such an excellent question, I explained that over a century later someone else remembered the poem and put it in writing. I talked about the poet's life and moved on to other major figures in black history. But by the time we got to James Meredith, Alonso was talking about Eugene's mother, and Harold and Curtis were roughhousing.

I sent them all to lunch, where they were under the security guard's supervision—they never went anywhere without him. Then I found my way to the office of Reginald's counselor, Miss Porter.

"We need to talk about Reginald Sheckles," I said. "Do you know him?"

"I know all your darlings, Mr. Merwin."

I explained how Reginald always hugged me.

"Is that all?" she said. "I mean, it's odd but not what I'd call a classroom emergency."

"Do you realize this kid hardly ever speaks? What's wrong with him, Miss Porter?"

She rolled her desk chair over to a dented gray file cabinet and rooted through drawers until she pulled out a folder.

"Here it is. 'Sheckles, Reginald. Seventh grader. Excellent attendance. But no academic credits earned. Reads on second grade level.'" She gave me a look.

"I get the picture," I said. "Reginald doesn't read well. Neither do lots of other kids in this school, but they're not in the Star Unit. Why do they call it that anyhow?"

"Somebody at the Board dreamed that up, I imagine." She put the file down.

"What's Reginald doing in the Star Unit?"

"His other teachers cannot control him," she said.

"Do you know he's been wearing the same clothes for weeks at a time? The other kids tell him he stinks, and he does. Now he's been absent ever since I asked him about it."

"Calm down. Did you contact his parents?"

"I tried to phone. Disconnected. I sent a note but got no response."

The counselor looked at the file again. "He qualifies for the free lunch program. Says here he lives with his grandmother." She picked up the phone and dialed. After listening briefly, she hung up. "Out of service."

"What are you going to do, Miss Porter?"

"Put him on the list."

"Is that all?"

"What more do you expect me to do?"

"You're his counselor, aren't you? Help him."

"Look around you. We have six hundred students here at Parkland, many with serious problems. We're overwhelmed."

"Do I have to go to the principal?"

"He'll tell you the same thing I have." She slid the file back into the drawer and shut it. "Let me offer you some advice. You're still a young man, only getting started in teaching. I can see you have a lot of passion and that's as it should be. But you can't save them all, Mr. Merwin. You can't."

I kept replaying my encounter with Miss Porter in my head, wondering if I'd been unfair to her. The woman was probably doing her best despite impossible odds, same as me. But if I followed her advice and cut my losses, where would that leave Reginald?

After school, I decided to stop off at the Ford dealership. The service manager was at his desk rummaging through invoices. I told him I needed to get my car radio repaired. He said they'd have to send it off to a specialist. It would take several days. I said okay.

While a tech was pulling the unit out of my dashboard, I recalled how disappointed Donald had looked when he found out my radio didn't work. I couldn't wait to see the expression on his face the first time he heard it play. If Deborah and I stayed together, I wondered if he could ever love me like a father. Or call me "Dad." I imagined helping him with his homework, coaching him in little league, offering him advice.

They tagged my radio and wrapped it in plastic. The technician tucked loose wires into the dash and covered them with a strip of hard plastic. If only human relationships could be repaired so easily, I mused.

That night, we planned to see a movie. Grownups only. But as I came home, Deborah phoned to say she had to work late at the bank. One of the tellers had made a mistake involving a large sum of money. None of them could go home until it was found. She said she didn't know how long it would take. Could I pick up Donald at day care and drop him off at his grandfather's? If so, that would save us time.

"Sure your 'old-fashioned' father is ready to meet me?"

That wouldn't be necessary, she said. I could let Donald out at the curb.

In this weather? Was she kidding?

She said Donald would be fine, and to steer clear of her father.

Tightening my collar against the cold, I collected the kid and chauffeured him to his grandfather's, puzzling all the way over Deborah's odd relationship with him. She talked as if she despised her father yet allowed him to babysit with Donald. I had to question whether she'd be willing to do that if her father had been such a lousy parent.

Despite the chill, Mr. Johnson was watching for us. As soon as I pulled up, he stepped out on the front porch in his khakis and a blue turtleneck sweater. His skin was bluish black, his hair snowy white. He resembled a retired accountant more than he did a railroad laborer.

When Donald saw him, he rushed toward the old man. Mr. Johnson picked up his grandson in a bear hug.

I pointed to a red whirligig suspended from the porch roof. "I like your cardinal, Mr. Johnson."

He didn't respond. I told him who I was, adding that Deborah had asked me to drop Donald off.

"You're the one she's living with now, huh?" He had a deep smoky voice. "What you want with her? Why don't you stick to your own kind?"

Well, that was direct, I thought.

"Deborah *is* my kind, Mr. Johnson. I care about her a lot. Do you know we've been talking about marriage?"

"Marriage?" He sounded disgusted. "Completing the disaster. The leopard can't change his spots."

"Am I the leopard?" I asked.

"Go on, get in the house, boy," Mr. Johnson said, and steered his grandson through the door. He closed it behind them.

The first words out of Deborah's mouth when she slid into my car were, "How did it go at my father's?"

Despite having to work late she seemed so happy. I couldn't tell her the truth.

"It went fine."

She seemed suspicious. "You talked to him, didn't you? After I told you not to."

"I just said hello and introduced myself."

"And what did he say?"

"Not too much. Something about leopards being unable to change their spots."

"Oh, Pate. Why didn't you listen to me?"

"Everything's okay. I dropped Donald off. They went inside. I came home." Disgruntled would be too mild a word to describe Deborah's demeanor. Time to change the subject. "And I dropped off the car radio to get it fixed, too."

"Donald will be thrilled."

Ignoring her sarcasm, I said, "Did everything get straightened out at the bank?"

"Finally. It was all Rhonda's fault. I swear that girl can't add up a column of numbers twice and get the same total."

"How do you do it?" I said.

"Do what? Long addition?"

"Manage to look so fresh at the end of the day."

"Are you kidding? I'm a mess."

"No, you're not." I leaned over and kissed her.

I sensed she had to force herself to respond.

At my apartment, I sprawled on the bed while she "freshened up."

"Aren't you going to change clothes?" she asked.

"What's wrong with these?"

"That's the same outfit you wear every day. Or looks like it. Why don't you put on that new shirt and jumpsuit I bought for you?"

"I'm saving them for a special occasion."

"What do you call this?"

"I call it going to the movies. What would you like to see?"

She continued doing her makeup. "How about *Airport*?"

"Not the one about a suicide bomber in flight?"

"You have something against action movies?"

"How about *THX 1138* instead?"

"Is that science fiction? I hate science fiction."

"Or we could skip the movie altogether."

"But then what would we do?"

"I suspect we'd think of something."

"You're such a naughty boy," she said.

On Monday after school, I was summoned to the principal's office. His door was open. I tapped on it anxiously, not knowing whether he wanted to give me a pat on the back or fire my ass. He was sitting behind his desk with his shirt sleeves rolled up and his tie hanging loose. His suit coat had been slung over his chair. He looked relaxed. That worried me.

"Come in and take a seat, Mr. Merwin," he invited. "How are things in the Star Unit?"

I said everything was fine. He seemed to believe it.

"I've noticed you never refer any discipline problems to me."

"I try to handle my own problems."

He said that was good. Very good.

"I see you remember what I said when I hired you. That I didn't want to have to come out there all the time. Well, by golly I haven't. And that's unusual. I feared you might be a babbling wreck by now, but you seem all right. Are you? Still happy at Parkland?"

I said I was.

"Good. Why?"

"Guess I just like my kids."

"Those kids? The ones everybody else likes so much we put them out of the building? C'mon, Mr. Merwin. Don't kid a kidder."

"I'm not kidding. They need my help. I respond well to that."

"Yes, you do. Your methods are unorthodox, but they seem to work. You and Mr. Thresher have made a good team. That's why I wanted to see you about coaching baseball."

"Coaching baseball? Me?"

"We have an opening for an assistant coach," Bloom said. "It's a great opportunity for the right young man. Coach Thresher's on the practice field right now, hoping that man shows up. And I believe that man is you."

"You want me to assist *Coach* Thresher?"

"Do you think you should be head coach?" Bloom chuckled. "Look, I'm sure you two will complement each other perfectly, like you do in the classroom. You can think it over if you need to, but I need an answer by tomorrow."

With that, he stood up. I was dismissed.

Thinking this was the craziest idea I'd ever heard of, I said, "Wait. There's something else we need to discuss."

"What might that be?"

"Reginald Sheckles." I told Bloom that I thought something was wrong at the kid's home.

"Have you phoned there?" he asked. "Sent a note home? Spoken to the student's counselor?"

"All three. The phone was out of order. No response to my letter. And Miss Porter . . ."

"What did she say?"

"That she'd put him on a list. What happens to Reginald in the meantime, Mr. Bloom? I want to do that home visit myself and get to the bottom of this."

"Bad idea, Coach. This neighborhood's a powder keg. Haven't you noticed the heavy police presence? It's dangerous around here. Leave this matter alone. Let his counselor handle it through normal channels."

I started to argue, but he cut me off.

"Did you hear what I said?"

I left his office more determined than ever to find out what was going on.

The following day I observed baseball practice before pulling my car out of the parking lot. Thresher was putting the team through some calisthenics. They were running in place, doing jumping jacks and pushups on what passed for the ball field. It was a ragtag group that included some of the school's most notoriously aggressive boys, meaning mine. The idea that a coach could have a positive impact on a player's classroom behavior was as old as school itself. My high school was full of kids like that, rough and undisciplined, looking for trouble, but often gifted athletes. There was no doubt in my mind that sports had kept many of them from dropping out or being kicked out. I wondered if that would work here.

A few blocks from Parkland, I looked back at the massive Greek Revival building brooding like an ancient monastery. It was easily the grandest structure in the neighborhood, and a stark reminder of the area's former glory, now lost apparently forever. On 18th Street, I passed an old man talking to himself in front of the Sweet Leaf Primitive Baptist Church. Farther on, a taunting pack of teens older than my students crossed the street right in front of me, another example of the simmering tensions Bloom had warned me to avoid.

He was right about the streets teeming with cops, as well. I passed a patrol car at 25th and Woodland. Saw another sitting near the old

Carnegie branch library with its motor running. And a third unmarked unit, recognizable by its spotlight, followed me for a few blocks though I had done nothing illegal. Guess I looked suspicious. I was relieved when they kept going straight as I turned on Wilson Avenue, where some old clunkers were parked with two wheels up on the sidewalk.

Many more twists and turns brought me to Reginald's block. I found the number on his grandmother's house, a one-story light blue frame with rat holes in the foundation. It stood next to a vacant corner lot. I wondered if there had been a house on it that had burned down during the riots.

Getting out of my car every day at Parkland required an effort, but nothing like what I felt here knowing I was in a war zone and strictly on my own. I took a deep breath and went up the front walk to the door. A heavyset woman probably in her seventies opened it, regarding me with misgiving. I was willing to bet that she hadn't laid eyes on many white faces around here in some time.

"Mrs. Sheckles? I'm Pate Merwin, your grandson's teacher at Parkland."

Her expression changed at once. "I'm glad to meet you, Mr. Merwin. You're his favorite teacher. Reginald talks about you all the time."

I smiled.

Mrs. Sheckles was wearing a baggy housedress and slippers. She had tubes in her nostrils connected to a wheeled oxygen tank at her side. She told me to come in and laboriously led me into a living room crowded with furniture that was new when Truman was president. She offered me the couch and sank into an exhausted looking high back easy chair with doilies on the arms.

"I'm sorry I can't offer you anything," she wheezed. "It's hard for me to get around with my emphysema and this old oxygen."

Emphysema. I told her my grandparents had suffered from the same ailment in their declining years.

A well-used Bible sat on a side table within easy reach. She picked it up and began leafing through the pages with knobby arthritic fingers.

"The Lord's always got an answer, if you know where to look," she said. "I tell Reginald that in this bad old world, we need all the help we can get. But you teach these children, so you know that. Now tell me what I can do for you."

"I need to ask you a few questions about Reginald. Are you his legal guardian?"

"Well, I raised him from a baby."

"Do you know his parents' whereabouts?"

"No."

All she could tell me was that her daughter Jean had Reginald when she was sixteen. Jean had tried to raise him by herself.

"Until that old devil liquor got hold of her. Since then, it's been up to me."

"What about his father?"

She just shook her head, indicating he was out of the picture and probably always had been. It was an old sad story, no less heartbreaking for the retelling.

"What's this about?" Mrs. Sheckles said. "How is Reginald doing in school? Is he behaving himself?"

"Yes," I said. "He's a sweet kid, very affectionate. I like him a lot. But there's one thing he does that puzzles me."

I described how he made a point of wrapping himself around my legs and hugging me every day.

She sighed. "I told him to quit that foolishness. What does he think he is—a boa constrictor?" Her laugh was sad. "That child always been sweet. But you shouldn't have to put up with that. I'll tell him again not to do it."

"There's something else," I said.

I explained that her grandson struggled with reading and how that made everything harder for him.

"I know he gets his words turned around," she said, "but he sure can memorize his Bible verses."

"Really? I've never heard him recite one. I'd like to some time."

"'For God so loved the world, that he gave his only begotten Son, that whosoever believeth in him should not perish, but have everlasting life.' John 3:16. Reginald knows that one by heart," she said.

I did, too. I remembered the verse from my old Sunday school days, before I realized I was being taught by hypocritical bigots. With war in mind, I now found the idea of fathers sacrificing their only sons over-rated. Far nobler for them to sacrifice themselves. Fathers had a lot to answer for, in my book. Reginald clearly needed one in his life. He'd apparently nominated me. And so far, I feared I was doing a lousy job.

God bless the grandparents.

Mrs. Sheckles was breathing raggedly. I didn't want to wear her out, but it was clear that she enjoyed talking about her grandson. Or anything. She probably didn't get many chances. Nonetheless, I need-ed her to get to the point.

"I'm concerned about Reginald, ma'am. He's been missing classes lately. In fact, he hasn't been to school in five days. I'm wondering why."

"Reginald's not been feeling well. I think he's been down with the flu."

I could tell from the change in her voice that Mrs. Sheckles was no longer telling the truth. It was agonizing, but I couldn't leave it there. I asked to see him.

"Oh, he's not here right now. He's feeling better today. He's mow-ing lawns. Got several regular customers. That grass money helps pay my medical bills, you see. Don't know what I'd do without that boy."

When would he be back?

She wasn't sure.

I told her Reginald could still make up any missed work. Otherwise he'd wind up losing all his credits and have to repeat the year. She thanked me sincerely for caring about him.

"One more thing. Before he started missing school, the other kids complained that Reginald smelled bad."

Mrs. Sheckles stiffened, obviously wounded. "Children can be aw-ful mean."

"You're right," I said. "But he wore the same clothes every day for a week. I don't believe you'd knowingly let him do that."

She blinked rapidly and used her hand to cover up her mouth, and her distress.

"Did you even know he'd been absent?"

She adjusted the tubes in her nostrils, as if breathing had become more difficult.

"How long has it been since you've seen him, ma'am?"

"Why you doing this, Mr. Merwin? My baby likes you."

"I'm on Reginald's side. But he can't keep missing school. Tell me where to find him. I'll do whatever I can to help."

She remained silent, probably wondering if she could trust me.

In the end, she said, "It breaks my heart to tell you, but Reginald got himself in trouble and had to leave for a while."

"Where is he? When will he be back?"

"He'll come back when it's safe."

And that was all she would say.

Unless I wanted to keep badgering her, I had to admit defeat. I'd need some other way to discover the truth.

I said good-bye and was walking back to my car when four teenagers appeared and encircled me. I'd been fumbling with my keys, my mind elsewhere, and failed to see them coming until they were already upon me. Very careless. Now I was about to pay for it. As the first punch was thrown, I managed to duck and even land a stiff uppercut of my own. But I was immediately nailed in the eye and another of my assailants drove a fist into my gut, knocking the wind out me. After that, the blows came fast and furious, slamming into me from every direction. There were too many of them for me. One sapped me down, igniting a psychedelic starburst in my head. As I fell to my knees, I heard a wailing siren in the distance. Then the ground rushed up at me.

9

July 1971

Shortly after sunrise, meditation and yoga completed, the Paraprosdokians pack their gear with the practiced efficiency of old deck hands. They're waiting with coffee when we stumble over, bleary-eyed. The road out of here, the same one we came in on, is lined with brilliant black-eyed Susans. Our next stop is Mesa Verde, the national park Nick says President Theodore Roosevelt designated in 1906 to protect what were said to be some of the best cliff dwellings in the world. This is the last leg of our journey with Nick and Iris, whose path will soon diverge from ours.

The flat landscape quickly changes into amber, gray, and white foothills. Then the hills grow into mountains. The grade up to Wolf Creek Pass is seven percent, a climb so steep it feels like you're going to flip over and fall off. A beast at any time, according to Nick, Wolf Creek is worse now due to major road construction. At the pass, a solitary flagman waves a few vehicles at a time through the only lane that remains open to traffic, which is soon backed up for miles. Although the view is spectacular—purple-gray peaks roofed with white cumulus clouds—we find ourselves wedged on a narrow strip of blacktop between soaring pines and a row of orange and white safety barrels.

Although I am frightened to death of heights, there is no way in hell I'm ever going to admit this in front of Stan and Matthew. To get away from the edge of a dizzying drop-off, I slide out on the driver's side of the Caddy. I need a way to distract myself. Maybe some of Iris's yoga moves will do the job. We're only twenty miles from the Continental Divide, so who knows? Maybe I'll find my center. What will people in the other cars think? I couldn't care less.

I began by trying to control my breathing. The idea is to clear the mind and relax the body. I focus first on relaxing my toes and then move upward. You aren't supposed to think while doing this, but I find that impossible. I cannot turn off my mind, or the fear I feel, but I can begin stretching and bending my body like Plastic Man. I keep at it for maybe twenty minutes before giving up and climbing back into the car, where I promptly fall asleep.

Half an hour later, I awaken as we're waved through, this time for a stomach-churning plunge. Our endless nightmare subsides as we reach the hills, then the valley of ranching and farming. By a wrinkled creek, Nick pulls over for us all to decompress. I walk down to the edge of the stream whose banks are lined with trees. Over the sound of rushing water, a guide can be heard barking orders. Paddlers in black wetsuit tops and orange life vests are backwatering here, each awaiting his turn to test the white water in an inflatable raft.

When Matthew and Stan catch up, they call my attention to a sign mounted on a post driven into a rocky outcropping on the other side of the creek.

"It is very easy to TIP OVER on the river," the sign reads, "but nearly impossible to OVER TIP the guide."

"Want to go whitewater rafting?" Matthew says. "We're here, so we might as well."

"I can't afford it," I say. "I'm broke. Besides, it wouldn't be fair of us to further delay Iris and Nick."

"It wouldn't take that long. What about you, Hicks? You were in the Navy," Matthew says.

"No thanks," Stan says.

"Why not? You're not afraid, are you?"

"I have no desire to go whitewater rafting with a shitbird like you," Stan tells him.

"Don't forget that this shitbird helped save your life."

They stalk off in opposite directions, leaving me to contemplate the sky's reflection in the water.

Shortly before noon, we arrive in the dusty old railroad town of Mancos, located between Durango and Cortez. Nick parks on a tree-lined street alongside the river so Iris can pick up a few items from the grocery store before we enter the national park. Nick says if we want to stretch our legs again, we must be back in fifteen minutes. Weary of the hostile silence between Stan and Matthew, I head off on my own to check out the town. It seems unremarkable, in need of both a cash infusion and spiffing up.

I've gone a couple of blocks when I come to a café with a shady patio area. It's full of customers. Even though I smell fried bacon and hot coffee, I can't afford to eat and am about to pass it by when I see a sign in the front window. "Help Wanted," it says. I open the door and go inside. We're planning to stay in the national park for a couple of days. Maybe I can make a few bucks while we're here.

An aproned young woman comes out of the kitchen carrying a tray of food. She's slim, round-faced, with braided long black hair and a light brown complexion suggesting she is at least part Indian.

"Back in a jiffy," she says.

I wait for her to return from the patio.

"What can I do you for?" she asks.

I nod at the sign in the window. "I need to make some money."

"It's minimum wage, and only temporary."

"You make it sound irresistible. What's the job?"

"Dishwasher. If you want it, talk to the bossman." She jerks her head toward the kitchen and starts off in that direction.

I follow. "What's your name?"

"Johona," she says, and pushes open the door.

Inside the tiny kitchen space dirty dishes are stacked high on a counter. A thick-set, gray-headed white man is flipping burgers on the crackling grill.

"Gus," Johona says. "This guy says he's interested in the dishwasher job."

Gus pauses to ask if that's right.

"Yeah," I respond, "but probably only for today, I'm afraid."

"Why do you waste my time?" Looking exasperated, Gus returns his full attention to cooking on the grill.

"Appears that you could use my help." I nod at the dishes. "I'm only passing through, but I'm a hard worker and I can start right now. Maybe at least get you over this hump."

Gus thinks it over. "Okay, but I'll need you again for the dinner shift. No pay until you do both. Still interested?"

"Give me five minutes."

"Thought you could start right now."

"I'll be back in five."

Flashing a smile at Johona, I hustle to the car.

When I relate my plan, Stan says, "You don't have to do this, Pate. I told you I got you covered."

I thank him but explain that I need to pick up some cash. It's for my own peace of mind, to help me feel more in control of my life. Everybody else is okay with it, though Nick expresses a concern that I'll have difficulty finding their campsite on my own.

"Mesa Verde's a damn big place," he says, adding that the campground is five miles from the entrance.

"I'll find it, don't worry."

Back at the café, Gus supplies me with boots, waterproof apron, and rubber gloves. Feeling a bit like Captain Nemo, I start digging my elbows in deep and "busting suds," as he puts it. There is no machine, only a large double sink. I fill it with steaming hot water and add detergent. As a layer of foam forms, I wash, rinse, and stack dishes on a plastic drying rack. Johona keeps bringing in plates, cups, glassware, and cutlery. Gus hands over pots and pans crusted with flour and burnt barbeque sauce.

I work fast. Too fast. In my haste, I jab a steak knife right through the rubber glove into my left index finger. "Oh, shit!"

"Let me see." Johona stanches the bleeding and puts a Band-Aid on the wound. "How do you like it here so far?"

"Pure torture."

"What does your girlfriend think about you suddenly taking this job?"

"Is that your way of asking if I have one? I don't."

"Your wife then?"

"I don't have one of those, either. How about you?"

"No wife," Johona smiles.

At one o'clock, Gus tells me I've done a good job and to be back at five.

I take off the apron. "I know I agreed not to be paid until after that shift, but I sure could use a small advance to tide me over till then."

"You must be flat broke." Gus opens the register.

I walk out into the sunshine with five hard-earned bucks in my hand only to find Johona waiting for me behind the wheel of an old red Chevy pickup with dented fenders and rust patches on the hood and doors.

"Need a lift, cowboy?"

I lean in the window of the white-top truck. "I am sore and scorched, and I understand it's a long walk to the campground, so yes, I believe I do."

"Well, get in."

"Are you working tonight?" I bang the door shut.

She nods. "Where are you from?"

"Louisville, Kentucky."

"Boy, are you a long way from home. What are you doing out here?"

I explain about hitchhiking to San Francisco. I try to impress her, but that seems easier said than done. I ask if she's from around here.

"I grew up in Cortez, about an hour from here."

"Ever wonder what it would be like to live somewhere else?" I'm wondering if Cortez is any bigger or more cosmopolitan than this sad little burg, with its windowless cocktail lounges and cinderblock motels.

"Why? Are you going to take me away from all this?"

"Got a sleeping bag?"

She drives us through heavy traffic, keeping the ancient pickup grinding along steadily five miles below the speed limit. She's loosened her thick hair, which now falls around her strong shoulders and blows in the breeze.

"Are you an Indian?" I ask, then immediately correct myself. "I mean a Native American?"

She leaves me hanging for a while before saying, "What I am is Ute. Americans are the ones who took away our land and put us on reservations."

When she sees my crestfallen expression, her lips curve into a smile.

"Don't worry. I won't hold you personally responsible. I'm really only half Ute. My mother was white."

"Was?"

"She died."

I'm afraid to ask how. This is no naïve country girl. What I want to do is ask her out. But where?

We stop at the ranger station by the entrance. The wiry young ranger, whose name badge reads "COLLINGS," is white, clean-cut. He greets Johona by name and says, "Who's your new friend?"

It sounds like more than a casual question. I wonder if there's something between them. It's a small world here in Mancos.

I introduce myself and mention that my friends are already here. He checks his records.

"Okay, you're good to go. Enjoy your stay."

"I plan to."

"See you, Johona," he says.

She gives him a wave and we roll on toward the campground, passing giant boulders and pines on our way.

"Old boyfriend of yours?"

"Something like that."

A few peach-colored houses are visible in the distance, blending in with similarly shaded slopes. At Iris and Nick's trailer, I introduce her to them and find out how to get to my own campsite, which they say is within easy walking distance.

"We're having drinks later, Johona. You should join us," Iris says. Nick repeats the invitation.

Johona thanks them both for the offer but remains noncommittal.

We get back in the truck and follow their directions to where Stan and I will be staying. It's a more primitive campsite similar to those at the Great Sand Dunes—piñon tree for shade, bear-proof trash can, fire pit. I look for Stan but he's nowhere in sight.

I wish I could think of a way to keep Johona around longer, but I can see that it's time to say goodbye for now. "I'll see you at five. Hope we can get together after work."

"We'll see," she says, her eyes probing mine. "Are you really as nice as you seem?"

"Absolutely not."

"Then I'm sure you can find your own way back to town."

Stan shows up as she drives away. And I'm left standing there with my mouth hanging open.

"Nice looking woman," he says. "You're turning into a fast worker, Pate."

"I'm afraid I just blew my chances."

"What makes you think so?"

"She doesn't seem to share my sense of humor."

"Look, man, she wouldn't have brought you all this way if she wasn't interested."

"Hope you're right. I should have just smiled and kept my mouth shut."

"Harder to put your foot in it that way."

"Where is Matthew?"

"He went off with a couple of ditsy chicks from Ohio. We've got to cut that shitbird loose."

"We'll cross that bridge when it's time to leave, Stan. Why ruin our stay?"

With that settled, I explain that I have a few hours free before going back to work. How about checking out the cliff dwellings?

"Thought we were going to score some magic mushrooms," Stan says.

"Can't do it sitting here on our butts, can we?"

The only way to see the most popular cliff dwellings is via ranger-guided one-hour tours. We'll have to buy tickets at the visitor center, which is a long hike. On the way, however, we run into the Paraprosdokians. When they hear our plans, Iris says we certainly are ambitious today.

"And ambition," Nick adds, "is the last refuge of the failure."

Nevertheless, they offer us a ride. Nick says they need to go into town to pick up some groceries anyway. Since I'm so desperate for money, he'll even take me to work afterward.

"What a guy," I say.

Nick grins.

At the center, Stan pays for our tickets to Cliff House, the largest of the ruins here. I promise to spend my five bucks splurging on a bottle of wine for tonight.

A tram takes us out to the ruins, where we learn that the ancients survived by farming on the mesa top while living in the somewhat climate-controlled alcove below.

"Mesa Verde means 'green table' in Spanish," our mustachioed ranger guide says.

We soon discover why the ranger warned us upfront that visiting a cliff dwelling at seven thousand feet could be strenuous. The trails to Cliff House prove steep and uneven, with steps and ladders sometimes required. I stumble often. By the time we get up to the multistoried village, which is constructed beneath an overhanging cliff, everyone is sweating.

Our guide explains that these pit houses, which are called pueblos, is where the Anasazi—or "ancient ones" in Navajo—lived. There are over a hundred and fifty rooms here. To get inside, we must descend on a primitive ladder through the roof. We see handprints and footprints where other visitors have gone before us. The walls are colorfully decorated with earthen plasters in pink, red, yellow, brown, and white.

I adore climbing down the ladder into the kiva, which is a large round structure built partly underground and thought to have been used for religious ceremonies. The ranger tells us that more than a hundred people would've lived here, and that each pueblo had its own hearth, fire hole, and storage room. We search the dusty corners, hoping to find a pot that everyone else has conveniently overlooked for the past seven hundred years.

After the tour, we catch a ride back to camp with a couple of long-haired Pennsylvanians, who share our exhilaration.

Back at the café, I keep busy as diners pour in until every seat is filled. It's so hot and noisy in the kitchen that it feels like being trapped in a burning room. While Gus is sneaking a quick smoke out back, Johona comes in with another armload of dirty dishes. I ask her to talk. Setting her tray down reluctantly, she says, "Go ahead."

"Earlier today you asked me an honest question. Instead of answering you properly, I wound up looking like a horse's ass by trying to be funny. I apologize and ask for a second chance. To answer your question, though, yes, I'm exactly as nice as I seem. And you're the nicest girl I've met in a long time. I think—"

"Shut up, Pate, and kiss me."

Gripping her by the shoulders, I kiss her gently on the lips. It's lovely and I want it to go on and on, but she pushes me away after a few seconds. "More later," she says, and it's back to work.

The rest of the shift flies by. At 9:15, after the crowd has cleared out, I pull on a fresh T-shirt and collect my pay in cash from Gus, who asks, "Are you sure you don't want to come back tomorrow?"

But I have no appetite for more work. I'm too busy thinking about that first kiss, and my first date to come with Johona, which will almost certainly be a one-night stand.

"Thanks, Bossman. This is some of the most beautiful country I've ever seen, but by this time tomorrow I'll probably be miles from here."

At her truck, I find Johona wearing a sleeveless denim vest over a purple and gray T-shirt. I tell her she looks great and thank her for forgiving me.

"Much as I like to hear men grovel," she says, "we Utes are a forgiving people."

"Say something in Ute."

"*Mique wush tagooven.*"

"That's beautiful. What does it mean?"

"It means, 'Hello, my friend.'"

She laughs at my halting effort to repeat it.

Previously, Nick had offered to pick me up after work. But hoping Johona might have a change of heart, I'd declined. Now I'm glad I did. As we're leaving, Gus steps out on the porch for a smoke. We wave good-bye to him and it's off to Iris and Nick's place. On the way, I want to tell Johona how fascinating I found my visit to Cliff House. But there's nothing I can say about the place or its history that she doesn't already know, so I leave it at that, hoping for a better opportunity later.

After showing my Mesa Verde camping pass to another ranger, we breeze through the main gate. The air is crisp and fragrant with blue columbine and mimosa. As we corkscrew toward the camping areas, Johona asks why I'm hitchhiking around the country.

"I was tired of my life, I guess. Why did the Anasazi move on seven hundred years ago?"

"The fact that they'd just endured a twenty-four-year drought might have influenced them," Johona says. "But personally, I think they were on a mysterious quest."

"What sort of mysterious quest?"

"I think it's possible that a spirit encouraged them to leave their homes and seek out new meaning in a new place."

We swerve at that instant, to avoid a pothole.

"Maybe a spirit encouraged you, too, Pate."

With my earlier flip reply still fresh in mind, I remind myself that this is a serious person and resist the temptation to answer her immediately. When I do reply, it's only after what I hope seems like a thoughtful pause.

"I like this idea, Johona. I suppose I am inspired by the idea of the Summer of Love. I missed it the first time around, but maybe this summer I'll be luckier. What about your mysterious quest? You must have one."

She shrugs. "Not really. It's tough enough to make even my ordinary dreams come true without throwing in all the mysticism."

"I don't understand."

"I've always wanted to be a national park ranger," she says.

"You strike me as the kind of woman who gets what she wants."

"I was working toward it, had good grades, won a partial scholarship. But when my father got disabled, there was no money for school. Now I have to work so my family can survive."

Our bouncing headlights pick up a sword-shaped yucca cactus. A fine grit whistles through the open windows, stinging our cheeks.

"Actually, that's not quite the truth," Johona says. "What really happened is my father is an alcoholic, my mother has emphysema and can only work a little, and I have to stay and help take care of my little brother and sister."

"Sounds like a hard life," I say, as the last of the sun fades from the sky.

"What is life?" Johona says.

In answer, she quotes a Blackfoot warrior whose poem marshals a trio of comparisons to reflect the fleeting nature of existence. Included are the winking of a lightning bug, a bison's brief exhalation, and a moving shadow that fades away as the sun sets.

"That's beautiful."

"It has helped me through some rough spots. I try to draw strength from the ancient ones."

I wonder what other rough spots, but we're at the camp now, where there's a party going on.

Music blares from a red Mustang with Ohio plates, parked on the edge of the road. Smelling the crushed-leaf scent of creosote, we step through the shadows into a pool of light. On one side of a flickering campfire, I see Stan and the Paraprosdokians. On the other, bathed in amber glow, it's Matthew with two women. He says they met at the lodge and, with a straight face, introduces them as Summer and Autumn.

Autumn is tall and dark, Summer shorter and blonde. Both are young, long-haired, and dressed like farmers in flannel shirts, bib overalls, and mud-flecked brogans. Matthew says they've been living in a farming commune for the last six months in Eureka, north of San Francisco.

"What was that like?" I ask, wondering why they've changed their names.

"It was really groovy," Autumn says. "Everybody worked in the garden and shared everything."

Everything?

When I tell them that this is Johona and we worked together —"well, at least for today"—they act surprised.

"Thought you were hitching across the county with Matthew," Autumn says, staring at me through tinted granny glasses.

With Matthew.

"With Stan," I say.

"We're thinking about hitchhiking, too," Summer says.

"I doubt you'd have any trouble getting rides," I say.

"Why do you want to do that?" Johona asks.

This strikes me as an excellent question since both seem so deadly serious about the commune. If it's so great, why are they here?

For a moment, I'm back in Ward. Were the hippies there trying to live off the land? I realize that I know next to nothing about them or what really might have been going on. Despite the clichés, I want to believe it's possible to only eat the food you've grown or harvested yourself. To live free and share in peace and love. As Marx said, from each according to his ability, to each according to his need. That's a big part of my quest. But as always, I have doubts about everything and everyone.

Lost in thought, I miss their answer. Now they're asking Johona lots of earnest questions about what it's like to live as a Ute in today's world. Who knows, maybe they're thinking of joining the tribe? I'm being sarcastic because I sense that in their hearts, these two cherish a belief that they are superior. That they have learned the secret of life. But what if there is no secret and they're just two dummies as lost in the world as anybody else?

To avoid being unpleasant, I whisk Johona away, leaving Matthew to entertain them. Nick and Iris generously provide us with a couple of margaritas. Hearing that they're in the rug business, Johona reveals that her mother is a weaver. This triggers a long discussion, during which Stan draws me aside.

"Iris and Nick are pulling out first thing in the morning," he says. "They're going to meet a buyer in Pagosa Springs, which would've been a hundred miles out of our way. So, tonight is definitely good-bye." Jerking his head at Matthew, he adds, "So we'll finally get rid of him."

Back at the fire, I tell Iris and Nick, "I hear you're leaving. I'll hate to see you go. We're grateful for everything you all have done for us."

"You boys have made this trip fun and exciting for us," Iris says. "Now as a little going away present, I'm going to do a reading for you."

I'm not sure what that means, but it sounds like something a gypsy fortune teller might do. And so it proves.

"Nick and I are about to turn in for the night, but first, would you like me to tell your fortunes?" Iris announces. She gathers everyone around the picnic table, where there's just enough fire light to read a deck of playing cards, and starts with Matthew. "Because we met him first." Matthew draws a card from the deck, looks at it, and lays it face up on the table. Iris adds two more cards. After looking them over, she closes her eyes.

"To you, getting dressed in the morning is like preparing for a role in a play," she says dramatically. "With each item of clothing, you're assembling the character you'll play. The one animating this guise is the real you."

"It's not *like* preparing for a role in a play, Iris," Matthew says. "It is actual preparation. That's what an actor does."

"I wasn't finished. Draw another card."

He does.

"You're good at getting what you want," she says, "but you're equally likely to throw it all away."

"You're probably right about that," Matthew says.

Iris slips the cards back into the deck. While she shuffles again Autumn says, "You're an actor, Matthew? What have I seen you in?"

"Only stage plays so far, but I'm on my way to Hollywood."

"Hollywood! Oh, how exciting."

"Your turn, Stan," Iris says.

She repeats the process of selecting cards. "They tell me you are on a quest."

"A quest for what?" Stan asks.

"It's hard to say. It's personal to you. Most people wouldn't understand."

"Should I continue with my quest?" Stan asks solemnly.

"You'll decide for yourself," Iris says. "What others think doesn't matter to you."

I realize it's all true. She has described Stan perfectly. All at once, what seemed like harmless fun turns serious indeed. Given Stan's dangerous behavior out on the dunes, I must take exception to Iris's advice that Stan decide for himself whether to continue his quest—if it means anything other than getting to San Francisco in one piece.

"Your turn, Pate," Iris says.

She shuffles the cards. Picks mine. Deals me two more.

"Strange twists will happen," Iris says, "and you must twist right along with them. It's your ability to do this that sets you apart."

She deals another card.

"You wish to go forward, Pate. Yet to do so, you must hold back. That is very Zen."

The Zen allusion is flattering, though I have no idea what she means by it. Before I can speak, Matthew interrupts:

"You're starting to sound like a fortune cookie, Iris."

Stan and I bristle, but Iris ignores him and continues, saying that Zen is a paradox. When we're ready, it will help us discover truth that logic cannot. Sometimes by doing nothing, we allow the murky water to clear and reveal what was hidden there all along.

Do nothing? How do you do that?

On that cryptic note, the reading is over, and Iris puts the cards away. Folding up their lawn chairs, she and Nick bid us all an extended Southern-style farewell.

10

March 1971

I heard somebody groan. Then somebody else saying, "He's coming around." I opened my eyes and saw the street in extreme close-up.

"Hey, buddy. You okay?"

Whoever had asked clearly was not a close observer. I felt like I'd been tenderized by a mallet. My head was spinning, my face ground into the asphalt. He turned me over and pulled me up into a sitting position. Two young cops stood looking down at me and, boy, was I glad to see them.

"We'll get you to the hospital," one said. "But first tell us what happened."

"I think you guys saved my ass." I tried to sketch the events in a few sentences but each attempt to catch my breath made me wince.

"It's okay. Take it easy."

Hearing the other cop say into his static-filled radio, "Looks like a mugging," I reached for my wallet and car keys, but my pockets had been turned inside out. When I looked around, I saw that my car was gone as well.

"We don't think you're seriously hurt," one guy said, and both helped me into the back seat of the cruiser.

Odds were on my assailants still being in the neighborhood. If I could identify them, the culprits might be apprehended. The police wanted to drive me around the area and see if we could find any of them. I felt I owed my rescuers that much. Every few minutes, they'd point out someone at random. But I couldn't identify any of them as my muggers.

"Are you sure? Take another look." They kept trying until I begged them to stop. Then they took me to General Hospital. Before turning me over to the medical staff in the slammed emergency room, they said I'd have to come downtown later to look at mug shots and give my statement. I said I would, but they made a point of emphasizing that the longer I waited, the less chance there would be of apprehending my attackers. I repeated that I'd come. I thanked them for their help.

When they left, a nurse eased me out of my blood-speckled work shirt and a doctor with a New York accent poked and prodded me. What happened? Does this hurt? Does that hurt? What about this?

Everything he did hurt.

After further examination, he said he didn't think any bones were broken. Mainly I had bruises and contusions, but also possibly a concussion. They wanted to keep me overnight. He gave me something for pain and cleaned up my scrapes and cuts. As I was being shipped off to X-ray on a gurney, I persuaded a sympathetic nurse to call Deborah for me.

Since the downtown medical complex wasn't far from the bank where she worked, I wasn't surprised to see her there waiting for me when I got back from X-ray. She hugged me and started asking questions. What was I doing here in the hospital? Had I been in an accident? Was I hurt badly? When I told her, she asked what I was doing out there away from school. I explained that, too.

She shook her head. "You can't help everyone, Pate. We're the ones who need you. Why can't you just help us?"

At least I think that's what she said. I was pretty drugged up. She drove us home.

Next morning, I awoke with war drums pounding in my head, and feeling sore and swollen all over. With my trembling fingers I extracted two pellet-sized pills that the doc had given me to tide me over from a bottle on the bedside table. I nearly knocked it over in the process but got them down with a sip of water.

Climbing gingerly out of bed, I noticed a rainbow on my bedroom wall. It took me a moment to realize that the window was acting as a prism. After a hot shower, the ache in my muscles ebbed and my head felt clearer. I wiped a patch of fog off the mirror. I couldn't believe my face—swollen nose, welts under the eyes, puffy blood-crusted patches of skin. Deborah had left a note on the kitchen table advising me to take it easy today. She wrote that she'd called my school for me. There was food in the fridge. She hoped I was feeling better and would see me later.

As I slowly swallowed a small glass of orange juice and some toast, I decided to phone Stan and tell him what happened. I called his mother. She told me he was not living there anymore, but she would pass along my message. I was stumped about where he might be staying, but I figured he was with some girl he'd met in a bar.

Part of my concern stemmed from my guilt over putting him out of the apartment. I had the right to evict him, though. He would've done the same if our positions were reversed, wouldn't he? Well, wouldn't he? I didn't know the answer and that bothered the hell out of me. I went back to bed, intending to read the newspaper. But the words were too blurry. I let the paper fall on my chest as my last shred of consciousness vanished.

I heard keys, or a key, rattling in my front door. I looked at the clock. Still too early for Deborah to be home. I heard the lock screech, the door groan.

"Pate?"

"Stan, thank God. You scared the living crap out of me. What are you doing here?"

"I got your message." He came over and set a six pack on the mattress. "Looks like you could use one of these."

"I'm not supposed to mix my pain meds with alcohol."

"Yeah, you are."

He must be kidding, I thought. But nope, he was popping a beer and offering it to me.

"Got any more pills?"

I told him he could have one if he really wanted it.

But he said no thanks and sat down at the foot of the bed. "What the hell have you done to yourself, Pate?"

"Put some music on and I'll tell you all about it."

Stan nodded, selected an album from the storage rack, and put it on the turntable. B.B. King began to sing "The Thrill Is Gone."

"Ah, the blues. Good choice."

"I thought so, considering the way you look right now."

"Black and blue you mean?"

He chuckled. "You know where the blues came from?"

"The Mississippi delta in the 1870s, I believe."

"In the navy, the blues can refer to something else," Stan said.

When a ship's captain died at sea, the crew would follow an old naval tradition by flying blue flags and painting a blue band all along the hull.

"Not exactly your standard twelve-bar blues progression," he said, "but it did symbolize their feelings of loss. Now tell me what happened."

By the time I finished describing being mugged, we'd finished our first beer. The bitter taste lay on my tongue, just the way I liked it.

"Show me what they did to you," he said.

I pulled up my shirt.

"The bastards. Why do you do it?"

"Teach, you mean? Besides the grueling work and low pay? Would you believe to have a chance to change a kid's life? Or improve the world, one person at a time?"

Stan said he'd drink to that.

"Where are you living?" I said.

"Here and there."

"Are you still pissed at me?"

"Damn straight, I am."

"So how come you're here?"

"I dislike drinking alone. They say it's a sign of alcoholism."

"You drink alone all the time."

"Doesn't mean I have to like it."

"Hey, guess who is Parkland Junior High's new assistant baseball coach," I said.

"Not you?" Seeing the look on my face, he added, "Why are you digging yourself in deeper when you should be trying to get out of there?"

"The cops who came to my classroom to arrest my students would agree with you."

"Just because they were pigs didn't necessarily make them wrong," he replied.

I said although I was worried about Braxton and Lamont, there was just nothing I could do for them. They weren't my only students at risk. When I described how Reginald greeted me every day, Stan laughed. But the more I told him about the kid, the more his attitude changed.

"Sounds like he really needs help," Stan said.

"I agree. I just don't how to provide it." We remained silent a moment. "But if I coach, I might be able to get closer to the rest of them."

"Maybe," Stan said. "On another subject, what are you going to do without your car? I mean without it you're going to need help yourself."

"I don't know. I'll figure something out."

"Want to borrow mine?"

"Thanks, but I couldn't do that."

"Why not? I don't need it."

"Why don't you need it?"

"My old lady got me on second shift at Philip Morris, so I ride to and from work with her."

So, his mother had lied. She must disapprove of me.

"How can you work for the same cigarette company you say ruined her health?"

"Money."

"What about your GI benefits? Won't you lose them if you aren't enrolled?"

"Yeah, but I'm burned out on school right now. I need a break, so I'm taking one. That's why I had to get a job."

Thinking back over the past semester, I realized how restless and bored with his classes Stan had seemed. Maybe taking a break was for the best. On the other hand, maybe he'd never go back.

"Stan, are you sure about this? Don't you want to earn a degree? I mean, once you drop out, getting motivated to re-enroll can be really tough."

"Yeah, I'm sure. Maybe there's a reason going back is so tough. Maybe I'm better off doing something else, at least for a while. You want to borrow my car or not? Here." He tossed me his car keys. "Use it until you're back on your feet. And try not to wreck it."

"I saw Stan's car parked out front," Deborah said, coming in the door. "What's he doing here?" Before I could explain, she added, "Have you been drinking?"

"Just a beer."

"I might've known."

I explained that Stan was lending me his car.

"Why would he do that?"

"Because mine was stolen and he's my friend."

She chewed that over. "For how long?"

"As long as we need it."

"That's really nice of him."

Later, while she was washing the supper dishes, Deborah said, "Are you listening to me?"

"It's the pills," I said from the table. "They make me groggy."

"I asked you to tell me why I don't ever buy anything at Stewart's."

"Because we can't afford to shop there?"

"But this afternoon I saw some items on sale that I thought would be perfect for going out. Let me show you."

She left and came back wearing a laced peasant blouse and a gathered skirt.

"What do you think?"

"You look like you just stepped out of the pages of *Ebony* or *Vogue.*" I was guessing. I didn't read those magazines.

Plucking at the hem of her skirt, she said, "This outfit's kind of white, isn't it?"

"Why do you always do that?"

"What? Dress white?"

"No, I mean why must you always put everything in racial terms?"

She gave me a tight smile. "Everything *is* racial."

"It doesn't have to be."

"You are so naïve sometimes."

"Maybe I am."

At bedtime, I read *The Little Prince* to Donald. We were at the point in the story where he and the fox "tame" each other, which I explained means to establish ties and therefore become "unique in all the world" to each other.

"Tame me, Pate," Donald said.

"I already have."

"Tame me again."

Feeling a twitch in my heart, I hugged him. Then I read the part where the fox tells the little prince his great secret: "It is only with the heart that one can see rightly. What is essential is invisible to the eye."

On my way to school, I wondered if the cops would ever recover my Falcon. The car's book value was practically zero, so I couldn't expect much from the insurance company. Living from paycheck to paycheck, as we did, it would be a long time before I could even think of buying another one. Whoever said two can live as cheaply as one clearly had never tried.

When I signed in, the school secretary's eyes widened at the sight of my discolored face, but she said only good morning. The sub had left a mess in my room. That's what happens when you're out for several days. I aired the portable out, cleaned the blackboard, and stood by the front door to await the students.

"God almighty, Merwin," said Thresher, on time for once. "What happened to you?"

I told him I ran into a door.

"Man, somebody bust yo' face," Eugene said, under his breath.

No sooner did they arrive than the kids were bickering and insulting each other. Having a sub had upset them, which was my fault. The order I'd carefully put in place had been disrupted. Now I had to get it back. Not easy for a man one hundred and six years old, the age I was feeling this morning. By reading stories, and making up other ones, I got through the day.

After school, I trekked out to our so-called ball diamond. No raked dirt on the weedy infield. No chalk-lined base paths, dugouts, or grandstands. Not even a bench. Only the chain link backstop made it recognizable as a ballfield. For bases, we used four pieces of cardboard.

In gray sweats and a blood-red ball cap with PARKLAND stenciled on the front, Thresher took the mound. Or rather where the mound would have been if we'd had one.

"Coach Merwin," he yelled. "Grab a bat and work with the outfielders. Have them catch some flies until it's their turn to hit."

Out here, his brusque, overbearing manner seemed almost normal. Every coach I'd ever known was the same way, all ship's captains, all tyrants at heart. I selected a bat and a couple of balls from a battered naval sea bag, probably Thresher's from the Corps, and had half the team spread out down the right-field line. I tossed a ball up and drove it two-handed high into the air, wincing as my rib cage and other hurting parts reminded me not-so-gently of my forgotten injuries. Breathing slowly and deeply, I hit another fly ball, which Harold called for and dropped.

"Two hands," I yelled. "And get your glove all the way down on grounders. Follow through on your throws. Touch your nose with your thumb if you have to."

"Man, Eugene, you can't throw worth a shit," Curtis yelled. Eugene, whose throws were way off the mark, chased him.

Not the most promising beginning. Easy to see we were undisciplined and weak on fundamentals. When a team falls behind by nine runs in little league, the umpires will call the game. I hoped there was a mercy rule at this level, too.

No spare mitts in the equipment bag, so some of the other kids had to catch the ball barehanded. And they wouldn't share, until I threatened to cut anyone who wasn't a team player. Thresher might not back me up, but it seemed like his kind of despotic edict, and it worked. Midway through practice, he blew the silvery whistle he wore on a string around his neck and called the kids in.

"You guys throw like girls and swing like old washerwomen," he said, behaving exactly like he did in the classroom—yelling, berating, intimidating. But out here on the diamond, the kids laughed.

He wanted me to work with the pitchers. "Who wants to pitch?" I asked. The four biggest kids on the team responded. Alonso, the only one of them I knew by name, threw the hardest but with little accuracy. Nobody had a curve or any other pitch but a fastball, so we focused on location. Later, I tried to teach them how to throw a changeup. The results were not promising. These kids hadn't lived and breathed baseball the way I had growing up, and it showed. They obviously had athletic ability, but it had been channeled in other directions.

At the end of our hour-long workout, Thresher called the team together again.

"We're going to work and train you gentlemen until we make men out of you. Anybody have a problem with that? All right now, give me twenty-five wind sprints, and I mean asses and elbows. Double-time it."

I was relieved he hadn't threatened to make everyone run until somebody quit, as was common at pre-season football practices. As we loaded gear into the equipment bag, he turned to me.

"What do you think, Coach? Should I get you a hat?"

We'd exchanged precious few words during practice, but I had to admit he knew how to run one. "If I stay, what would my role be?"

Whatever I wanted it to be, he said.

In that case, I told him, I wore a size seven and three-quarters.

*

The next day right after lunch, the phone on the classroom wall rang. Bloom said he was sending Mr. Green over to babysit my class. The principal needed me in his office right away. When I asked what it was about, he told me to ask the police. I arrived to find the two cops who'd bailed me out with the muggers sitting across from Bloom at his desk. More than ever, the principal's office felt like a locker room rather than an administrative eyrie.

After we exchanged greetings, Bloom said there were more suspects for me to look at.

They'd spread out a dozen mug shots on the desk. It was a real rogue's gallery, but I didn't recognize any of the unsmiling young Afro-American males. Was I sure? Take my time, they said. When I still couldn't ID any of these, they gathered up the mug shots and put them in a folder. They'd saved one more for me. When they laid it out, I saw a familiar pair of googly eyes staring up at me.

"How about this one?" they said.

"He's not one of them. That's Reginald Sheckles, the student whose home I was visiting when I got mugged. Why do you have his picture?"

"He was swept up in a drug bust near the Beecher Terrace projects. Neighbors had been complaining about traffic there day and night, so narcotics set up on the house. After an undercover made a buy, they got a warrant, forced entry, and seized four pounds of pot. While they were making the arrests, they discovered this thirteen-year-old."

"Is he in jail?"

"He's underage, so he's with Child Protective Services."

When I asked what would happen to him next, they said it was up to the judge.

"Kid doesn't have a record, so he'll probably be released back into the custody of his legal guardian."

"His grandmother."

The cops stood up. They told me to be sure and let them know if I saw any of my attackers again. I said I would. When I asked if my car had been found, they shook their heads. As they left, Bloom told me to stick around.

"You don't listen so good, Mr. Merwin," he said. "Didn't I tell you not to make that home visit? Didn't I warn you it was too dangerous? But you had to do it anyway, didn't you? What were you thinking?"

"At least now we know where Reginald is," I said.

"We would've found that out without all this aggravation."

"Yeah, but when? Except for me, Reginald thinks nobody cares about him. I had to try to help him."

"Merwin, I have six hundred Reginald Sheckles. We wouldn't be having this conversation—and your job wouldn't be hanging by a thread—if you had done what you were told."

"My job's hanging by a thread?"

"Maybe this is partly my fault. I gave you too long a leash. If I'd insisted from the start that you dress and groom yourself more professionally, this wouldn't have happened."

"Right. A coat and tie would've made all the difference."

"Listen, smartass, we have big challenges here. We need the best teachers we can find, and that's not easy. From what I've seen so far, you've been doing mostly good work. I understand your students actually turn in their assignments."

"Some of them," I said, "some of the time."

"Which tends to make me think you're the right person for the job. But if you want to keep teaching here, there are things you can't do anymore. Like no more meddling outside your classroom. No more home visits. Understood?"

"What about Reginald?"

"You're a teacher, not a social worker. Worry about your other students. Let the system handle Reginald. Promise me you will."

"I don't know if I can."

"You have to."

We locked eyes. His were dark as an eight ball.

"Now think hard about this before you answer."

I'd put a lot into this job. Besides trying to roll the same rock up the same mountain every day, I'd been beaten, robbed, and had my car stolen. I'd been chewed out repeatedly for trying to help a student. Then I thought of the kids' faces when I read to them, the way they responded to even the smallest show of love and support. Could I really desert them?

"I'm sorry, but I can't promise."

"Then clean out your desk. Leave the keys with my secretary."

For once, I followed his instructions—to the letter.

Driving home, I couldn't believe that I had thrown it all away. There was nothing else to fall back on. But I had to be the kind of teacher I thought I should. I could still go back to itinerant subbing, but I knew my teaching career was over. What would I do with the rest of my life? Of more pressing concern as I pulled into a parking place on Saint James Court, what was I going to tell Deborah when I got home?

I sat in Stan's car a while, morosely staring at turrets and towers. Then I got out and, in a daze, wandered the streets. At 4th and Kentucky, I came to a massive columned Greek Revival building, Memorial Auditorium. Across the street, in front of another impressive building, I noticed a large "Help Wanted" sign. But what help would a church need? Nevertheless, drawn by the sign, I crossed the street.

They were looking for a janitor.

I walked on, thinking surely, as a trained journalist with a college degree, I was qualified for better than that. What about advertising, public relations, sales? As a younger man, I'd once worked at a grocery store. Another time, I'd toiled in a factory all summer. Maybe Stan's mother could get me a job at Phillip Morris.

Half a block later, I turned around and went back to the church.

"I have some news," I said

Deborah was fixing her hair in front of the bathroom mirror. She turned to me and smiled. "What news?"

I'd poured out two glasses of white wine. I handed her one.

"Is it that bad?" she said.

"Come join me at the table."

When we were seated, I said, "I quit my job today."

Her smile faded. "You what?"

I said it again.

She put the glass down. "What do you mean, you quit? How could you quit such a good job?"

As I tried to explain, her expression hardened.

"Don't worry, it'll be all right," I said. "I've already got another one, here in the neighborhood. I won't even need a car."

"What new job?"

"You're looking at the new janitor of the First Christian Church on 4th Street."

"A church janitor? You can't be serious."

I held up my new keyring.

"Oh, my God," she said.

"It's only temporary."

"You did this without even talking to me about it? Go back to that principal and beg him for your job."

"I can't."

"Why not? The great Pate Merwin cannot admit making a mistake? Not even if it ruins our lives?"

"Come on, it's not that bad."

"It is. It is. If you care about me, you'll do what I say."

When I didn't react, she stamped her foot, once, twice, and vanished into Donald's room.

I'd never seen her so angry. I wanted to offer reassurance, but she wasn't in the mood. For hours, I lay awake. Everything was coming apart.

11

July 1971

We're sitting on top of the knobby picnic table, talking about our fortunes. When I say mine seem murky to me, Johona says, "I think that was the point, Pate. Iris was telling you to be patient until you find your true path."

Which path? I wonder.

Before I can speak, Matthew interrupts. "Thank God Iris and Nick are finally gone."

It makes me furious, but I don't say anything. He'll soon be gone, too.

"I have a surprise," he says.

He wants us to make a circle around the fire. I only want to be alone with Johona. But I play along, hoping this might be the quickest way to make that happen. Summer steps into the ring holding up a plastic bag full of what appear to be gel capsules.

"Magic mushrooms, anyone?"

"Around here, we call them 'sacred mushrooms.' And we only take them to visit the spirit world. Is that what you're planning to do?" Johona says.

There's some nervous giggling.

"My ancestors were forced here at gunpoint. This land is all we have left. And we truly believe it is the path to the spirit world. Be sure that's where you want to go before you take those mushrooms. Oh, and by the way, where did you get them?"

"What does it matter?" Summer says. "It's good shit. And free."

"How do you know they're not poisonous dried toadstools?" Johona asks.

"Because I spent the last six months hunting them on the farm. If you don't want any, that's fine. But I promise you these are the right little brown 'shrooms."

Summer shakes out four caps. She and Autumn swallow two apiece.

"Would we do this if they weren't safe? It's going to be a great, spiritual trip. They're pure psilocybin and very mellow, like mild acid with none of the usual side effects like having a nasty taste in the mouth. But they can still kick your ass."

Matthew and Stan opt for the 'shrooms. I assume Stan intends to go off on a side trip with one of the two seasons.

"How long before we start getting off?" Matthew asks.

"Fifteen or twenty minutes."

"We'll leave these on the table," Autumn says, "in case you change your minds."

We step away to speak privately.

"Were you serious about visiting the spiritual world? Or just messing with their heads?"

"Of course, I was serious." A hint of a smile. "Messing with their heads is good, too."

We decide to wait and see what happens. Meanwhile, we rejoin the others around the fire. As more sticks are added, the blaze grows. Autumn suggests that we all share our previous tripping experiences. This seems like a good idea, since the people you trip with really matter a lot. I know that much. The stories we hear do not seem memorable and tell me little that I don't already know, or infer, about my companions. Then it's my turn.

"Okay, my first hallucinogenic experience was in college on mescaline. I didn't really know what to expect. To tell the truth, I was a little scared of possibly losing my mind."

"So that's where it went," Stan says.

"Wow! Really?" Autumn says. "That's heavy."

"Why did you do it then?" Matthew asks.

"It seemed a risk worth taking. I was totally alienated, about to get drafted, so what did I have to lose? It was like a rite of passage, I guess. By then, I'd read a lot about drugs: *The Doors of Perception, The Teachings of Don Juan. The Electric Kool-Aid Acid Test.* And I'd smoked"—looking at Stan—"as we like to say, 'copious quantities of weed.' So, I understood about being stoned. What that was like. But I wanted to get heavier, to dig the very essence of reality."

"Whatever that means," Matthew says.

"Anyway, I'd found the perfect place to do psychedelics without fear of being hassled. That was important, of course, because as everybody knows the drug itself makes you feel paranoid. So, you want a safe, pleasant environment and friends you trust."

"Where was this?" Stans asks.

"A friend invited me and half a dozen others—some of them you might know, Matthew—out to where he was house-sitting for a prof away on sabbatical. The house was secluded in the middle of the woods."

"Sort of like out here," Summer says, "only not as beautiful."

"Except we hardly know each other," Johona says.

"True," says Autumn, "but we're all cool, aren't we?"

After letting the question hang for a moment, I continue my tale.

"It actually was quite beautiful in its own way. It was a fall afternoon and all the leaves were in full color. The house itself was impressive, had a lot of stone and steel and glass walls. It was a contemporary geometric design with cathedral ceiling, odd angles, open flights of stairs. Trippy, in fact. It reminded me of an Escher print—the one that creates the illusion of an endless staircase, like a Möbius strip."

"Möbius strip. Wasn't that the name of a band?" Summer murmurs.

"You're thinking of Moby Grape," Matthew tells her.

"Or Moby Dick," Stan adds, with a sly expression.

"That was a book," Autumn points out.

"Anyway, there was a massive deck on the back of the house that extended maybe ten yards deep into the trees. Looking out from inside, you felt like you were outdoors in the middle of the forest."

"Hey, that sounds like Paul Kimball's place," Matthew says. "You know, the art prof who lived out Glen Lily Road? I've been there. My wife had a class with him. She's an artist as well as an actor, you know. I think Paul was trying to get in her pants. Half the art department was. He invited us out there for a little party."

This information doesn't surprise me.

"So, we dropped some mescaline. For the first twenty or thirty minutes nothing happened. Then I started feeling dizzy and nauseated. At the same time, all the colors of the leaves became so intense, *vibrant*. And the music on the stereo was so vivid."

"I'd say you were getting off," Autumn says.

"We were listening to the Moody Blues, who are pretty cosmic even when you're straight. That funny song about Timothy Leary being dead, according to one voice, while another claims not so. Instead Leary's daytripping around in his astral *plane*, which of course is a pun, trying to find the key to cosmic perception. In my head, I see this cartoon figure zooming around in his Sopwith Camel like Snoopy, babbling about experiencing the direct, total awareness that love is the fundamental fact of the universe. Or some such. And suddenly I got it. I mean, I *grokked* it, like in *Stranger in a Strange Land*. But as soon as I tried to voice the thought, the words slipped away like in a dream you know you'll never be able to remember. This sort of thing went on for about eight more hours, and included seeing purple and green water, before we crashed."

After a pregnant pause, Matthew says, "I'd like to take that trip myself. But so far, I still don't feel a thing. Are you sure these 'shrooms are any good, Autumn?"

"Just be patient," she tells him. "Any minute now they'll kick in."

And they do. We can tell from our fellow travelers' comments as the mushrooms' effects begin to manifest themselves.

"Wow!"

"What a rush!"

"I am zonked out of my mind!"

And so on.

They tell of seeing flashes of light. Or moving geometrical patterns. Visuals with eyes open or shut.

"Time for us to go now," Johona says.

"Where?" I ask.

"Where would you like to go? It's a big desert."

"You lead, I'll follow."

The light of the campfire fades behind us as we follow a hidden path upward. I worry a bit about getting lost in the desert. Johona won't, I know, but what if we get separated? Then there's always the possibility of stepping on a rattlesnake in the darkness. What then? We file though the cacti and mesquite for ten minutes and reach a mesa. From here the surrounding canyons are lit by the moon's glow.

We find a smooth rock to sit on together. "Perfect," I say.

Johona tells me she enjoyed my story and asks if I was alone at the time, or with someone.

"You mean did I get laid? Unfortunately, no."

"Maybe you'll have better luck next time."

"This is next time."

"I know."

She shows me four mushroom caps she snagged as we slipped away from the others.

"Now I'm ready to visit the spirit world," she says, taking two and offering me the rest.

After swallowing the mushrooms, we sit in quiet contemplation of the desert's vastness, its shapes and shadows illuminated by the moon. This goes on for quite some time as we listen to the desert sobbing and keening. I know that this is the hour when burrowing denizens like the antelope squirrel come out to hunt for food. Larger animals, too. Although the sand feels cooler, I am fearful of brushing against sharp-needled plants that could pierce my skin.

To lose my apprehensiveness, I say, "Tell me about your tribe."

"I am of the Weeminuche, one of the seven original Ute bands that inhabited all of Colorado."

She goes on to describe how in 1868, both the Ute and Navajo tribes were removed to reservations and what has happened to them since. It's not a pretty picture, similar in many ways to the fate of the Indian tribes back home—Shawnee, Cherokee, Chickasaw, Iroquois.

Then Johona stops abruptly. "My mouth has gone dry. Do you feel it?"

I nod, conscious of the heightened awareness with which I'm experiencing each phantom moment.

"We must be getting off. Oh, my God," she says, pointing to the canyon walls.

They seem to be melting, leaving only a pool of hot wax behind.

Johona begins chanting softly in what I assume is Ute.

As the moon slips below the horizon, she stops and says, "Look, there is a sight that most people will never see."

I stare up in wonderment at a glowing band of stars arching across the sky.

"It's the Milky Way," she says. "This is one of the best places for star-gazing in the whole Four Corners."

And then something truly extraordinary happens. The stars and the pitch-blackness of the night suddenly disappear in a blaze of high-wattage brightness as if stadium lights have just come on. And in the dazzling glow, a massive eagle appears hovering before us.

I close my eyes, but the visual remains. It's still there when I re-open them. It's impossible but seeing is believing.

"Can you see that?" I sputter, staring at the bird's seven-foot wingspan and predatory yellow eyes.

"The eagle is the spiritual guide of the People and of all things," she says.

In my astonishment, I begin wondering if this could be what Johona was chanting for earlier. Was she praying to the grandfathers to send us this enormous creature? And for what purpose—perhaps to carry us off to the spirit world? Forever?

Slipping my arm around her, I hold Johona tight for a long, long moment. Then the hooked beak and sharp talons begin to fade back into the night. And then the bird is gone.

"Probably just a hallucination," I say, heart palpitating, as I take a deep breath.

"Or a vision."

"If that's what it was, what did it mean?"

Johona smiles. "A blessing, maybe?"

I cling to her, realizing that I could easily spend a lifetime with her under this huge remote sky.

At daybreak, I awaken on the sand by the rock with the sun still below the horizon, its reflected rays lighting up the sky. Johona is still beside me, her hair streaked golden. I lay still, feeling her breath against my cheek, the heat in her skin.

"How are you feeling?" she asks.

"Like I've fed on honeydew and drunk the milk of paradise."

"Poetry, so early in the morning?"

The truth is I'm both overjoyed and completely wrung out. My night with Johona was fabulous, but now my mouth feels numb and my joints poker stiff from staying in one cramped position. As we brush off the sand and start back to camp, I'm suddenly overcome by a feeling of loss—knowing that when we come down from this mesa, retracing our steps along the narrow trail, my time with Johona will soon be over. And I don't want it to be. But how could I stay here in Mancos forever?

I start to speak, but the words catch in my throat before finally tumbling out.

"Come traveling with me, Johona. Let's go to San Francisco together. No matter how wonderful it is there, it will be even better with you."

"I'd like to," she says. "I really would. But I couldn't leave my family."

"They can't expect you to stay here forever."

"It is not what they expect that matters."

I know intuitively that I won't be able to change her mind through argument or persuasion. I also know she is someone who I could spend my whole life with. But in the space of a single breath, I'm about to lose her.

Approaching camp, I hear Jim Morrison waxing prophetic about the future being uncertain and the end always near, so naturally he has a beer. Last night's campfire has burned down to ashes. From the way the sleeping bags are arranged, I assume everyone's had a good night. I've been feeling guilty about ditching Stan, so it's a relief to find him still in Summer's embrace.

"Hey." He starts to get up but grabs his ankle instead and sinks onto the picnic table.

"What's wrong?" I ask.

"Tried to climb that." He indicates a nearby escarpment at least forty feet high. "Fell."

"You tried to scale that in the dark while you were tripping? Unbelievable. Let me take a look."

The ankle is puffy, with reddish marks both around and below the bone.

"Looks like a bad sprain." I've had enough of them to know. If this were a basketball game, the trainer would simply tape him up and let Stan finish the game. He'd be fine—until the compression of the tape was removed. Then the ankle would balloon up. But we don't have any tape and it's too late for that anyway. If Stan tries to walk on that ankle now, he might wind up on crutches for days. Not that we have any crutches.

The ranger I met the first day at Mesa Verde arrives in a dusty Jeep. As soon as he gets out, he goes over to the Mustang, leans through the window, and switches off the music. Noticing Stan's ankle, he says, "You should get that X-rayed. It might be broken."

Stan thanks the ranger, but I know he won't do it.

When the ranger sees Johona, he seems affronted. "I'm surprised to find you here. What are you doing with them?"

"This is none of your business, Ben," she says.

"You're wrong about that." Ben is red-faced. "This is a family campground, with rules set by the National Park Service that must be followed. We're investigating reports of lewd conduct and suspected drug use."

"Oh, come on," Johona says.

"I want to talk to you in private, Johona," he says.

When I step in front of him, he orders me out of his way, then tries to push past. We wind up in a shoving match.

"Stop it. Please." Johona tries to push us apart.

I let go of Ben. I even pick up his hat, which came off in the struggle, and brush it off. He snatches it away.

"You just made a huge mistake," he tells me.

"Don't you like the hat?" I say.

Johona talks to him quietly and earnestly.

He keeps glaring over at me and shaking his head.

Somehow, she persuades him to let us all go.

"For Johona's sake," he says, "I'm going to give you a break. You've got twenty minutes to clear out. After that, we'll start arresting you."

He walks stiffly to his Jeep. Pulls out a first aid kit, takes out an elastic bandage, and tosses it to Stan. Again, he advises elevating the injured ankle and putting some ice on it.

"You were truly amazing, Johona," I say once Ben is gone.

We gather up our belongings and stow them in her truck. As I bandage Stan's ankle, he nods at Matthew.

"I can't wait to see his face when we drop the hammer on that shitbird."

Before we can depart, Matthew once again tells me we need to talk. I say I can't imagine why, but give in.

"Look, I know we planned to go to Hollywood together," he says, "but with the Paraprosdokians out of the picture, things have changed. Summer and Autumn are offering me a ride."

I laugh.

"What's so funny?" he says.

"Tell me something, Matthew. Do you really have a soap opera role waiting for you? Or was that all bullshit, too?"

"No, man. I'm playing a hippie. Can you dig it?" He gives me his little sneaky, in-the-know snicker.

"You son of a bitch," I say. "You've been using us as guinea pigs all along."

"Then I ought to be pretty convincing, right?" He turns and marches away. I watch as he slings his gear into the Mustang. Slamming the trunk, he climbs into the front passenger seat beside Autumn. Summer waves to us from the back seat as they drive off.

"What the hell just happened?" Stan says.

When I tell him, Stan's eyes light up with mischief. "I'm all broken up about it, but as long as we're really rid of him—"

"Hurry up, you two," Johona calls. "Get a move on before Ben changes his mind."

I carry our rucksacks to the pickup. Stan hobbles over and slips in beside Johona.

"Where's the nearest hospital?" I ask, as she begins covering the four miles back to the park entrance.

"Southwest Memorial. That's about ten miles east in Cortez."

"I don't need a doctor. It's only a sprain," Stan says.

"But you're in pain," Johona tells him. "My cousin Ignacio could make it better. He's a *poowagudt*—"

"A what?"

"A healer. He uses natural medicine to help people. He could conduct a healing ceremony for you."

Stan turns to me. "What do you think?"

I turn to Johona. "What about your job? You'll miss work."

"I'll call a friend to cover for me."

"Must be a good friend," I say.

"She needs the money."

"Well?" Stan says.

"I say that the Ute have been taking care of their own forever. If Johona trusts her cousin, maybe we should give him a try."

And Stan says okay.

We head west on Highway 160. It's a twenty-minute drive to Ignacio's place, Johona says. On the way, I'm fretting about Stan's medical care. I'm the one who said supplanting modern medicine with folk remedies would be all right. But what if this *poowagudt's* poultices and potions make Stan worse?

We leave the highway behind for hardpan dirt through riverbeds, mesas, and buttes. Among a stand of cottonwoods, we find a small house and Johona dashes inside. A moment later, she returns. Ignacio is not at home. He's at the "sacred place communing with the spirits," according to his wife.

"Can we get out there?" Stan asks.

"We'll need horses," Johona says.

She drives us to a rough wood-rail corral, where half a dozen horses are milling around. She tells me to come with her while Stan waits in the truck. Inside the small barn, we're assailed by strong smells of hay and manure and oiled leather. We pass darkened stalls until coming to a tiny tack room. She selects what we'll need from the riding gear hanging on wall pegs. I carry our saddles and stirrups out to the corral. I watch in admiration as she saddles the horses.

"Mount up," she says.

Despite being from Kentucky, I've only ridden a few times and don't know if I'll be able to stay in the saddle. Nonetheless, I take the reins and haul myself aboard a bay mare named Smokey. With his sprained ankle, Stan has a much harder time getting on a black gelding. The horse snorts and snuffles and moves around a lot. But Johona strokes his mane and talks to him. Then she mounts a frisky reddish-brown stallion.

The first twenty minutes are an easy ride over flat terrain. At a canyon rim, we dismount. The way to the bottom is via a slash-cut trail. Meanwhile, Johona herds all the horses. The drop, according to her, is a dizzying one thousand feet. I don't know how I'm going to make it to the bottom myself, let alone Stan. But game as always, he picks up a walking stick and sets off. I follow my surprisingly nimble pal. We slide on loose rock, grasp at boulders, and slowly make our way.

At the halfway point, we stop to rest.

"Stan, this *poowagudt* better know his stuff. Otherwise, we'll never get back up."

"We'll make it," he says.

At the bottom, we mount back up.

Our destination lies about forty-five minutes away. From this point on, Johona warns, we must be on the lookout for quicksand and flash floods. The trail winds through sandy washes, crossing and re-crossing the same muddy stream. Our horses know the way and do pretty much as they please, stopping to drink or eat sage growing along the trail whenever they feel like it. The pace is slow, which is okay by me, but Johona keeps the horses moving with a switch.

"Don't let Smokey eat sage or she'll become impossible to control," she warns.

"She's already impossible to control."

I can't keep the beast away from the brush no matter what I do. My only consolation is that Stan is having similar troubles. Of course, he has a bum ankle for an excuse. What's mine?

Shafts of sunlight partially shadow the narrow canyon we're passing through. At the foot of a cliff, we come upon a partially buried pile of bleached bones and a skull.

"Horse skeleton," Johona says. "That's the only animal big enough around here for those bones. Probably chased off the cliff by another stallion."

Looking up, I imagine a horse flailing through the air, twisting and turning as it falls.

"They fight over the mares," she explains.

We find a second skeleton at the bottom of another precipice, this one with tufts of wool still attached to the bones.

"It's a sheep, probably killed by coyotes."

Encountering dead animals in this way, where they're allowed to remain out in the open until disintegrating and sinking into the sand, is another reminder of the desert's unforgiving nature—something to ponder while riding on, for life is short and precious. Isn't that why I evaded the draft—to avoid killing or being killed for no good reason? Are there any good reasons to die? Life is also fragile—I think of Stan stubbornly collapsing out on the dunes—and could end at any moment. What if mine were to end right here, right now? I imagine myself stretched out back there at the canyon's lowermost point with tufts of my own wool still attached to my bones, slowly disintegrating and sinking into the sand. Would my life have meant anything? Or is Matthew correct in believing that life is absurd, a meaningless joke? And what happens to us after death? Is there really a spirit world, as Johona believes? Did our vision of the eagle really mean anything?

It's almost more than I can bear to think on for very long. My mind wanders until at last we come over a rise to discover a multistoried cliff dwelling. It's built under a massive overhang at a canyon rim and seems carved into, rather than built on, the ledges. A towering wooden ladder leans against the cliff. I assume we must climb it if we want to reach the sacred place where the *poowagudt* communes with the spirits—if spirits exist as other than delusions of minds frightened by the Ultimate Unknown.

Johona tethers our horses next to one she says is her cousin's.

"Think you can make it up to the top?" she asks both of us.

I find the question irritating. Sure, it looks dangerous. But I'm not injured like Stan. If Johona and her *poowagudt* cousin can make it, so can I. But it is a long way up, which triggers my fear of heights, and that old ladder looks shaky. I wonder how trustworthy it is. Conditions six hundred years ago must've been really threatening for the cliff dwellers to daily have risked such a perilous climb.

But Stan's fine with it. "Piece of cake," he declares, and begins pulling himself up hand over hand, one rung at a time.

I take a deep breath and follow, eyes riveted to the square foot of cliff face in front of me, determined not to look down however strong the temptation might prove. Johona brings up the rear, as if she's going to catch us when we fall. As part of the climb, we must traverse a narrow gap where there's nothing between us and a scary view but the ladder. Nevertheless, we all make it to our destination without further incident.

While Johona presses on ahead to find her cousin, the two of us catch our breath seated in shade on a wide rocky shelf.

"You okay?" I ask.

"Yeah," Stan grunts. "Are you?"

"Hell yeah." But talk is cheap and we both know it. Just being in such an ancient, eerie ruin has us pumping adrenaline.

I think Stan is as relieved as I am when she reappears a few moments later, accompanied by her cousin. He doesn't bother with introductions, getting right to the business at hand.

"Johona tells me of your need to be healed," Ignacio says, peering at Stan's bandaged ankle. "Do you wish for me to perform a healing rite?"

The cousin is a lean man with braided hair. But with his tasseled robe and bead-fringed necklace, he might've stepped out of a six-hundred-year-old wall painting. Strapped across one of his broad shoulders is a bag made out of animal skin and decorated with ornate beadwork. His medicine bag, I assume.

"I do want you to perform the healing rite," Stan says, very formally.

"Come with me then."

We follow the *poowagudt* through a recess in the wall. This pueblo is divided into perhaps two dozen rooms. Like the Anasazi ruins at Mesa Verde, this one was built of sandstone blocks and mud. Fingerprints are still visible in the thousand-year-old mortar. Ancient artifacts—shards of pottery, a piece of an urn, one small crude broken arrowhead—are everywhere. I'm tempted to pick them up, but don't.

In a dim chamber we encounter stone enclosures in various stages of decay, collapse, or disintegration. A whole history of the Anasazi people laid out for us to see. I feel a heaviness pressing upon me, as if the too-dense air in here has not been disturbed for centuries. That can't be true, I know, especially considering Ignacio's familiarity with the place. Yet the feeling lingers.

I'm expecting a kiva, but there's no underground room here, only a circle of stones, which Ignacio tells Stan to enter. But first he must remove his shoes and socks, and the elastic bandage. As Stan takes them off, I see despite the dimness that the skin on his knotted ankle has turned a deep purple and seems stretched tight. A shiver of fear runs through me as I wonder if we've made a mistake by coming here instead of rushing to an emergency room. Too late now, in any case.

The medicine man spreads the contents of his medicine bag, which include deer tails and feathers, on the ground. When he beckons for Stan to rise, Johona nudges me.

"Time for us to go," she whispers.

"But I don't want to leave Stan. Aren't we going to watch the ceremony?"

She squeezes my hand. "I'm not allowed to. Wouldn't you rather be with me?"

Talk about a hard choice. But I elect to follow her through several more rooms until we come to a low, dark tunnel. This triggers my claustrophobia. But I can see a proverbial light at the end, and it isn't stuffy, meaning there must be a source of fresh air. So, when she drops to her hands and knees and starts inside, I do, too. It's spooky in the tunnel. I worry about bats, which are plentiful in this neck of the woods, but don't encounter any. Also, the surface is smooth, making it easy going. At the end, it widens into another room. But it's a dead end.

She turns to me and we lock eyes.

"This may be our last time alone together. Even though we have known each other only a short time, you have touched me deeply, Pate. I will always carry your memory with me."

I gaze at her feeling simultaneously overwhelmed by joy and dread. Joy because no woman has ever spoken to me in this way before. Dread because of the certainty that our short happy dream together is about to end. Whatever the cause—an unhappy childhood, rejection, disillusionment—I've never dared to believe in true love or happily-ever-after endings for me. All you need is love but you can't always get what you want, as Deborah Johnson recently taught me, a lesson to be learned all over again.

When I start to speak Johona says, "Don't talk," and closes her eyes. I kiss her lips, taking the bitter with the sweet and knowing that the course of true love never did run smooth.

12

April 1971

At first light, I dressed quietly and walked to work. My new employer, the Rev. Bailey, had given me a set of keys. I used one to unlock the basement door. It felt odd to be inside a church after all these years. It was silent, except for a low electrical humming. The Star Unit had never been this quiet. Classes there wouldn't commence for another forty-five minutes. By now Deborah would be getting Donald ready for daycare. After a day of butting heads with my kids from another planet, I'd return to an evening of domestic bliss with my beautiful lady. But the world had changed.

When I opened my padlocked "office" located at the end of a long murky corridor, I was greeted by an oily cedar smell. I saw, by the harsh glare of a single naked bulb, shelves stocked with floor polish, cleaning products, and tools.

I spread out the morning paper I'd purchased on my way to work. Read the sports until hearing footsteps as the first daycare workers arrived. Time to look busy. Grabbing trash bags, I went outdoors to the rusty green dumpster with the creaking lid situated behind the church. Traffic was honking, car doors slamming, waking up the city as I dragged the bags toward the alley. I scoured the shrubbery for wrinkled plastic bags and cigarette wrappers, not to mention empty beer cans and bottles left behind by winos.

Back inside the sanctuary, I admired the tall stained-glass windows lit by morning sunbeams. What a stark contrast with the darkened stone walls and floor. Feeling drawn in by the decidedly medieval feel of the place, I briefly became in my mind a monk, proving my devotion by humbly mopping the floor and dusting the fine oak pews and pulpit. Perhaps later I'd continue copying an ancient manuscript of the Holy Bible. Fit work for a medieval writer.

Trying out a variety of occupations was supposed to be an honorable endeavor for aspiring young writers in modern times, though. Perhaps like Hemingway, I'd make the leap from journalism to fiction. But other writers had performed many other jobs. Hawthorne and Melville were surveyors, Faulkner a postal clerk, Steinbeck a migrant farm worker. Were there any who'd started out as church janitors, I wondered?

None came readily to mind.

I parked my bucket and took a break in the church kitchen, where I could read while brewing myself a cup of coffee. Earlier, I'd found a smudged church bulletin stuffed inside a hymnal.

"For meditation," it read. "'Are you lonely out here?' asked a visitor of a lighthouse keeper on an isolated reef. 'Not since I saved my first man' came the swift reply."

An obvious spiritual metaphor, but one I admired even though long ago having given up on saving my own drowning soul. Part of it was recognizing through the eyes of a child the fanatical elders of my church as hypocritical bigots. The other part was feeling no joy—none whatsoever, only anxiety—when I'd succumbed during a service and come forward to "accept Jesus Christ as my personal savior."

I didn't miss the people at my old church, but sometimes I felt a lingering attachment to the building itself. Places of worship were quiet most of the time. I respected their historic role as places of not only religious but political sanctuary. If the draft board ever caught up with me while I was in here, they'd have to drag me out kicking and screaming.

Around 3:30, I locked up and went home.

From the moment I entered the apartment, I knew that Deborah and Donald were gone for good. I rushed through each room, calling out their names. The beds were made, no wet toothbrushes or uncapped tubes on the sink. None of Deborah's feminine beauty products on the shelf. Bare hangers in her side of our closet. I opened her drawers but found none of her silky undergarments. Donald's room had been emptied, as well.

In the kitchen cupboard, the envelope where I kept the grocery money was gone.

Seized by a flurry of feelings, I hurried down to the bank where she worked. Only one teller's window was open. I asked the middle-aged woman behind the counter if she'd seen Deborah today. Told she had not, I asked for the manager. She pointed out Mr. Burris, a fiftyish man in an expensive looking suit sitting behind a desk in his office.

"What can I do for you?" he asked.

I didn't mince words. "You can tell me if Deborah Johnson reported for work today." As he hesitated, I added, "It's personal."

"Ah. Well, I'm sorry, but I can't give out private information about our employees."

"Come on, help me out here, Mr. Burris. Deborah's my lady. I'm worried about her. I haven't been able to reach her, you see."

Burris tapped a fountain pen on his desk blotter. The surface was cluttered with family photos and bric-a-brac.

"Normally, my lips would be sealed. But I suppose there's no harm in telling you that Miss Johnson is no longer with us. She resigned today without giving notice. Shocking behavior, especially after all we've done for her."

I didn't like his tone, but I disliked his message even more. I pressed him for more details but couldn't get anything else out of him.

Next, I went to see her father. He was sitting on the stoop reading the Bible.

"What do you want?" He seemed much older now than when I first encountered him.

"I'm looking for Deborah."

"She's not here."

He got up and went inside, shutting the door. I opened it and followed him into the living room, where he'd taken a seat in an armchair facing an ancient television. Books and magazines lay scattered on a side table marred with cup rings.

"When I got home from work today, all her stuff was gone. I need your help, Mr. Johnson."

"Why should I help you?"

"Because I love her."

"This kills my soul," he said. "You had no business in the world involving yourself with that girl. I told you to leave her alone, but you wouldn't listen. Now look what's happened."

"I understand you want to blame me, but I'm not the one who walked out."

"They're still gone, aren't they?"

I had no answer for that. When I asked him to let me know if he heard from her, he didn't reply. I left him sitting with the Bible still in his hands.

I went back to the Falls of the Ohio and wandered aimlessly along the river's edge, stepping carefully among boulders and crunching pebbles underfoot. The area was deserted. Not a single footprint in sight, supporting the illusion that no human had ever walked this beach before. But dogs had. Or at least one dog. I found paw prints in the mud. The ground was too wet to follow them. At one spot, I came across an incredible plethora of tangled light gray to creamy tan driftwood. Some of it was shaped like mammoth tusks, or skeletal sea monsters who'd crawled onto the sand to die.

Though a cold wind was kicking up out in the channel, I sat down beside the exposed roots of a tree. For a while, I studied the bent driftwood that had washed up recently and wondered if any of it had potential as a repository for beverages and magazines.

It was starting to get dark but the longer I stayed, the harder it was to move.

I went back to the car, opened the trunk, and wrestled out the big piece of driftwood that I'd been attempting to sculpt. I carried it back where I'd found it originally and stood there thinking that, despite all the hours I'd spent shaping and sanding it, the project remained incomplete. Now it always would. Taking a breath, I heaved it as far as I could out into the Ohio. After a huge splash, it bobbed along, partly concealed beneath the surface like an iceberg. Maybe it would wind up in New Orleans, or Brazil.

I turned toward the parking lot, finding the going up easier than the coming down.

For weeks, I went through the motions, seeing no one outside of work, losing my appetite, hardly sleeping. And when I did doze, I dreamed of Deborah—tortured smoldering visions always ending with her disappearance. The empty chairs, silent bedrooms, bare shelves—everything reminded me of her. Each day, I opened the mail, hoping it was from her. Each time the phone rang, I prayed I'd hear her voice.

But I never did.

Time supposedly heals all wounds. And winter eventually began to loosen its grip on the world. Nothing like spring in Kentucky, nowhere prettier. I felt heartened by the early blooming forsythia, then the redbuds, dogwoods, azaleas, and rhododendrons. As the trees flowered and leafed out, the robins returned. The air seemed fresher, blown here from warmer climes. On the first Saturday in May, Canonero II won the Kentucky Derby. A couple of weeks later, he won the Preakness as well.

But through all the seasonal change, my dull monotonous work remained the same. As did the darkness in my soul. Lonely and embittered, I longed for a relief from the heartbreak that continued to plague me.

One Friday early in June, I heard footsteps echoing through the church basement. I knew that the Rev. Bailey sometimes took it upon himself to try and catch me slacking off, so I made sure to appear busy for his benefit. But the effort was wasted. It wasn't him—it was Stan.

"What are you doing here?" I demanded, putting down my oily rag and rusty grass clippers.

"Place reminds me of a dungeon," Stan said.

"It's the maid's day off."

"I thought you were the maid. Aren't you going to invite me in?"

I didn't really want to. It was too embarrassing. Not that I minded doing menial tasks—work is work—but I didn't want him to see me doing so in these surroundings. It just felt wrong.

"Shouldn't you be at work, Stan?"

He ignored the question, saying he wanted to talk.

We went across the street to a little park with a low wall where I sometimes lunched under a blue jay sky. I hadn't seen Stan since I returned his car. At the time, my old friend had hinted about moving back in with me. My emotions were still so raw at the time that I'd said no, even though I could've used the money. Had he come to revisit the subject?

He pulled out a red, white, and blue pack of Winstons.

"Patriotic smokes now. But aren't you the same guy who told me that his mother was slowly being killed by smoking?"

"I've tried to get her to quit. The habit's just too hard to break."

"So now you're a smoker, too? How does that work?"

"They give you free cigarettes on breaks at the plant. Big tubs of them. You can take as many as you want."

"The first one's always free."

"Don't mock me, Pate."

Seeing the anguish in his eyes, I said, "Sorry, man. Who am I to judge?"

"It's okay," he said. "You're right. I'm going to quit right now."

With that, he tossed the pack into a trash bin.

"Good for you, man," I said, feeling a bit like a street evangelist. What irony, me saving Stan from himself. I wished somebody would save me from myself. And then, as if in answer to my unspoken desire, someone did.

"Listen, I'm going on a trip to San Francisco. You're coming with me."

I felt a wild surge of ecstasy at the very thought of escaping what had become my life. But it seemed impossible.

"Stan, I don't have the money."

"No problem," he said. "We'll hitchhike."

"To the west coast? Have you ever hitchhiked anywhere before?"

"Not that far, but sure. It won't cost us a cent."

"Yeah, but we can't live on nothing. I'm still broke."

Stan said he'd quit his job after putting together a grubstake big enough for both of us.

Clenching my jaw and trying to settle my fidgety hands, I listened intently to what he had to say. At the same time, I was mentally running through everything I knew about Stan himself, the current state of hippiedom, and weighing the danger level of riding with strangers who could be anything from armed rednecks to serial killers.

"You and I are going for the Summer of Love," Stan said, and held up a hand. "Don't say it. I know that was four years ago, but so what? There were a hundred thousand flower children who made the scene in Haight-Ashbury in '67. A lot of them are still there. I want to see what's become of them. And I want to turn on, tune in, and drop out, man. It's still the Age of Aquarius. Put aside your broom and your doubts and your excuses, and let's go."

"You should be an evangelist," I said. "I think you've got the gift."

"What I've got is a bankroll that I'm willing to share and a strong desire to blow this scene. What do you say?"

I felt jumpy, my heartbeat racing. "When are you leaving?"

"Monday morning, first thing."

"Thanks for all the notice."

"That gives you two whole days. You need to start living in the present tense."

Still, I hesitated.

"She's not coming back, you know."

"You mean Deborah?"

"No, the Queen of Sheba. Don't snooze on this, man."

And he walked away, whistling. I'd never heard him whistle before.

For the rest of the afternoon, I couldn't shake the idea out of my head. What would it be like to hitchhike two thousand miles? I'd never done anything remotely like that before. This was a huge leap. And what would it be like in the Haight after all this time had passed since it first became the epicenter of the counterculture? I had other questions, more disturbing ones, such as whether this eventually meant a complete break with reality as I knew it. That's what it felt like. Leave the known world behind for a strange new one. Cast my fate to the wind like Columbus sailing on the *Pinta, Niña,* and *Santa Maria*? Put the slogans I espoused to the test. What if they were found wanting? What might become of me?

I was still turning all this over in my mind when the Rev. Bailey surprised me by dropping by and inviting me to join him in his study at the end of my shift.

For brandy and cigars, no doubt. Ha.

At quitting time, I found him seated behind his antique walnut writing desk surrounded by floor-to-ceiling bookshelves and leaded glass windows. The room, like the reverend himself, seemed old but comfortable rather than ascetic.

"Come in, Pate," he said.

When I was seated, he continued, "I'm concerned about you. A man who spends as much time inside the Lord's house as you should appreciate the gift he's been blessed with."

Stung by his words, I felt like making a quick retort. But I bit my lip because he had given me a job when I truly needed one. Instead, I said, "I appreciate those gifts."

"I don't mean your job, if that's what you think," he said, and steepled his fingers. "How long have you been with us now, a couple of months? And I'm pleased with your work, but in all that time you haven't attended a single worship service."

All at once, the purpose of this meeting became clear. Time to try and save the soul of the help.

As if in response to this thought, Rev. Bailey said, "If you give the Lord His share of your time, you won't regret it. God's talking to you. Won't you listen?"

Despite my gratitude and good intentions, I couldn't help saying, "I think He's telling me to go West, young man, go West."

"I believe that Horace Greeley said that, not the Lord."

I didn't contradict him. After all, he was right.

"Let Him come into your heart, Pate."

With a frozen smile I cleared my throat and said, "Reverend, I'm sorry for the short notice, but it's time for me to turn in my mop and broom."

"Why?"

I told him about our plan of hitchhiking to California.

"What if I offered you a pay raise and a promotion?" he said.

"Are you offering me a raise and a promotion?"

He leaned forward, resting his palms on the desk.

"I would hate to lose you, Pate. This old building needs a makeover. I'll soon be hiring a crew of painters and other workers to do the job. We'll need someone responsible to supervise them. I'd like that person to be you."

Licking my lips, I said, "But I'm only the janitor."

"You'll do. If anything, you're over-qualified."

A better-paying job with bigger responsibilities. All I had to do was say yes and start showing up for church. I would need more time to think this over.

"Monday then, shall we say?" Rev. Bailey smiled. "You've been doing a fine job, Pate."

I thanked him. Before leaving, I picked up my paycheck for the week. It came to $97.32.

13

July 1971

Stan is still sitting inside the circle of stones when we return. But the ceremony is over and the *poowagudt* gone. Since the swelling and discoloration of Stan's ankle looks no different than before, I assume the ceremony has failed. I wonder if that's what I really wanted to happen. Perhaps I am fearful that the spirit world might exist.

"You okay?"

Stan nods.

"Tell us what happened."

Stan draws himself up as if on the witness stand, promising to tell the truth, the whole truth, etc.

"It was heavy, man."

First, Ignacio had lit a fire in the center of the circle. After burning some herbs, Stan says he'd sprinkled powders. Then he'd waved deer tails and an eagle feather.

"That, um, was to scatter the evil spirits to the wind. Then he started chanting in some other tongue—Ute maybe. The chanting lasted a long time."

Ignacio had played strange, atonal sounds on a wood flute. They'd seemed to conjure up haunting images.

"I can't describe them," Stan says.

After a while, the "poo" had started beating out this complex rhythm on the medicine drum. Slow, steady beats that grew faster and more emphatic. Then he'd added rattles and bells and started shouting.

"It was different than anything I've ever heard before," Stan says.

The music had lasted a long time. When Ignacio finally stopped drumming, he'd asked the spirits to bless Stan and strengthen his ankle. At least that's what Stan assumed.

"Was he speaking English?" I ask.

"I'm not sure. All I specifically remember is him saying that now I must meditate on what the spirits said to me."

"How long are you supposed to meditate?"

"He said I'd know when it was time."

"I think you've meditated long enough," I say. "Can you stand on that ankle?"

Stan pushes himself up off the ground slowly and steps out of the circle of stones without showing any obvious signs of being in pain.

The ride back to Ignacio's farm goes quickly and without incident.

"Did you pass out during the ceremony?"

"I got a little dizzy at one point," Stan says.

"Could he have given you peyote? Maybe in the smoke from those herbs?"

"I don't know."

Stan has no trouble climbing the slash-cut trail. When the horses are taken care of, and the tack put away, and there's nothing else to keep us, we get into the pickup truck and set off on our last ride together.

"Johona, do you really believe Stan was healed by the *poowagudt*?"

"Oh, Pate," she says, "I hoped you would be, too."

"What do you mean?"

But I get no answer. Only the distinct impression that I've failed an important test.

At our agreed-upon drop-off point on the main highway, Johona pulls onto the shoulder. This is it. After she and Stan say farewell, I ask him to give us a minute. I watch him carry his bag across the highway, miraculously showing no signs of injury.

"I don't know what to say, Johona, but I wish this was not goodbye.

You could still come with me. You and I have something special. We can't just throw it away."

She smiles, but with sorrow in her eyes.

"The same spirits who want you to go," she says, "want me to stay."

"To hell with the spirits."

She places her palm against my cheek and gives me a long, lingering kiss.

"You and I are shadows who will lose ourselves in the sunset."

"This really is the end? All right. Tell me how to say goodbye in Ute."

"There are no words for goodbye in Ute," she says. "We say, 'Until I see you again.'"

As if such a time will ever come, I think, as her rusty Chevy rolls off into the afternoon sun.

We stand with our thumbs out, once again hoping for a long ride soon.

"You okay?" Stan asks.

"Yeah. Fine."

But I continue torturing myself until a white '61 Dodge Lancer crunches to a stop on the roadside gravel. From the open window as I lean in comes a whiff of mild pipe tobacco.

"Looks like you guys could use a lift," the driver says, blowing nutty burley-scented smoke out the side of his mouth. He's alone. His carbon-caked pipe reminds me of the curved briar type my favorite uncle smoked. How can anyone who favors such a pipe be anything but good?

As we climb in, the driver says we're in luck: he can take us all the way to Flagstaff, where getting a longer ride should be easier.

He introduces himself as Otis Feldkamp, a geology professor from Northern Arizona University, in Flagstaff. Feldkamp's in his mid-forties, wears khakis and a blue oxford cloth shirt. As we speed southwest toward Tuba City along the edge of the Navajo Nation, Feldkamp tells us he's been in Mesa Verde researching an article, an assertion made to seem more credible by his leather briefcase resting on the floor behind the driver's seat.

"Are you students?" he asks. "You look like a lot of mine, with the hair and the beards."

"Not students," I say.

"Well, what are you fellows doing out here? Sightseeing or what?"

"More like what. We're hitchhiking to the West Coast," I tell him.

"Trying to catch up with the Summer of Love," Stan adds.

Puffing on his pipe, Feldkamp says, "That's quite a goal. A bit quixotic, perhaps, but none the less noble for it. I always wanted to do something like that but never had the time. Got married. Graduate school. Don't get me wrong. I love my life and the decisions I've made. But I've always had a little wanderlust, an itch I couldn't scratch. That's one reason I like coming to Mesa Verde."

"What's your article about?"

For the next fifty miles, Feldkamp talks of his research project, which involves the formation of Cliff House Sandstone some hundred million years ago. It's not riveting, but when he's talking, I don't have to. A voice in my head keeps telling me that I know in my heart that my relationship with Johona would never work. There's no place for me in Mancos, or Cortez. I'd never be anything but an outsider in either town. And unsure I could ever believe in Johona's spirit world or the *poowagudt*'s miracle cures. All the way through the gray-and red-banded Painted Desert I brood.

I actually feel relieved to hear a scientific voice when Feldkamp says the landscape's vibrant colors are caused by iron compounds in the sandstone.

Stan says as a scientist, our driver must know this area well.

"Enough to know that these buttes and sage brush have appeared in many Western movies."

"I thought this looked familiar," Stan says.

Meanwhile, I'm thinking about Matthew and wondering if his mug will ever grace the West on celluloid, or whatever films are made of in the future.

After a few more comments about movies, Stan introduces a segue: "What do you think about medicine men, Professor Feldkamp?"

"Not my area of expertise." Feldkamp says. "But I can tell you all about pictographs and petroglyphs, if that's any help."

"Know anything about natural healing ceremonies?" Stan asks.

"Interesting stuff. Too bad Rosa's not with us. She's an anthropology colleague who's interested in shamans and that sort of thing. She could probably tell you whatever you wanted to know. Why do you ask?"

"What would you think if I told you I sprained my ankle," Stan says, "and a *poowagudt* healed it instantly?"

"I'd think you were pulling my leg—so to speak." Feldkamp laughs.

"Pate," Stan says. "Tell him."

"I was there, too, Professor," I oblige.

"You witnessed this?" Feldkamp glances over at me.

"Not the ceremony itself. Only before and after."

"You weren't by any chance on a different *plane of consciousness* at the time, were you?" the academic inquires casually.

"Not then," I say, smiling while thinking of Leary's astral planes.

"Take a look." Stan bares his injured ankle. "It still looks bad, but I can walk on it without pain. How do you explain that?"

"I'm not sure I can. Like I said, anthropology is not my field. I'm a geologist. I believe in facts. Sprained ankles take time to heal. I can't really tell by looking at yours if you should be able to walk on it or not."

Feldkamp speeds up to pass a slow-moving RV.

"But if you like, I could arrange for one of the university's doctors to examine you. And I'm sure Rosa would love to talk with you."

"Sorry," Stan says, glancing at me. "No time for that, I'm afraid."

But Feldkamp is into it now and keeps trying to convince us to reconsider.

"All my training tells me that this cure of yours is impossible. There's something mystical about this part of the world, I know, and strange things have a way of happening that can't always be explained away. I sure wish you'd think about it."

As we reach the intersection of I-17 with I-40 Feldkamp reaches for his wallet and pulls out a business card, which he gives to Stan.

"You guys need to get back in school. You might find Northern Arizona is just the place for you. I'd be glad to put you up. And you could talk to my friend. Who knows where it all might lead?"

Stan and I look at each other. With darkness looming, it's a somewhat tempting offer. Stan shakes his head, though. After thanking Feldkamp, we resume hitchhiking. We pass the time discussing the prof's surprising proposal.

"He must've thought there was something to the healing ceremony or he wouldn't have made the offer," Stan says.

"Why didn't you want to do it?"

"Didn't want to be a guinea pig anymore, I guess. Talking to some professor wasn't going to do anything for me. I should've pressed Ignacio to explain when I had the chance."

"I don't know how you press a wizard," I say.

"Me, either."

After another hour, we're still in the same place. Finally, somebody stops to pick us up. That ride and another gets us to Kingman four hours later. Along the way, I keep thinking about Stan's decision to turn down Feldkamp. Somebody once told me that life bends one way or another, depending on decisions you make. They might seem small at the time but loom much larger later. I considered whether it was farfetched to imagine our lives being significantly changed because of this latest choice. No way to know, I guess. But I can't help wondering if we'd just passed up a watershed opportunity.

At midnight, we're still three hundred miles from Bakersfield and I'm ready to call it a night and slink off into the cacti, predators be damned. Stan insists that we keep trying, even as traffic thins out. Twenty more minutes pass and then there's a rumbling in the distance. When a '66 four-door hardtop Cutlass Supreme pulls over, the driver says he needs somebody to help him stay awake.

"We're the guys," I say. "We've done it before."

Stan makes good on the promise. I, however, soon fall into a stupor.

Five hours later, I awake on a darkened street in downtown Bakersfield where the Cutlass driver drops us off. In a café, we watch the sun come up while devouring ham and eggs and drinking gallons of coffee. We sponge bathe in the restroom and are ready to face another day on the road.

"It's a straight shot from here through the San Joaquin Valley to Fresno, then another two hundred miles to San Francisco," I say. "With any luck, we'll make it this afternoon."

"Write it down," Stan says. "We'll be there."

14

The next morning in San Francisco, we find the bus station and stash our rucksacks in lockers. It's early July but the temperature's in the mid 70s, perfect for wandering aimlessly through the hilly downtown area.

"I can't believe we made it," I say.

"Now let the fun begin," Stan says.

We begin by drifting into Chinatown through the Dragon Gate, then on to the Russian Hill neighborhood, and eventually to Lombard Street, whose switchbacks were featured as the setting for Steve McQueen's memorable car chase in *Bullitt*. Our downhill ramble brings us to the waterfront, where we find Ghirardelli Square and Fisherman's Wharf overrun by tourists. We board one of those famous little cable cars and stand on a ledge while clinging to a post as we chug uphill. Surprisingly, nobody asks for our fare. We don't know why, and we don't ask. Gazing down at the bay, I speculate on the possible availability of temp work on those docks for an enterprising modern young Jack London like me.

Reality sets in when I must ask for directions multiple times in order to reach Haight-Ashbury, possibly the world's most famous crossroads. On the way, we pass Buena Vista Park, a steeply forested hill where—according to an historical marker—a hundred thousand hippies built camps during the Summer of Love.

Oh boy, I think, now we've *really* made it! It's taken two weeks, but we're here at last. We high five each other and saunter onward through blocks of rundown Victorian houses, many inhabited by freaks, where clouds of heavy incense flow from open windows and the smell of pot is everywhere.

At first glance, Haight and Ashbury is nothing special. Two lanes wide, with cars and motorcycles parked under low-growing trees. Vine-covered brick buildings with apartments over ground-floor shops. But the colors are spectacular: mauve, tangerine, copper, pistachio. At 5:30, it's crowded with young adults wearing whatever they feel like, from loose flowing shirts and flared bell bottoms to Mexican peasant blouses, miniskirts, and veiled hats. This is it: the neighborhood where Jefferson Airplane, Janis Joplin, and the Grateful Dead live.

When the initial shock wears off, Stan rambles over to this weird looking storefront spiritual center, which seems natural after our Mesa Verde experiences. Meanwhile, I'm drawn to a bra-less woman with hair down to her waist who's selling macramé plant hangers. The dawning of the Age of Aquarius, all right, I think. Bring on the mystic crystal revelations.

"Those must be hard to make," I suggest, nodding at her plant hangers.

"Not really. Macramé is simple," she says, at once betraying her East Coast origins with a few lingering traces of her accent.

As she shows me how to tie several knots, I ask her name—Willow, she says—and I tell her that is a beautiful name, adding, "You are a long way from home. What's a New Yorker like you doing way out here?"

"I'm surprised you can tell," she says, touching her throat. "I came out here four years ago to visit friends and fell in love with the place. Where are you from?"

"Kentucky. Bet you could tell from my accent."

She brushes a strand of hair out of her eye while giving me a tentative smile. "Yeah, somewhat. You are a long way from home, too. Why are you here?"

"We, Stan and I—he's over there," I point him out, "we've come for the Summer of Love." I've gotten a lot of mileage out of that line up to now but her bored expression makes me decide it's time to retire it.

"The day I moved in was when they burned a hippie effigy in Golden Gate Park to officially declare the movement dead here," Willow tells me.

"Wow, then we really are way behind the times, aren't we?" I grin.

"But it's not," she laughs, "so maybe you're not."

We chat about the Haight and how great it is to be here. At some point, Stan joins us. A bit later, I find myself asking Willow out to dinner, even though I know damn well I have no money. But she saves me from embarrassment by saying, "I have a better idea. Why don't you both come home with me for dinner."

"Do you have a roommate?" Stan asks.

"I have nine of them," Willow says. "I live in a commune."

The magic words. Lafayette, we are here!

While Willow gathers up her unsold merchandise, I'm thinking Stan and I must be the luckiest guys in the world and wonder exactly what kind of commune she lives in. Not that it matters. At this point, we're not picky. Almost any kind will do.

On the walk to her commune, I divide my attention between the whacked-out people we encounter and the multistoried Victorian houses. Many of the dwellings still look great. Some have been painted outlandish colors—red, yellow, chocolate, orange. I love their steep gables, bay windows, and corniced eaves. But the farther we go, the scruffier the people on the street become.

Noticing our wonder, Willow volunteers that when the Haight became a haven for hippies, too many came at one time. Thirty might be living in a single room, she explains. The scene had deteriorated into hard drugs, homelessness, crime.

"But you're still here."

"I still love it here," she says.

When we reach a big two-story Italianate clapboard house on hilly Sanchez Street, I begin to understand why.

"This is it," Willow announces.

Once obviously a showplace, the house now seems as neglected as the surrounding neighborhood. But traces of its former grandeur remain. We go up the steps to a gracious covered front porch that offers a grand view of the area. An old Mamas and the Papas song is playing inside. It's the one about going wherever and doing whatever with whomever you want, which just about says it all, and it strikes me as the perfect musical welcome to this abode.

Instantly I detect a smell that seems to permeate the very atmosphere of this entire neighborhood. Beyond the front door, we enter a large parlor with built-in bookcases and decorative molding where two young guys in their twenties are sitting around, listening to the music.

One has shoulder-length sandy hair and wears jeans with stars painted all over them. He lies sprawled on the couch. The other has a black Fu Manchu moustache and dark sunglasses. He's sitting in a battered armchair in a half lotus. Willow makes introductions. Stars is Jude, Fu Manchu is Stormy Carl. What magnificent names, I'm thinking. But like the Two Seasons, I doubt those are their real names.

Willow tells Jude and Stormy Carl that we have come for dinner.

"They hitched here all the way from Kentucky," she elaborates, then heads off to help in the kitchen.

"Are either of you narcs? Sorry," Jude says, "but I got to ask."

Stan and I exchange grins. Paranoia strikes deep.

"No," Stan says. "Are you?"

"In that case," Stormy Carl says, "want some hash?"

With that out of the way, we flop on a frayed carpet as Stormy Carl pulls out a pipe previously wedged in the chair arm cushion and lights it to pass around. As we smoke, we begin to tell them a bit about our travels. In the process, we learn that Jude, who is from Minneapolis, is part of a coalition that provides free food and distributes free legal drugs.

"Some of them stolen off the backs of trucks," according to Stormy Carl.

"You mean *liberated* from the back of trucks," Jude corrects.

"What about you, man?" I ask Stormy Carl.

"I'm an actor," he says, "from Cleveland."

Oh God, not another one.

But it turns out that Stormy Carl is less of an egomaniac than some I've known and also part of an ensemble that combines street theatre with anarchistic action. Sometimes, he says, they organize concerts and art events.

Better than playing a hippie in a soap opera, I muse, wondering where Matthew Duncan is now.

Every so often, Willow pops in for a hit off the pipe.

When she calls us in for a dinner, the kitchen reeks of garlic and onions. A vegetable stew is bubbling in a huge pot. The cook, a woman with long slate-colored hair, is laying out bowls and silverware on a big wood table, which is the staging area for the meal.

"I'm Piper," she says.

We tell her the stew smells good and that we hope our staying for supper isn't a problem.

"It's not," Piper says. "People are always dropping in for dinner. In fact, we expect to feed about twenty tonight."

"I hope you like vegetables," Willow says. "We're all vegetarians."

She begins ladling out the stew. We help ourselves to sourdough bread. There's butter and peanut butter, too, and pitchers of water and cherry Kool-Aid, which I can't recall the last time I ever had. We pick up our plates and drinks and follow Willow out onto the back porch. We all eat the stew and the bread while sitting on the steps. It has an earthy flavor I can't quite identify but find appealing.

"How did you get into a commune?" Stan asks, biting into the bread.

"Kinda fell into it," Willow says. "I just met some people, and one thing led to another."

I hope this encounter may do the same. I also hope this talk leads to a more wide-ranging discussion of the setup here. But it doesn't, at least not yet.

"If you guys need a place to crash tonight, there's a room on the second floor," Willow offers.

We accept. After a lot more rapping with Piper and Willow, and smoking with Jude and Stormy Carl, Stan and I crash in our own bedroom.

"Can you believe it?" I say when we're alone. "On the same night we arrive in San Francisco we wind up in a hippie commune. It's almost too good to be true."

"Yeah, it must be fate," Stan says, with a touch of sarcasm.

"Guess I'm a little wide-eyed, huh?"

"You think?"

Our room has a double bed. Since I'm broke and relying on Stan for funds, I offer to sleep on the floor.

"Bet your ass you will," he says.

In the middle of the night, someone bursts through our door. "Who the bloody hell are you?"

"Who are *you*?" Stan says.

"I am Leland bloody Fitzpatrick," roars the figure standing in the dimness of the doorway, "and this is my house. I don't know how you got in here, but I want you out. Now."

"But Willow told us we could stay here," I say.

"Well, it's not her house. It's mine. And I want you gone in five minutes."

With that, Leland bloody Fitzpatrick pivots and disappears, leaving the door standing wide open behind him.

"What just happened?" I query, feeling totally boggled by this turn of events.

One minute, everything seems fine. The next, we're out in the street. I question whether this Leland character really owns the house. If the place is a commune, shouldn't everything be owned in common? Maybe he's just some loudmouth who wants the room for himself. But the real question is:

"Why would Willow ask us to stay if she knew this was going to happen?"

"She probably didn't know," Stan replies.

We pack up.

"Where the hell are we going?" I ask, as we wander through the fog on a deserted Sanchez Street.

"Buena Vista Park," Stan says.

"You want to crash there?"

"Unless you'd prefer the Fairmont." A famous historic hotel on Mason Street.

"Come on, Stan. We couldn't afford a broom closet there."

"You have a better idea?"

I don't, which is why we wind up at the park. We follow a path to the top of the wooded hill and crash under a big tree, hoping we won't get our throats cut.

In the morning, the fog has cleared off, revealing an awe-inspiring view of the famous suspension bridge that demarks San Francisco Bay and the Pacific. It's a nice wakeup after spending the night sleeping on bone-chilling hard ground. But the air is still piercing and we quickly drag ourselves up and break camp with minimal conversation before descending to the sleepy streets below.

We're looking for a place to get warm with facilities we can use at minimal cost. A nearby branch library seems to fit the bill, except for all the men, obviously vagrants, lined up at the front door seeking the same thing. Confronted by the possibility of a long wait and a less than friendly reception, we move on seeking a better alternative. We find what we're looking for at a bakery, where we fortify ourselves with chocolate doughnuts and coffee. We discuss our plans for the day. Stan wants to explore the city. I want to go back and talk to Willow about what happened. We decide to split up and rendezvous later back at the commune, even though we know we may no longer be welcome.

On my own here for the first time, I retrace my steps to where I originally found Willow selling her macramé. She's there today dressed in a sleeveless blue pullover. As soon as she sees me, she looks down, unable to meet my eyes directly.

"I'm sorry about last night," she says, with flushed cheeks and slumped shoulders.

"What happened, Willow? Who was that guy Leland? Does he really own the place?"

She nods. "He does. Leland and his old lady, Zoe Renee, met a couple who needed a place to crash. He offered them the room, not knowing I'd already put you in it. He can be a bear sometimes. I apologize."

"It's okay," I say, with a half-hearted shrug. "Not your fault, I guess."

"Where did you guys sleep?"

"Buena Vista Park."

"Oh, my God, that area's not safe."

Tightening her fists and clenching her jaw line, Willow says we should come back to the commune tonight.

"I promise to clear it with Leland, all right? Worst case, you can crash with me."

"Not what *I* would call *worst case*," I tell her.

She smiles up at me through her wind-blown hair.

That night, Willow greets us at the door. "Leland and Zoe Renee have gone off somewhere with the couple who took over your bed last night," she says. "I'll deal with him whenever he gets back. Meanwhile you can have the room again, okay?"

"If you're sure," we say.

She says she is and escorts us to the kitchen, where dinner this evening is brown rice and mushrooms, with a peanut butter sandwich on the side. We meet our dining companions, who include two more members: Lindsay, a redheaded dancer from Bloomington, Indiana, and Drake, who calls himself a cabbie, actor, and poet.

Everyone tells us how sorry they are that we got kicked out.

After the meal, I help Willow do the dishes. She tells me about her family of liberal Brooklyn Jews of Polish descent. She says her parents did well in business, which enabled her to get an art history degree at NYU. After college, she had a job in New York for a couple of years doing market research.

"But it felt dishonest trying to figure out how to sell people things they didn't want, or need," she says. "Of course, look at me now, selling macramé ·to tourists. Not sure it's all that different, I'm afraid."

"Even artists have to pay their bills."

She takes my hand, giving it a light squeeze and holding on longer than necessary.

"After Martin Luther King was assassinated, I thought the world was coming to an end. I came out here, hoping to find kindred spirits. Looks like I've found another."

"I know what you mean about the assassination. I felt kind of the same way myself. It was like that for both Kennedys, too. I doubt we'll ever get over all that as a nation."

"I think you're right," she says, rinsing a dinner plate and putting it in the drainer.

Time to shift topics.

"How does the commune work?"

"You mean like how we pay the bills."

"Yeah. And I don't know quite how to put this, but what about sex? Does everyone just sleep with everyone else?"

"If we did, would that be a problem for you?" she asks.

"For me? No. I mean, I'm not a member."

"What if you were? You sound interested. Are you?"

"Maybe," I say, but I am. I know this. It's one of the main reasons I'm here at all. Traditional monogamous relationships haven't worked out so well for me, as evidenced by my latest heartbreak over Johona. Maybe people aren't meant to live that way. I think I'd like to find out. Yet I hold back. A part of me is unsure.

"Well look, Pate. Here's some of what we believe in: peace and love, nature, art, sharing. Leland says we're all richest when we don't own, or need, anything."

Leland, who owns this house. "Sounds like communism," I say.

She frowns. "It's more of a mantra than a dogma. Our prime unwritten rule is that you have to do something to earn your keep. While you might not pay a portion of the rent, you have to cook dinner, or clean like we are now, or contribute in some other way. Speaking of which, by any chance are you a musician?"

"Don't I wish."

"Too bad. Sometimes musicians earn their keep by playing for us." She fingers a button on what must be a handmade flowered shirt. "As for sex, it just happens. Evolves. You meet someone who's nice, you sleep with them. It doesn't have any major moral overtones. Free love is free love."

I gasp a little at this but try to remain circumspect about revealing my emotions. Nevertheless, I'm certain that sleeping with Willow would be very nice indeed.

We finish the dishes and put them away. Drake's strumming on his guitar on the front steps. Stan and Lindsay are singing along with the Grateful Dead about how sometimes the way forward is clear, while other times it's not, and what a long odd journey it's been.

Then Leland arrives with a much younger woman on his arm. Zoe Renee, I take it. She's so thin and pale she seems almost transparent, and tiny in comparison to Leland, who is tall and broadly built. He's older than the rest, probably in his forties, with a full curly beard and nut-brown hair reaching down to his shoulders. He's not Indian like the Maharishi Mahesh Yogi, but otherwise he fits my profile of a resident guru perfectly.

"Sorry about kicking you guys out last night," he says, immediately coming to the point. "I guess by now Willow's explained the situation. Unfortunately, the room's still taken, but you're welcome to the sofa and floor in the parlor tonight."

Nonplussed by his demeanor, which seems at once both gentle and vaguely menacing, I remain silent as Stan accepts the offer with our thanks.

Leland nods with a certain element of noblesse oblige, then after a minimum of chat retires from the gathering along with his limpid companion, leaving me yearning for a private discussion with Stan about our status here. But there's no opportunity immediately available. And when it's time to bed down in the darkened parlor, Willow steps in and beckons for me to follow her. I do so, with a look back over my shoulder at Stan, who is grinning broadly as if in possession of knowledge of which I am unaware.

We go upstairs to her bedroom and there's a loud squeak when she opens her door.

"Sounds like your hinges need oiling," I say.

"Why do you think I brought you up here?" Willow asks with a lascivious smile.

She backs me up and pushes me down onto her double bed. Open-mouthed kisses ensue, followed by the shedding of our clothing. Soon all that remains between us is her peace sign necklace.

Sleeping in a real bed is a welcome change.

So is waking up in the morning alongside a woman like Willow. All I want to do is savor this moment and remember our lovemaking last night. She was fierce and demanding in bed, a woman who gave no quarter and took no prisoners. I felt a little afraid that I wouldn't be able to keep up with her, to tell the truth, but I did my best.

I doze off again. This time when I awaken, she's up and gone. I notice that her bag of macramé is nowhere in sight, so I assume she has already left to peddle her plant hangers. I'm puzzled as to how she can make ends meet by turning square knots into wall hangings. It doesn't seem possible. Perhaps she sells a little pot on the side. Who knows? This is Haight-Ashbury, where the hippie movement died and was resurrected. Miracles happen.

Yawning mightily, I notice that I'm sleeping under a thick wool Navajo blanket that looks handspun. Its red, black, and white geometric pattern reminds me of Mesa Verde and all that I left behind there. With a pang, I get up and shower.

I get dressed and slip downstairs to the parlor, anxious to confide in Stan about my triumphant escapades of last night, but he's not there. So, where did he sleep? And with whom? I weigh the possibilities. Piper perhaps? Or that redhead from Bloomington? With Stan, anything's possible.

Nobody seems to be around, either still asleep or gone. But someone's made coffee and I drink it happily at the kitchen table, thinking about what to do today. At a little after eight, with the sun warming my shoulders, I head for the same public library that Stan and I had scoped out yesterday morning, which now seems like such a long time ago.

I'm here to conduct a job search. I need money. Not a lot, just enough to get by for the next few days. After checking the job listings in the *Chronicle,* I wander around the streets of the Haight checking shop windows for Help Wanted signs. I recall my whimsy about becoming a longshoreman but realize those are union jobs now. The best I can come up with is to check in with the state employment agency, but when I do there's a flood of unemployed longhairs ahead of me.

I return to the commune disappointed, only to find Leland at the kitchen table clad in a gold silk bathrobe with red Chinese dragons embroidered upon it.

"Ah," he says, and puts down the thick book he's been reading. "You'll be glad to hear that my friends are gone, so you and your roadie can have the room."

I thank him.

"What have you been up to this morning?" he asks.

I tell him of my unsuccessful job search.

Nodding sagaciously, he says, "If you're looking for work, I may have just the job for you."

"Really? Doing what?"

"Since WWII, this house has been painted battleship gray. I'd like to add some pink and peach trim. It will require climbing a tall ladder, which I have, and a painter who isn't afraid of heights."

Which I am, but probably not the height of a tall ladder.

"The pay would be as an in-kind contribution in lieu of cash for staying at the commune. Still interested?"

So, no cash involved, but it would keep me busy while providing a roof over my head.

"How about some beer money?" I ask. "All painters drink on the job."

"Do you have any experience?" he counters.

"I once worked all summer for a painting contractor while I was in college. And I can begin right now this moment."

"Then the job is yours," Leland says. "I'll pay you a little extra, but not enough for you to get drunk and fall off the house."

"Deal."

I begin by examining the trim surfaces. There are dozens of them. Leland's house was built during the Victorian period, when people dressed up more and preferred lots of frills and laces and wanted the same thing in their houses. This one has so many parts to paint that I'll never even learn all their names.

I tell Leland that I know two simple rules for painting: prepare the surface well and buy the best paint you can afford. Since he's paying for this, it's important to convince him to let me buy excellent quality paint. I point out that he's getting a good deal on labor, paying me only an extra pittance for "beer money." I also assure him the paint will last much longer with quality materials.

Impressed by my apparent expertise, Leland drives me to the paint store in his van and allows me to select whatever I need. I tell him that the prep work and cleanup will require as much effort as the labor of painting itself. Also, that more trips will be necessary as the work progresses. He doesn't seem to mind.

"No problem," he says.

With the proper tools in hand, I'm ready to begin the project. I decide to work in the mornings when the air is cooler. There's a lot of intricate fancy work—gables, corniced eaves, carved corbels, lathed railings, dentil trim molding—that needs painting. I figure it might take me the rest of this summer if I should last that long. Will I? Hard to say.

Knowing that booze and dope—along with falling scaffolding— are among the most common occupational hazards for house painters, I resolve to stay sober while I'm up on the ladder. Despite what I told Leland I'll only spend my beer money at the end of the day. I explain all this to Willow, wondering how she'll take the news. I hope she'll be happy and see this as a positive step. Why shouldn't she if it keeps me around? But if I've learned anything from the women I've known, it's to never assume you know what they're thinking or why.

Willow does seem happy, though. So happy, in fact, that she presents me with one of her hand-made macramé bookmarks as a gift.

"That's so you won't lose your place," she smiles.

Lose my place. I sense that there's possibly more to this than meets the eye, but I can't fathom what exactly. I thank her and begin looking for the right book to put it in.

When I tell Stan about my job, though, he doesn't seem to understand my need for employment.

"For beer money," I say, unwilling to go further into it, though I'm pretty sure we both know there are deeper reasons, as well.

Reflecting on this later, I realize how far apart Stan and I have grown in such a short time. Travel seems to have been the glue holding us together. Now that we've settled down at least temporarily, we don't seem to need each other as much. I regret this and vow to find more time to be together and share our experiences. After all, that's a big part of why we're doing this.

Believing that the job itself will take my mind off these other concerns, I'm eager to start. First, I remove the planters, mailboxes, and shutters and stack them all up against the back fence where they'll be out of the way. Second, I cover all concrete surfaces with canvas and use plastic drop cloths to protect the few foundation plantings.

Now it's time to set about preparing the surface, which is the hardest part of the job. Once that's done, the painting itself will be relatively easy. I'm using a twenty-four-foot long adjustable aluminum ladder. It's light enough for me to carry around and manage. It's also sturdy enough to support my weight along with the paint without collapsing under me.

Carefully balancing it against the wall, I start scraping away the paint with a curved flexible blade. As I work, I'm on the lookout for rotting or stained boards that will require replacement. But I don't see many. The wood's underlying condition seems good. I wonder whimsically if this is a metaphor for the commune's condition as well.

As I keep scraping away, the house begins to take on the aspect of a ruin more than a precious antique whose former glory is being restored. Some passersby gawp at me, others smile and wave their hands, and a few cheer or jeer. At dinner each evening, commune members offer advice and quiz me on when I'll be done. Possibly a few bets have been made. The one who counts, though, is Leland, who signifies his satisfaction simply by sitting back and smiling.

As the work progresses, I see close up how the trim is beautifully carved, but also covered with multiple coats of oil paint. There's an uneven pattern of cracks, chips, and flakes because the paint can't expand or contract with the wood. Even inanimate objects seem to have a hard time getting along together. The deeper cracks will require a preservative, but I can probably feather out the rest with sandpaper. Once that's done, it'll be time to prime the bare spots. And then finally I'll topcoat it all.

To me, this work is fun. It feels great to do something that I know is useful.

I like it so much that I tell myself that I'd almost do it without being paid.

Almost.

15

One afternoon in mid-to-late July when I'm not painting, Willow and I take a long walk around the Haight, which she says became a suburb after the great earthquake of 1906 because of the cable cars. And, of course, there are all those wonderful old Victorian homes to see. But there are also rows of two- and three-story commercial buildings, the same kind you'd find anywhere, except here many have "Love" scrawled across the front. Upper floors are reserved for professional offices, but the ground level shop windows are full of psychedelic posters or R. Crumb's underground comix.

We talk about anything and everything, getting to know each other better, and I discover Willow has both a wicked sense of humor and a strong disdain for daytrippers and weekend hippies. When one excursion bus full of gawking tourists slowly passes by, she turns into an overenthusiastic tour guide and announces via her imaginary microphone that the Grateful Dead used to live right here and the Hell's Angels just across the street.

"You crack me up, Willow," I chuckle.

"I'm afraid we've almost become a cliché. That's why they burned the hippie effigy in the park."

"What do you mean?" I wave at a throng of our fellow longhairs occupying the streets and sidewalks. "There are still plenty of goddamn hippies around here, if you ask me."

"I didn't," she smiles, "but I'm sure you'll tell me anyway."

Thus encouraged, I quote my fellow Louisvillian Hunter S. Thompson on what three sights you supposedly could never miss in this neighborhood: a long-haired wood piper with sunglasses, a bongo player in a cowboy hat, and a dazed braless girl wearing a blouse.

Willow collapses into laughter because, she says, Thompson's not off by much.

We walk on.

"Willow," I say, pretty much out of the blue, "I'm thinking about hippies and communes. They seem intertwined, but there's a lot more hippies than communes."

"That's indisputably true, Pate."

"So, you can be a hippie without living in a commune. But can you live in a commune without being a hippie?"

"That's an interesting question. I've only lived in one, but I guess you can. They're obviously not all the same."

"So, what is the Sanchez Street Commune all about?"

"I don't think it has a name actually."

"But what would you say it's all about?"

It may sound casual, but it's a deadly serious question, and she takes a moment to think it over before answering.

"We don't have a credo," she says, tugging at her earlobe and adjusting her blue peasant blouse. "I guess I'd say we're all in the commune because we want to be free and to love one another. That, and to live simply. Eat organic food. To oppose war, the oppression of minorities, or the destruction of nature. And to expand our minds."

"Sound like a pretty good credo to me."

"Of course, it is."

And we bop along, holding hands and expanding our minds. I'm thinking there are worse things you could do.

*

Other activities besides painting and going for walks are taking place in the commune. From time to time, I help Jude and others provide free food through his coalition, which also distributes free legal drugs "liberated" from the back of trucks. Handing out food with the guy who has stars on his jeans is pretty sad work. I've never seen so many down-and-outers, especially young ones, fifteen-year-olds, some of them. They flocked here without a clue about how they were going to make it and ended up living on the streets. I wonder if they'd started out like Stan and me, looking for adventure, a good time, maybe some insights about their life. We might not have found our answers yet, but at least we're not lining up with these innocents on the corner.

As I hand out a hunk of cheese and some canned goods, I look across Mission Street and see Stan coming out of the Stairway to Heaven Spiritual Center.

That night at the communal dinner I ask him about it.

"Don't laugh," he says, "but lately I've been going through a spiritual growth thing."

"Nothing funny about that," I say.

"I was never a churchgoer growing up. When I did go occasionally, it left me cynical. I know you can relate," Stan says to me. "But all my life I've wanted to be a more spiritual person. And ever since the healing ceremony back at the ruin, I've wanted to know more about what happened to me out there."

"How come this is the first that I've heard of it?" I ask.

He spreads peanut butter thick on sliced wheat bread. "You already seem to have a lot on your mind."

"Not that much. You can talk to me. That's what friends are for."

"Okay, from now on I will."

Stan tells me there are numerous spiritual centers in the area. He's been checking them out. Many are about yoga, meditation, inspirational talk, or some combination. I realize that he's talking about achieving higher consciousness without drugs, a noble goal. But are these spiritual centers trustworthy? Stan says the Stairway to Heaven Spiritual Center has a licensed Spiritual Practitioner. Whatever that means.

"Her name is Adra," he says, "and her workshops can change your life."

"Is that what you want?" I ask, "to change your life?"

"Don't you?"

"Of course, I do. I've come all this way to live in a commune, for chrissake."

"I'm talking about an inner change," Stan says. "Filling the void where the soul used to be. You'll probably laugh, but Adra says introspective stillness can do that."

"Introspective stillness, huh? Sorry, I didn't know your soul was missing. Where do you think it is?"

"I knew that's how you'd react, Pate."

"You must admit it sounds a little fanatical."

"I'm not brainwashed, if that's what you mean. I've been going there for a while now, and it seems to help."

"Okay, man," I say. "I'm happy you've found something that gives you peace of mind."

But inside I'm worried. I've never seen Stan like this before. He glows when he talks about this woman. Is he in love with her or . . . brainwashed? For his own good, I hope he'll lose interest in her, as he has in so many other women.

On a perfect day that is not too cool and with plenty of sunshine, Willow and I catch the cable car down to Fisherman's Wharf, which my unofficial tour guide says dates back to the Gold Rush when immigrants from Italy and China sold their catch right off their boats. It's also inundated with tourists.

At the wharf, we stop outside a restaurant where a guitarist in a stovepipe hat is playing. His hair is tucked inside a pink T-shirt, but one braid falls all the way below his knees. With a German Shepherd at his feet, he sings that Youngbloods tune about how love is a song and we're but a moment's sunlight, so we should all get together and love one another immediately. Who could argue with that, I wonder?

We applaud and praise his playing. I drop some change into his guitar case. We move on to the wharf for a chance to view Alcatraz through heavy-duty mounted telescopes. While we wait our turn to view the abandoned federal prison, Willow points out that it was only months ago when a year-long occupation by American Indians who had "reclaimed" the island was ended when the government forcibly removed them.

After scanning the sheer cliffs through magnified lenses, we take to the shoreline. At Aquatic Park, sea lions and seals are foraging. Clouds of birds startle us with their beating wings and high-pitched calls. Among them, I recognize only gulls and pelicans. Sea birds swoop, fishing in the bay, while stick-legged shore birds troll tide pools for shellfish.

We walk on hand-in-hand all the way over to North Beach, which no longer actually is a beach, but does have lots of bars and cafés. As we stroll, we go for long stretches speaking only with our eyes. At one of the cafés where Willow says the Beat Generation hung out in the fifties, we buy a cup of coffee and talk about Kerouac, Ginsberg, Ferlinghetti, and in a lighter vein, Maynard G. Krebs. And how the Beats had disappeared by the Sixties, replaced by the new bohemians—meaning us, the alleged hippies—but in Haight-Ashbury this time, where the rents were even lower. I tell her a joke, which is not particularly funny, but Willow laughs anyway.

We wind up at—of all places—Jack Kerouac Alley, located next door to a famous bookstore. In the window, I spot a paperback copy of *The Electric Kool-Aid Acid Test*. I ask Willow if she's read it and I'm surprised to hear that she has not.

"How is that possible?" I ask. "You used to live practically next door to Jerry Garcia?"

She shrugs. "Seen it, heard about it. Just haven't gotten around to reading it."

I tell her that she should, that it tells the story of Ken Kesey, the guy who wrote *One Flew Over the Cuckoo's Nest* while starting the whole West Coast psychedelic drug movement practically by himself.

"I've heard of him, too," she says. "Just haven't read the book."

"Kesey is a funny guy. Communes are not for him, he says, for two very good reasons. One, who can think seriously in a crowd? And two, how can you go visit your friends if they're all already living with you?"

"Never thought of it like that."

"If I had any money, I'd buy you a copy of the book."

"You're sweet, Pate." Willow plants a kiss on my lips, during which we're almost run over by a bare-chested, long-haired bicyclist wearing only jeans and fancy suspenders.

We move on to Washington Square Park, the center of Little Italy, which proves thick with dog-walkers and artists taking part in a fair. Their paintings are displayed on sawhorses. We watch them chatting among themselves under white umbrellas. Across the lawn is Saints Peter & Paul Church. Willow says that's where Marilyn Monroe and Joe DiMaggio had their wedding photos taken. "But they had to marry at City Hall because they were divorced."

I think I know how Willow feels about marriage, so I don't ask.

Across the park, two police cars arrive, inspiring her to tell me just how badly the cops mistreated the May Day anti-war protesters here earlier this year.

"It started off peacefully," she says, "with live music and people flying Frisbees or coffee can lids. In the financial district, there was even a street theatre performance by an ensemble similar to Stormy Carl's. But when that ended, the situation turned ugly. There was hysteria when the horse pigs backed into the jam-packed sidewalks and started indiscriminately clubbing both protesters and office workers who were at lunch. It was horrible."

As I scrape the curved molding overhanging the sides of Leland's house I think about Willow and the time we're spending together, hopefully deepening our relationship. I don't want this one to end like all the rest. But I know full well that Willow still believes in free love. We never fight. In fact, it's all smooth sailing and good times. But I worry that's not enough. That we need to experience conflict and challenge, just to see how we'd handle it. Not enough for me to pick a fight, though.

On the other hand, I find my work satisfying beyond expectations, especially being my own boss. I'm paying my own way now, for a change, and I intend to see this project successfully through to the end. Not my strong suit lately, as my failures with the Star Unit and Deborah Johnson will attest. Thinking back on all that now, I'm sure it wouldn't have worked out with Deborah. Her needs were too different from mine, and I just wasn't ready for all the responsibilities involved with raising a kid.

I strip the cornices, fill holes, and caulk cracks. I realize I need to have a heart-to-heart with the only person out here I can truly trust— Stan. But that proves easier said than done. Stan has been off somewhere, doing something, I know not what, but I suspect it involves a woman. Most likely Adra, whose workshops he believes can change his life.

I finally catch up with him one night at Inagodadavida, a funky little dive on a side street not far from the commune. The interior is mobbed, so we sit under a tree at a long table on the open-air back patio and sip cheap draft and smoke some weed.

"So, what have you been into lately, Stan?"

Turns out he's found a wage-paying factory job himself. It involves breaking down heavy-duty steam irons used to press wash and wear clothing. Once disassembled, the irons are shipped to the Philippines, where they're reassembled and sold to Third World countries.

"Weird," I say. "Why are you doing this?"

"The money." Stan reminds me that as a non-student he no longer has any income from the GI Bill. And as for what he saved up for this trip, that is long gone.

Partly, I think, because of me.

He works in this big industrial warehouse where it's dusty, dark, and hard to breathe. "They have these wide bay doors that they keep open for ventilation," he says, "but no way it would pass any kind of government health and safety standards."

"Jesus, Stan."

He shrugs. "It's not so bad for me, but these other poor bastards have to support their families. Injuries are pretty common. If you get sick, you're fired. We stand for ten hours a day in the same spot doing the same thing."

"Sounds like something out of Dickens. Listen, we came out here to rekindle the Summer of Love, not slave away in some sweatshop. You need to quit."

"Soon," he says, "as I've put a couple hundred bucks together. Meanwhile, we're living in a commune in Haight-Ashbury, aren't we? How much closer can we get than that?"

We drink to it.

I mention being worried about Willow sleeping around. I'm still bunking with her every night, although officially I continue sharing the second-floor bedroom with Stan. But she could decide at any moment to take up with somebody else. I tell Stan that I hate the thought but feel I *must* respect her position. Not so long ago, I thought it was my position, too. But lately I've come to question the whole notion of free love. Is it really love? Is it really free?

"Whenever I try to bring this up with Willow, she avoids it. She's probably already laid practically everyone in the commune, and maybe not just the guys."

Stan listens in silence.

"Well, aren't you going to say anything?" I ask.

"Look, you've known from the start that chick was going to screw whoever she wanted. Now you expect her to change?"

"You don't think she will?"

"I think you might have picked the wrong girl."

One night before dinner, we're all in the parlor smoking grass, rapping about The Concert for Bangladesh, and singing along with Drake on his acoustic when Willow brings in two vagabonds off the streets. They have hair down to their asses and Day-Glo swirls on their skin and clothes. They look like a couple though somewhat mismatched since the guy—Oak, as he is known—is short and skinny, whereas the girl—Stoney—is tall and a bit overweight. Oak's got a rainbow-colored headband. Stoney is wearing flowers in her hair.

Stan rolls his eyes. I know what he's thinking: we're close to self-parody here. I'm guessing that Leland, Zoe Renee, and Jude share our take on these dewy-eyed novices. But I notice that when Willow makes the rounds—smiling, hugging, and kissing everyone on the cheek—she takes scant notice of me, continuing to smile and nod at the newcomers while using their names in every other sentence out of her mouth. None of this is unusual. Willow's always kind. I've seen her give away a whole day's macramé sales to some pregnant stranger, and she's always volunteering at one health clinic or another. But I want more of her attention and can't help feeling a bit jealous.

Drake asks the newbies if they are narcs. When they shake their heads no, he says, "Good to know," and breaks out a fresh joint and passes it around. Stormy Carl sticks his head in long enough to grab a toke before breezing back out to the kitchen, where he's supposed to be helping Piper and Lindsay cook tonight's meal.

As Drake starts picking out the chords to "While My Guitar Gently Weeps," Leland says, "I just heard that Tim Leary's out on bond in Switzerland."

"What was he doing in Switzerland?" Stan asks.

Zoe Renee, who hardly ever opens her mouth, says, "Just trying to start a new life and find peace, I imagine. He was a fugitive, you know. Drug charges."

"Leary tried to lead us to a profound new experience, but anyone who tries to illuminate the world will inevitably pay a steep price," Leland opines.

I believe he's right about this, of course. Think Jesus, Abraham, Martin, and John. I'm also convinced that, although most decisions in the commune seem based on consensus, Leland in fact is our resident guru. His authority behind the scenes is unmistakable. Maybe it's because he seems wise—and owns the house.

Piper appears: "Ladies and gentlemen, dinner is served."

We troop into the kitchen where despite a dozen candles Lindsay has lit around the room, the odors of garlic and onions remain ever-present. There's a low hum of symphonic music, too, something that I don't recognize but it feels oddly right for this moment. Despite its reputation for balancing the yin and yang of food and cookware, I'm heartily sick of the commune's wretched macrobiotic diet. Nevertheless, I fill my bowl. Maybe I'll slip out later for a burger and beer.

I grab a seat next to Willow and immediately sense that something is amiss.

"What's wrong, Willow? You're not mad at me, are you?"

"Why should I be mad at you, Pate?"

I'll be damned if I know. But she won't say another word about it. Well, I've been wanting a conflict to test our relationship, haven't I? Maybe this is it. But I'm far from sure about that and, in the end, I chicken out. Like Nick said, no need to go seeking trouble when it'll find you on its own.

16

Toward the end of July, Stormy Carl's guerilla theatre ensemble decides to stage an event at the University of California Berkeley campus. Willow wants me to take part. Everyone else in the commune is going, she says. What the ensemble does, she explains, is show up unannounced in a public place and stage a satirical sketch targeting the war, or capitalist oppression. They swear a lot, wear silly symbolic costumes, and even include a little nudity.

It's not the sort of thing I've ever seen myself doing, but out here it doesn't seem nearly as outlandish. But this time the setting is a place where recent protests have been met by police in full riot gear. If I get involved, it won't be my first protest. Two years ago, I took part in the first anti-war sit-in in my university's history. I remember the electric moment when the dean of students ordered us off the administration building lawn and we didn't budge, despite fear of dire repercussions. I've also marched on Washington once, but never been gassed or hit with a truncheon.

The risk of something like that happening this time seems high.

When I ask Stan what he thinks, he surprises me. "Not interested."

Asked why, he adds, "I don't want to see anybody get hurt. It's easier to put yourself at risk when you've never seen first-hand what a heavy caliber round can do to soft human flesh."

"It's supposed to be nonviolent," I say.

"Tell that to the kids at Kent State."

I wonder if this is the same guy who went on without any water on the Great Sand Dunes.

"Willow wants me to go."

"Fuck it then. Let's go," Stan says.

When the time comes, we take Leland's van but with Drake behind the wheel. He parks far away from the campus. Before we begin, Leland says a few words.

"Zoe Renee and I are proud to join you today in this noble endeavor. But remember, my brothers and sisters, that the pigs will have itchy trigger fingers today. If things go wrong, keep your heads down and run back here."

We make our way into the heart of the sprawling campus. In a square surrounded by Beaux-Arts Classical architecture, students sun themselves or throw Frisbees. Others read *The Berkeley Barb*. Hare Krishnas dance. An African combo pounds out a beat. It's as calm as Pearl Harbor before the Japanese attacked.

As usual, the costumes and props are simple: some face paint, and a few cardboard replicas of traffic signs. We unroll them. They read: STOP, YIELD, NO PARKING. Once the performance starts, I try to relax and play my part. We have no sound amplification and must depend on our own natural vocal ability as actors. "Come join us," we chant, and a crowd forms to watch us perform a skit highlighting the irony of black soldiers killing yellow Vietnamese on the orders of white imperialists.

Campus police stand by, outnumbered, making no effort to stop us, as we yell our lines, wave our signs, and ridicule authority. The outdoor setting helps. The audience grows quickly, with passersby voicing their approval and more knots of supporters arriving. We're having an impact, making a point, waking people up.

And then someone sets an American flag afire. Not one of us, but that doesn't matter. Now everything changes. The skit stops when sirens blare, drowning us out. Columns of real police armed with clubs, mace, and tear gas approach. Protestors we don't know begin taunting the police, charging their line, but staying just out of reach. When a couple of idiots start throwing rocks, it's obvious that the situation is about to spin out of control.

As the riot police put on their helmets Stan says, "Let's get out of here," and motions for us to follow.

I grab my sign, take Willow by the arm, and run.

He moves forcefully and seems to have a plan. Maybe his military training has kicked in. Moving away from the cops seems like a good idea, in any case. But before we can put a building between us and them, they start firing tear gas. Fights break out between police and half-blinded protesters. We're caught in a stampede of coughing, crying young people. My lungs burn. Tears stream from my eyes.

"This way," Stan yells.

I drop my sign, probing for a way out, dodging the mounting mayhem. This is nothing like nonviolent civil disobedience. This is a riot, with the cops chasing people down and beating them. Blood is everywhere. Close to me, Drake gets knocked down and kneed in the throat by a cop. I try to stop another from clubbing him but get a nightstick in the gut for my trouble. While I'm doubled over, another cop tries to club me. But Stan blocks the blow with his forearm and maces him. I'm breathless for a moment. When I look up again, Willow and Stan are gone. I begin racing with the herd toward the edge of campus, but more police block our way. Then I see Leland just as he sets off a series of smoke bombs, producing enough confusion for us to stagger away.

At the van, everyone's there except for Drake, who has been arrested. I thank Stan for saving my ass. He refuses medical attention for his ballooning arm. As Leland drives us back to the Haight, I can't stop shaking.

The next day, it's back to painting the house. Scraping is hard work, a physical grind, but the place is slowly recovering its lost grandeur. As I strip old paint all the way down to the bare wood, I think about Willow. I can't stop wondering how she manages to get by just selling her macramé creations. At lunch, I ask her.

"I can't," she says.

She explains that she's been living off savings from her New York job. She also has a part-time gig at a garden shop a couple of mornings a week.

"What kind of herbs do they sell?" I ask.

"Medicinal." She smiles. "Come see for yourself."

When I'm done for the day, I accompany her to a street-level shop located five blocks away in a neglected purple Victorian storefront. A sign over the door says the shop specializes in "traditional Western Herbalism and natural medicine." A table with green plants is set up on the sidewalk out front, while display windows of what might once have been a pharmacy showcase everything from holistic plants in powdered form to teas and sage hair tint. Inside, exotic scents and notes played on a flute provide atmosphere I believe is intended to have a calming effect.

It does not work on me. I am pretty uptight when Willow introduces me to her employer, a crusty old grandfatherly type named Merritt. After greeting me, he recommends trying some of the shop's "essential oils and flower essences," which he claims are natural remedies for everything from insomnia to sugar cravings. I thank him but say I'm just looking.

As I begin to wander around, Willow and old Merritt exchange wise looks. There are compartmentalized counters, which are filled with seed packets and tiny green plants. In one corner, I notice gardening tools, bags of fertilizer, and planting soil. The soil's loamy fragrance and the humidity in the shop remind me of home.

When I come to a row of particularly fragrant herbs, Willow says, "Those are our most popular and exotic aphrodisiacs."

"Get out of here," I say.

But no, she's serious. She pulls out some little plants in paper cups and offers me an envelope, which I sniff and find particularly pungent.

"Ginseng's a customer favorite, partly due to the root shape," Willow tells me. "But personally, I like the horny goat weed best."

"Horny goat weed?"

She nods. "According to folklore, a Chinese goatherd noticed increased sexual activity in his flock after they ate this weed."

"I've never tried anything like that before," I say.

"Oh, but you have," Willow says. "You've been taking it in your evening tea the whole time we've been together."

I'm in shock for the rest of the night.

I fall asleep thinking of potions and spells. Then later I wake up from an erotic dream to find Willow spread-eagled beside me in the quasi-darkness of the bedroom. The sheets are strewn about and her thin gown has ridden up, baring her legs and the tops of her thighs. Quite a sight. For a moment I wonder if I'm still dreaming. I start to reach out for her but pull back at the last minute when my mouth turns dry and my stomach queasy. A horny goat weed hangover?

Not wanting to awaken Willow, I slip out of bed quietly and creep downstairs to the kitchen, where I find Leland sitting at the table in that silly Chinese silk robe, spooning Cheerios and milk into his mouth.

"Want some?" he offers.

Not really, but I pull up a chair anyway and fill up a bowl of my own. We focus on eating our cereal and don't talk for a while. That's not surprising. Since the night Leland threw Stan and me out of the house, I've never felt comfortable around him—not even after we both survived the police riot over in Berkeley. Since the day he hired me to paint his house, Leland has hardly said two words to me. Now, though, he breaks the silence:

"Something tells me you've been in the herb shop with Willow."

"What makes you think that?"

"The funk of horny goat weed—and the fact that she works there."

"I can't smell it. You know what she told me? That horny goat weed is love sold over the counter. What do you think of that?"

"Willow's got a marketing background," he says.

"That's what I hear. Have you ever tried horny goat weed yourself?"

"I have," he says.

"Did it work for you?"

His only answer is a wry grin.

"Have you ever been in love, Leland?"

"Why do you ask?"

I don't think—I just blurt it out: "Because I think I am, and I don't know what to do about it."

"Interesting," Leland says. "Only one problem. Love's an illusion."

"What do you mean?"

"Love is just another way to make us feel better. What you really desire is not love but to control and possess another."

"That's not true."

"Sure it is. By definition love is unselfish. True?"

"I guess so."

"But we are selfish creatures. In fact, everything we do is selfish. Therefore, love and human beings are incompatible."

"Well, that's just plain crazy."

"No, Pate, that's philosophy."

"Not everybody is selfish like you."

"Yes, they are."

I'm getting angry now. "What about martyrs, who sacrifice themselves? How are they selfish?"

"Martyrs find fulfillment by sacrificing themselves. That makes it a selfish pleasure."

"Jeez, if that's what you believe, why live in a commune?"

"All I can say is that for some reason it feels a bit less selfish here than anywhere else."

He puts down his spoon and wipes his mouth on the back of his hand, ending the discussion.

As the days slip by, I focus on the front of the house where the trim work is the most elaborate, its face to the world. Hour after hour I scrape off loose paint, brooding all the while on the face we show others, along with the meaning of life, love, and human nature. I find attempting to grapple with such profound matters overwhelming, which is why I suppose most people avoid doing so. Surely, it's pure arrogance on my part to think that I can succeed where others, including even the greatest minds, have failed.

A bleak thought as I wipe the sweat from my brow and attempt to break the bond between paint and wood, in the process spraying myself with chips and flakes. This craggy clapboard seems as resistant to my efforts as the universe to my questions. But does that mean I shouldn't make the attempt? I don't think so, but I can't avoid it in any case—it's *my* human nature. I want to believe that Leland is wrong about love. And what about Zoe Renee? I should have asked if she agrees with his views on love.

All I can say is that, despite all my personal failures, I want to believe that love is real and more than merely fodder for a slogan, that it really means something deep and abiding. This sparks an idea just as I scrape off another big fleck of paint and send it flying into space. Everybody knows love is a feeling. But it's also a *word*. Wouldn't the most obvious place to seek its meaning be in the dictionary? I know there's one resting on the bookshelves in the parlor. On my next break I ought to clean myself up enough to go look it up without tracking paint all over the house. And that's exactly what I by god do.

What I find is hardly unexpected. Love is defined as a feeling of strong or constant affection for a person; an attraction that includes sexual desire; and the strong affection felt by people who have a romantic relationship. The *strong feeling* part I get; it's the *constant* aspect that has eluded me with Deborah, Johona, and other women I've known. Why haven't my loves endured like this old house? Maybe I should consider my relationship with Willow as a work in progress, rather than a finished product, and patiently keep sanding and filling nail holes until we both agree that the time for a topcoat is nigh.

Believing I've made some progress today, I turn the garden hose on the house trim, then leave it to dry and put my tools away.

I'm on my way upstairs to shower when I spot my best friend coming out of Willow's bedroom.

"What are you doing here, Stan?"

He freezes with his hand still on the doorknob and glances at me briefly before raising his gaze above my head. He stares out the window behind me, then at the gray-flecked wallpaper. Everywhere but at me.

"What the hell?" I say, but the silence between us grows and I begin to absorb the enormity of this monstrous betrayal. "No, man. Don't tell me you're . . . balling Willow. You can't be—not after I've asked you not to."

Again, my faithful friend can't meet my eyes.

"You can't," I say. "Tell me it's not true."

But he can't, apparently. What he says is, "Take it easy, Pate."

"You take it easy, you son of a bitch."

"Come on, man." He reaches out in a pleading gesture.

"Go to hell," I yell, and shove him hard.

Just as his head bangs off the wall, Willow opens her door wearing nothing but a half-buttoned blouse.

"Oh my God, Pate," she says, "What is wrong with you?"

"What do you think?" I scream.

I step toward her—Caesar betrayed by Brutus, Othello made mad with jealousy by Desdemona—and stop only inches away from strangling her.

"How could you do this to me, Willow? How could you screw my best friend?"

Fixing her eyes on me, she says coldly, "You've known the score, right from the start."

I'm crumbling like a tenement in an earthquake.

"Okay, you had to get it on with someone else, but did it have to be him?"

"Who I bed is my business, not yours. I thought you understood that, but I guess I was wrong. I've never seen you like this before."

"What do you expect when you're screwing my best friend?"

She turns and goes back into her room, shutting the door in my face. I pivot toward Stan, but he's gone. I chase after him, intent on running him down. But he's disappeared. Where could he go? I check the bars he frequents, but no sign of him. I ask myself where I would go if I were him. An image appears before my fevered eyes. It's a small lake in a dusty wood, with grasshoppers and fish. That's a thousand miles away, but I know a spot closer where he might gravitate.

Ten minutes later, I arrive at the intersection of Haight and Buena Vista West and begin climbing the stairway where at least a hundred thousand hippies have gone before me. Steep footpaths wind through secluded groves of oak trees. As I take them to the top, I hear the N Judah rumbling through the tunnel under the park and know in my tortured heart that I've come to the right place. I find Stan sitting cross-legged on a bench there looking out at Sausalito.

"I'm going to kick your ass," I yell.

I crash into him, knocking him off the bench. I'm up again while he's still down on his knees. As he tries to rise, I launch a solid kick into his ribcage that doubles him over.

"Get up so I can give you the beating you deserve," I say, as he huddles there groaning and holding onto his sides.

Infuriated even more by his failure to fight, I draw back and slap him with the palm of my hand hard across his face. It rocks him, but he still doesn't get up.

"Fight back, god damn it."

When I punch him in the eye, his head snaps sideways.

"On your feet, damn you. Or I swear I'll beat you to a pulp."

He still won't get up.

I start raining blows on him around his head and shoulders. Some he blocks with his arms while others slip through to find their mark. Blood is flowing from his nose now and his left eye is staring up at me like the wild eye of a fallen stallion.

"Why?" I scream. "You could have any woman you want. Why take mine?"

I realize he won't resist, no matter what I do. I've never been in a fight before where I was so enraged that I could have killed my foe. The thought unnerves me. I wait till Stan slowly gets up and wipes blood on his sleeve.

"I'll answer your question," he says, "after you've bought me a beer at Inagodadavida. For once, I know you've got the money."

I think twice about refusing his request but then recall that it wasn't so long ago when Stan had shielded me by absorbing a cop's vicious blow with his own body.

"Okay."

We tromp slowly down the hill and out of the park to the dimly lit dive. It's nearly deserted. We sit at one end of the bar. I order a round while Stan dabs at his nose with a paper napkin.

"So?" I say.

"You should thank me."

"Thank you for what—fucking my woman?"

Our drafts arrive. Stan gulps half of his down.

"For saving you from a relationship with someone who could never love you back. You deserve more, you son of a bitch. Unlike me, you're capable of love."

"Funny you should mention that. Leland has proved to me that love's not real."

Stan wipes his bloody nose on a blood-soaked napkin. He then takes a piece of paper out of his shirt pocket and drops it on the bar. It appears to be an official government document. I unfold it. After reading what it has to say, I comment, "Your orders. You've re-upped. Are you insane?"

Stan leans back on his barstool, staring at me wearily. He's blood-crusted and swollen already.

"I've been thinking it over for a long time. I've come to the conclusion that I have more in common with other veterans than I do with civilians."

"I'm a freaking civilian, Stan."

He drains his beer.

"I can't make it out here anymore, Pate. I need lines drawn, even if I keep trying to cross them. There are some things I can live without, and some I can't."

I don't know what to say. To buy time, I tell him that I need to hit the head.

"Don't go anywhere. I'll be right back." I stop. "When do you ship out?"

Stan folds his orders and slips them back in his pocket. "Today on the 3:30 Greyhound to San Diego."

The fact that he's leaving so soon hits me like a Mack truck, but I'm trying not to show it. In the restroom, I peer at myself in the mirror and wonder what the hell I'm doing. I'm furious with Stan for betraying me with Willow, but I'm even madder about this harebrained scheme to re-up. No matter what he's done, he's still my best friend.

I splash my face with cold water and return intending to talk him out of this military nonsense and get ourselves back on track. But I'm too late. No Stan in the bar. No Stan back at the commune. No Stan, period.

17

A couple of weeks later in early August I get my first letter ever at the commune. The return address on the envelope reads: U.S. Navy Medical Center, Box 14, FPO San Diego.

Dear Pate,

Hey man, how is civilian life? Thought I'd drop you a few lines. Sorry I left SF the way I did. Hope you're doing well and are not too mad at me. I'll be out of here soon. I was having some problems adjusting, but now I'm looking forward to being back aboard ship.

There seems to be about a two-year "void" in my life. But things are looking up. I've met some nice people and seem to be adjusting even though I'm back in the military.

Please say hello to everyone on Sanchez Street for me. And take care. Hope to hear from you soon.

Your buddy,
Stan

I read Stan's letter several times. Problems adjusting. No doubt. But a two-year void?

If Stan's mental health required a stay in the hospital, I question why the Navy ever allowed him to re-enlist. But that's foolish of me. Nobody in his right mind in our generation is going to volunteer for Vietnam. That alone made him attractive to recruiters so desperate for manpower they'd go back to impressment if they could get away with it. Add to that Stan's naval experience and they'd have themselves one plum prize.

I stuff Stan's letter into my pocket but keep taking it out and reading it over again. I write to him but receive no reply.

18

A few days into September, the weather turns cooler as billowing white fog rolls into San Francisco Bay. They say this is the best time of year here. Not for me, though, while nursing a broken heart. I try to compensate by avoiding Willow and throwing myself into my work. And I drink vodka from half-pint bottles alone at night in my room. Call it a mild oblivion.

This changes when I get a long-distance phone call, my first at the commune.

At the time Piper summons me, I'm up on a ladder running my hand over the newly smooth surface of the trim. I can't imagine who's calling since no one but Stan knows I'm here. The voice on the other end, however, is not Stan's.

When the caller says he's a chaplain at the naval hospital in San Diego, beads of sweat collect on my forehead, and sweat starts to trickle down my back.

"How did you get this number?" I ask.

"From a piece of paper found in Seaman First Class Stanley Hicks's wallet . . . after the accident."

A wave of dread washes over me. "What accident?"

"Mr. Merwin, I'm sorry to have to tell you this over the phone, but Seaman First Class Hicks was struck by an automobile yesterday while out hitchhiking.”

“Oh, no. I thought he was in the hospital.”

“He was. He’d just been discharged. I’m sorry, but it’s my duty to inform you that he died this morning from his injuries.”

“Stan’s dead?” I’m light-headed, dizzy.

“Yes, I’m afraid so. I was with him at the end, sir. His dying request was that I convey to you a message.”

“What’s the message?”

“He wanted me to tell you that he loved you like a brother and he hoped that someday you’d forgive him.”

“Is that it?”

“Yes, sir.”

I’m quivering. I can’t believe that Stan is dead, killed by a car. He didn’t even make it back to the war. When someone asks me what’s wrong, and I fail to respond, they snatch away the phone. I go to lie down and get my head together, but I can’t do it and after a while, I leave the house. I walk instinctively to the park, hike up to the summit, and sit on a bench.

The news is horrifying enough, but I wonder if this truly was an accident—or suicide. He hadn’t made any threats or dropped any hints that I knew of. At the sand dunes he’d exhibited dangerous, self-harmful behavior by pushing too far into the desert. If he had been thinking of suicide, then perhaps the military hospital had discharged him too soon.

And then there’s his funeral, which I assume will be held back in Louisville. If so, I ponder whether I should go. It’s not only a long way, but his parents—especially his right-wing father—might well blame me for his death, even though our journey west was Stan’s idea all along.

That night I have a dream. I’m at Stan’s funeral. The chapel is filled with mourners, but I don’t know any of them. And they don’t see me, as if I’m invisible, a ghost. A man of the cloth is waving the Good Book while giving the eulogy. This should be interesting, since he's never even met Stan. At least he admits it: I didn't know Stanley personally, since he wasn't a regular worshipper, but I'm told he was a sensitive person. A sensitive man who suffered for his sensitivity. We all know Stanley loved his country and served it well. Only recently he had re-enlisted in the United States Navy. Then the clergyman brings the service to a close with a reading . . .

> How blessed is the tie that binds
> Our hearts in lasting love
> The comradeship of kindred minds
> Is like to that above . . .

followed by an invitation to file by the casket for one last look, which I do. An American flag is draped over the coffin. Stan is lying there in his naval uniform, shaved and shorn, and I hardly recognize him without his beard and long hair. I wish he'd sit up and tell them this is not who he is. But he can't, so I shout it out myself:

You didn't really know Stan like I do. My Stan is a completely different person than yours. My Stan is the guy who saved my ass more than once, the kindest and most gentle soul I ever met.

But they're not hearing me.

I turn to Stan himself to say my goodbyes.

Oh, Stan, I remember you sitting on top of the hill, staring out at Sausalito, your hands on your knees. Distressed. I wish you'd told me more about what was going on. I wish I could have talked you out of re-enlisting. I wish I'd never hit you. Forgive me, old friend. That hangdog smile. How blissful you seemed after the medicine man did his thing, released your ankle from pain. We were both lost in a dark place when we started out on the road. Weren't we?

The scene dissolves into a cemetery and, with a hard wind blowing in my face, I watch them as they lower Stan's coffin into the grave that will be his final resting place. And then it's over and I'm pulling out into traffic, stopping at a light to mop my brow and wait for permission. And wait for permission to move again. Permission to move again along the seething pavement.

The next day, while gathering up my belongings, I run across the macramé bookmark that Willow gave me. My first impulse is to drop it into the trash. But then I take it out again, thinking it may help me find my place in the book of life when this adventure is long behind me.

Leland is sitting at the kitchen table once more when I find him, sipping tea while doing paperwork and perhaps paying bills. He looks up at me and, noticing my gear, says, "Hey, you're not leaving us, are you?"

"I'm afraid so, Leland. I need to move on."

"I'm sorry to hear it."

"I hate asking, but my wallet's a little light, and I wonder if you could spot me a few bucks for bus fare. I'll pay you back when I get settled."

With Stan gone, he's the only one I know who might lend me money.

"Well, you know my philosophy," Leland says. "What do I get out of it?"

"My thanks. The satisfaction of doing a good deed. And the room back."

He thinks it over before reaching into his pocket and pulling out a wad of cash. He peels off five twenties and hands them to me.

"You'll get it back."

"Don't worry about it. Where will you go—up north to Portland, Seattle, Victoria?"

All fertile ground for hippies and wanderers. But I'm not sure I fit into those categories anymore.

"I read a book once that said you can't go home again, but maybe you can."

He raises his eyebrows, offering a questioning gaze, and it strikes me that Leland would be equally at home living on a mountain or in a cave or any remote place where an old master might stoke the flame of enlightenment to pass on to others.

"You know, before you go," he says, "you might want to think this through."

"I have. You see, I've come to believe that you're at least partly right about love being an illusion. Not because humanity is rotten, but because it's impossible for human beings to do anything that can't be construed as selfish. But selfish or not, we all need each other and sometimes despite our baser natures we're capable of astonishing feats of self-sacrifice and, well, love."

"What brings you to that conclusion?"

"The realization that while Stan might've slept with Willow simply because she was there and willing, it also might've been a perverse act of freeing himself from me so he could go back to life in the Navy. In the end, I prefer to think of what he did not as a betrayal, but a gift." I take a breath. "Or maybe I'm just full of shit."

Leland nods sagely, as if gratified he hasn't entirely wasted his time on me. "Finding the pathway to attaining a state of inner peace and higher consciousness is seldom easy, Pate. But these hard-won nuggets of truth speak well of your inner progress. Somehow I don't think you're quite there yet."

A scoffing voice inside warns me not to be taken in by this extravagant prattle, that Leland is having entirely too much fun playing spiritual guide at my expense. What does this false prophet really know about the profundity of life? What qualifies a middle-aged landlord in a ridiculous robe to teach me the way to purify my heart and mind?

Nonetheless, here I stand, seeking not only his money but his blessing and words of wisdom.

"What do you mean I'm not quite there yet, Leland?"

He sighs as if deeply fatigued. "You seem restless. In a great hurry to separate yourself from your present surroundings as if this will somehow magically lift your burdens and solve your problems. But you'll never overmaster emotions and all the setbacks of life by running away."

"So, you're telling me I shouldn't leave?"

"I'm saying you are making a choice based on an unsound principle."

"What principle? I don't understand."

"It's hard to find satisfaction or live a meaningful life. I'm suggesting that you reconsider the idea that traveling can do you any good when you carry yourself around with you."

Slowly I realize he's right. I've already come two thousand miles and look where it's gotten me. But it hasn't been all for naught. My life is so much richer from journeying with Stan. How I'm going to miss him!

"What should I do, Leland?"

"The Greeks tell us that the unexamined life is not worth living. Maybe you ought to stick around and think about that while finishing what you started."

"Ha! You just want me to finish the paint job before I leave."

"I do," he admits, with a benign smile. "Don't you want to do that yourself?"

I consider this carefully, visualizing every trim piece on the house, from the elaborately curved gingerbread molding on the gables to the tall shutters. Forget about enlightenment. I've already scraped, primed, and top-coated so much of this place it would be a shame not to see it through.

"Okay, I'll do it."

Back to my room. I put on my work clothes and get ready to resume my task. But first I pick up the phone and call Deborah's father in Louisville. I'm halfway expecting him to hang up on me, but he doesn't. Instead, he tells me I'm wasting my time calling. Deborah's found somebody else.

"Someone more suitable and a better job, too. She's happy. Leave her alone."

"Tell her I wish her the best."

"Don't think I will," Mr. Johnson says, and puts down the phone.

I don't know whether to believe him or not. Maybe I should call the bank and ask for her. If he's lying about the new job, he might be lying about the rest. But what if he is? Will my call make anything better? Some things, once broken, can never be fixed.

19

By early October, I'm standing on a ladder all the time. A small scraper gets me into tight corners. A wide-bladed putty knife helps me smooth missed edges. I knock off dirt, sawdust, and other debris with a garden hose and scrub brush. And I keep remembering the women I've known this year, and what I love and appreciate about each of them.

Deborah tried to make a good life for herself and her son. Could our relationship have lasted? I don't believe so anymore. I hope Deborah got what she needed: a secure home for her son, something I could not provide.

Someday Johona is bound to find another who shares her bond with the tribal land. My most permanent bond is this paint smudging my shirts and pants.

Primer leaves a surface rough. But a light sanding can do wonders once the dust is wiped off with a tack rag. Three days to allow proper drying, then comes the most rewarding part of the whole process—applying the finish coat.

As I do, I envision Willow selling macramé at Haight and Ashbury, serving me soup, slipping horny goat weed into my tea. I'm not as free-minded as I thought. I need someone, and some solid underpinnings, I can depend on. There are lines that I, unlike Stan, don't want to cross. Willow gave me a taste of summer wine, and for that I bless her. I doubt she can go on this way forever, but that's up to her.

In the late afternoon with the sun in my eyes, I paint the fanciful flamboyant designs that the old-time carpenters were so proud they'd created. Long, smooth brush strokes find a rhythm of their own, leaving the mind free to wander. The house has changed, but what about me? Am I still the same person who set out with Stan on this journey?

No. But also *yes*.

Yes, I've changed. I recall what Hemingway said about morality: the only way to judge a choice is whether you feel good or bad afterward. Nothing could make me feel worse than Stan's untimely death. But the choices that led up to his death were his, not mine. I know that I loved my friend, and about *that*, I feel good.

And now, high up this ladder on top of the hill, with the sun on my back and a salty breeze coming off the bay, I look out and see people moving around below. And I'm ready at last to brush the final strokes of paint on this gorgeous old house.

acknowledgments

This book was a long time in the making. It began when I was a college student in the late Sixties, trying to come to terms with the prospect of dying in Vietnam along with thousands of others. I protested the war, which made no sense to me, and did whatever I could to resist it. My whole life was changed forever by that terrifying but also exhilarating experience and its aftermath. When someone asks, "Did you really do all those things in the book?" I answer, "Some I did, and the rest I made up." That's fiction. But real people died because of a senseless war. That's reality. May it never happen again.

I am more grateful than I can express to Sena Jeter Naslund, my long-time friend, mentor extraordinaire, and literary champion for believing in my writing and bringing *Journeyman* to life. My heartfelt thanks to Sena, Ed McClanahan, Eleanor Morse, and Kenny Cook for their generous endorsements of *Journeyman*.

My thanks to the Fleur-de-Lis publishing team, especially Jonathan Weinert for his fantastic design and artwork, Kathleen Loomis for her excellent proofreading, and Chip Norton for his outstanding photography on the cover photo. I thank Corie Neumayer for her beautiful painting on the cover. I thank Bette Levy for generously telling me about her life in Haight-Ashbury during the 1960s.

I am very grateful to all of my Spalding University MFA mentors—Eleanor Morse, K.L. Cook, Robin Lippincott, and Silas House—for helping me become a better writer. My deepest thanks especially to Eleanor for her wise guidance and encouragement in crafting this novel. I am also deeply grateful to my talented and insightful writer friends—the late Joe Peacock, Michele Ruby, and Bob Sachs—for many years of invaluable critiques and nurturing support, especially for *Journeyman*.

I thank Neela Vaswani, Kirby Gann, and Mary Clyde for being terrific workshop leaders. I thank classmates and friends Drēma Drudge, Cindy Lane, and Margery Gans for workshopping *Journeyman*. I thank all the students, faculty, and staff of the low-residency MFA in Writing Program at Spalding University, for creating what is truly a remarkable creative community and a home for writers.

I am grateful to my wonderful family members for their love and support in so many ways, including as readers of the manuscript in progress. I thank my endlessly patient wife Corie for listening, advising, and commiserating, my amazing daughter Caroline Rouse Neumayer, late aunt Rita George, late uncle Henry Valentine Neumayer, Sr., sister-in-law JoAnne Rouse, and brother-in-law Ed Wong. I also thank my friends and readers Alan Naslund, Charlie Merkel, Dave Caudill, and Marianna Schakel-Metcalf.

about the author

Rick Neumayer has published short fiction in many literary magazines, and three of his full-length Broadway-style musical collaborations have been produced. *Journeyman* is his first published novel. Rick co-edited *River City Review* literary magazine and has reviewed books for the Louisville *Courier Journal*. The Louisville native, resident, and Male High graduate has had a wide variety of experiences, including working as a newspaper reporter. After retiring from a thirty-year teaching career, he began writing full-time while earning an MFA in creative writing at Spalding University. He also holds degrees from the University of Louisville (MA) and Western Kentucky University (BA). Contact the author at RickNeumayer.com.

Fleur-de-Lis Press is named to celebrate the life

of Flora Lee Sims Jeter

(1901–1990)

9 780996 012041